Whisper of
KINGS

Debbie Skye

Table of Contents

I:
Iyah: Surrounded By Light

Why am I running? From whom am I running? No, am I the one chasing? That explains this sharp gold spear in my hand. It's sharp enough to pierce even the skin of a grizzly bear, but then again, why in the hell would I chase anyone with the intent to kill? I hate even the sight of weapons. All I know right now is I haven't killed anyone, as my spear perfectly mimics the light of the full moon. But here, right now, even the moonlight does me no favors, as all I see in front of me is darkness. I am panting and out of breath, yet I also sense within me calm, like a lake that sleeps in between the mountains, devoid of ripples… absent of life. I am at peace, yet I want to escape. I am tired. So tired that I need to catch my breath.

I feel cold, which is strange since it's summer. Why am I feeling so cold? Oh shit! I am dressed like a complete slut. This is not even my style, a gold cap merely covering my breasts. Was I held captive? This is neither the place nor the state I am supposed to be in. Think! Recall. How did I end up here… Bingo! I get it. It's dark. I am alone, almost naked and running. It's sleep paralysis. I am in a state of dream from which I cannot seem to wake up. But I see no demons. It's just me. Still, that's a relief. The last thing I want is to be dressed like this, all out in the open and holding a spear on top of it. I'd be a laughing stock.

I catch my breath. I feel better and calmer, quite a lot calmer. The rock that I am sitting on feels like a chair that my ass has sat on before. The Oak tree, the giant one, is right before me. I have seen it before. How big and old it is, I have had this thought before, too. It's been struck by lightning once, I remember. The left side of its woody stem was black, with a huge hole. I get up and walk around it to see if it is still there. There it is. The left body of the oak tree that homes a huge, cruel scar from nature, the same one I've seen before. How strange to be in the same dream. Tiny sweat beads form above my forehead, and my scalp becomes moist from the sweat, causing my natural curly hair to shrink half its size within seconds. In the darkness that has barely any light coming across, something catches my attention. It glimmers in the dark, calling me. I walk up to it, a head-shaped object with grey hair on it. I sit in the corner and gently stroke the hair. It's beautiful, gray, and shiny with a soft, smooth touch. As I reach the end of the hair, there is blood on the tips of the end of the hair. I know it's blood. It has a thickness to the feel. What a strange dream! I even recall my emotions, the tiredness, and even the scent of soil as it had rained just a few hours ago. I can feel it when the wind passes by me. I can even hear the whistling sound of it as it wisps past my ears. It's like a déjà vu. I have been here before.

A twig breaks, and I stand, my spear aimed right where I heard the sound, all ready to kill. A gushing wind sends shivers down my spine, and the goosebumps on my naked body make me look like a cat who stands against dogs she knows she has no chance to win against.

Iyah. I hear someone calling my name from a distance. It's coming from all directions. I move around in circles, and my name keeps on getting called, and every time it gets louder, closer, yet I cannot see who calls my name.

"IYAH!"

I jolt myself awake. The strange faces in the classroom stare at me like I am some alien, except for some girls who are giggling, probably because I have embarrassed myself or the one who awaits me. There she stands, at the front, glaring at me.

"Good morning, Iyah," Mrs. Ramaz mocks me, my history teacher. Her face clearly has an annoyed look, and I don't blame her for that. After all, I am the one who dozed off during her class while I ran naked with a spear in my hand in my weird dream. With dazed eyes, a small headache is about to present itself. I look up at her and smile, knowing what's to come for me. A loud mouth, a scornful look, and taunts mixed with complaints about my attitude.

Mrs. Remez is a slender, somewhat pretty lady, but only if she would smile just a little more. I often wonder why the most beautiful women seem to have irritated faces. I understand that, in this case, it is somewhat understandable, but still, she can be nicer. You are blessed with divine beauty, yet you do everything to make it look ugly. If only she would just smile more. Why is it always the prettiest ladies who do everything to make themselves look mediocre? Is she trying not to make herself look attractive? My mind starts to wander. Who hurt her? Who broke this beautiful lady's heart?

"This is the third time you have fallen asleep this week. What is it? Is history too boring for you?" She began with her jeers. "Or perhaps someone had a pretty busy night."

I rolled my eyes. Here she goes. This is the last thing I want right now. I feel like my head is going to explode, and my repetitive dreams are really annoying me at this point. I have so many questions, and I feel so different, but I am really tired at this point. I'd rather have someone explain things to me and not Mrs. Ramaz asking me questions.

"Would you care to share with us about your endeavors? You know, help and make this class less boring?"

Mrs. Ramaz, not today. Wrong time. You're really testing your luck and pushing my patience; you are already on very thin ice.

"Mrs. Ramaz," I sighed. Tired obviously. "It's not that your class is boring. I just am not interested." My reply was met with her smirking and the entire class laughing. I don't think I made a joke, but I'll take their compliment.

"Oh, and," yes, I am not done. She asked for it, after all. "My night was very exciting. I watched a show on how to make tacos." I gave her my attitude. Take that, Mrs. Ramaz. I hope you don't find this *boring*. It was an insult, one that she did not take lightly, but being the teacher, she knew her job was to remain composed, and this wasn't much of a surprise for her, as this wasn't the first time I had slumbered during her lectures.

"Nothing new from Iyah, always wants to be the smart ass."

Mrs. Ramaz walked away, ignoring my mockery but giving me only a look of disappointment. She resumed her teaching to those who were still listening while guilt consumed me. Unable to cope and feeling uneasy about what I had just done, I got up and walked up to her as she sat at her desk after she was done assigning students' reading classwork. "I am sorry, Mrs. Ramaz," I awkwardly murmur while avoiding eye contact.

"I can't hear you," she responds, her eyes fixed on the book she is reading. I take a deep breath and look at her with sincerity. "I apologize. My attitude was inexcusable, and I will work on myself."

Mrs. Ramaz closes her book and looks up at my guilt-ridden face. She nodded her head in approval but didn't utter a word. It was a look of understanding as if she knew that I was fighting some battles in privacy, the battles that were mine and mine alone. The ones I wasn't ready to share with anyone. She has known me for a while now, so we do have some understanding, and I appreciate how she respected my privacy. With that, I walked back to my seat, now feeling a lot better and less guilty, and got on the reading task assigned to the class.

But it wasn't over for me. My self-sabotaging behavior was yet to come. Now was the time to question my existence and ask the big question: What the fuck is wrong with me? Why do I always have to be such bitch? The routine mantra that I love saying out loud in my head whenever I act like a bitch. I've been acting like this for months now. I'm sick of having dreams at least three times a week for almost a month. I want to rid myself of these stupid dreams that seem to disturb my already miserable reality. I've changed my diet, read books, done exercise, and even looked over the internet for help. *Sleep Paralysis.* That's what the internet has to say for me. But I know well it's not. Oh, and sleeping pills. I have trouble sleeping as I sleep. Therefore, I dream. So, to have a dreamless sleep where I don't feel tired upon waking up, I take sleeping pills. But these pills help people who have trouble sleeping, and I sleep. It's just a nightmare on Elm Street for me. But nothing has seemed to aid me so far. I suppose I am taken over by some sort of ghostly curse. I am beaten.

Now, if these dreams remained only dreams in which I did crimes undiscovered by humanity, I would not have minded, even though I am a pacifist. But the lines between the two are blurring. I am slowly losing myself. I find myself more irritated by people around me who question me. I hate people, the things they do, the words they speak, the opinions they hold. I am becoming an object with nothing but malice in my heart. I remain unsurprised. Excitement and enthusiasm are now alien to me. I once loved the attention. I cared what people thought of me. This wasn't the same as seeking people's validation but being part of others' lives, even strangers. I no longer yearn for any of that, not anymore.

I'm tired of the old stories being told about my childhood that make absolutely no sense. Same old, same old. *"When you were a child, your mother left you to make a better life for the family,"* My 76-year-old aunt loves reminding me of that. What better life? As far as I remember, I live in a hellhole. I barely have any friends. The people I live with look at me as if I am some sort of an imposter. *Where is the better life that was supposed to be some grand sacrifice she made in exchange for deserting me?* This is what I want to tell my aunt, but instead, I'm yawning, rolling my eyes at her, who thinks that this story is brave and exciting. *"Your grandmother said that it's your sister so that the baby will drink your breast milk. I used to get up every morning at 6 am to breastfeed you."* She never shies away from telling me this, either. Thank you, I guess? What am I supposed to do with that? Her stories seem too old. And lately, I think these are just made-up bull stories they tell me so they don't feel bad about treating me the way they do. Frankly, I feel no connection to this story. I wonder if she is even my aunt.

There is this sad distance between my family and me. This inescapable prison I can't seem to escape, no matter what I do. Every time I enter a room, they all observe this hush silence as if I have intruded on their secret meeting. They look at me, and their eyes talk to me. They told me that they were enjoying it until I came into this room. But I also sense pity. The eyes that say, *Here comes the poor thing.* But I have grown quite accustomed to it. This pathetic and lonely life of mine has done me no favors but has made every attempt to make me feel alone.

I mean, they are great people, just no personality, complainers, whiners, and gluttons. Sisters complain and whine about why their boyfriend broke up with them, or my boss is such a total loser who doesn't cherish my work. "Try waking up and getting to work on time. That might help!" Uncles drink and criticize. Every word is about which big-ass girl is on Instagram. Perhaps I am no different either, hating on them. Oh, and no family is a good family without those two aunts who come to dinner and bring the plastic containers to pack food before everybody else eats, but overall! They are funny as hell to watch. Either way, I do not belong among these people. I could swear on that. Not because of the things they do that annoy me. I am certain this is life, how every family is. I feel that way because I have this gut feeling that they, to me, are complete strangers with whom I just share my life. I can tell it like a guard dog that can tell whether a bag has marijuana in it. I am that confident. Or maybe I am just losing my mind. Overthinking because I have no answers to the things that bother me. But that's how I feel every day, like I dumped my nose in a good bag of weed, just sniffing all day long until I get a daze and just crash. Burnt out, exhausted from all the bull life has to offer.

Well, this is me. All this has been going on for the last five years. I wonder if it's about damn time I seek some professional help. I guess the garbage man will clear out the mountains of trash that's been stored inside my head. Or else, I fear, I'll succumb to my fucked-up dreams and turn into a serial killer and wipe out these phony people. Or worse, I'll find myself running naked in the streets, dazed and confused. Maybe I have that mental illness. What's it called? The one that every *fucked neglected* person usually has. Oh yes, Schizophrenia. I am seeing things. I am angry all the time. It does make sense. A tasteless word no one wants to talk about. I am pretty sure that I have withdrawal symptoms.

When I am not dreaming, these are the thoughts that haunt me. So, I don't prefer to be left alone with my thoughts. I like to do things and work all the time. And this family is testing my patience by having me wait at the dinner table. Why can't this family be at the dinner table at six on the dot like Michele's? Everyone sits there and just eats without saying one damn word, the food on the table beautifully laid out, each person waiting their turn to be served by mom. Dad looks tired from the office, so he sits there with his glasses on, tapping his cigar gently on the side of the table. But no, good fate has never been on my plate. My Family has all these silver trays with every flipping meal on one table, looking like a buffet of meat. Just pass me the Kellogg's cornflakes. That's all I need. Please, one cup to satisfy my sugar needs for the day!

I guess I shouldn't complain. They do feed me well, and yes, sometimes I think I live in a beautiful fantasy world—well, at least my dreams seem that way. I always awaken with a pain-filled feeling in my chest. It doesn't hurt, but it's as if someone has pelted my heart with stones. Painless but buries me beneath a mountain. To feel something. I thought it to be beautiful. And in some way, it is. It makes me feel less lonely and less different. Having to feel what others feel. It scares me, too, but I delude myself, saying it's all part of growth into becoming something wonderful. To appreciate the beauty of something, one must know the horror. How else would you cherish it? It's satisfying yet scary at the same time. My hands don't feel alive, always with numbness, and some wake up with a bitter-sweet taste inside my mouth, craving something. I just don't know what it is, so of course, I run to the kitchen and grab the box of Kellogg's cornflakes.

I remember once I woke up crying uncontrollably. Probably from a nightmare I no longer remember, but I am sure it was one of *those* dreams. I panted and breathed heavily, wishing someone would comfort me. Tell me it's alright. Isn't that what parents do when a child wakes up from a nightmare? Am I mentally ill, or all of this is part of the human experience I don't know of since I am farthest from being a human? Where do I turn to? Friends? That I don't have. Family? I question if they are real. A psychiatrist who will say I have anxiety and put me on medications? I am anxious, anxious to find love. I need that. I deserve that. I was robbed of it. I have people come and say that I am attractive. I also am aware of it. But being pretty and good-looking doesn't give you love.

I am a 5'7 dark-skinned girl with curly hair that swings across my hips and eyes that are blue. Yes, blue eyes. How beautiful. How rare. Yet, on my black skin, people have only judged me. I think I'm skinny, but I've been told that I look like a perfect white girl, only with black skin. I still have no clue what to make of that. Sometimes, I let people talk because it's something that is beyond my comprehension, or it's just their sheer stupidity. And when I do that, ignore them; they accuse me of being some phony bitch who is looking for attention with fake eyes and hair. *You can't be black with blue eyes and long hair. They must be fake.* They say this, waiting for me to say that they can grab my hair, throw me around, and see if they still remain glued to my head.

But hell, I cannot blame them for wanting to try that. My family has dark skin and dark eyes. It kind of makes sense. Knowing that my mother was adventurous enough to leave her daughter behind. I assume during her secured marriage of 35 years, she may have ventured off one of the nights and may have stumbled upon some blue-eyed, probably a Caucasian guy with curly hair. That's a possibility. Did I ask my aunt this? Absolutely not.

II:
The Misery that had No End

I waited patiently for my misery to end, and when I ran out of it, my anxiousness only grew. My days were exhausting, but I wasn't the only person in the world. The world, time, and fate were cruel to everyone. Obviously, my battles were unique. I was alone, but I also felt what everyone felt. I sought what everyone sought: a place to escape. A place where time did not exist. A place where only one body lived, mine. But that was a dream, a fairytale, a hope on which I clung dearly to. Until then, I had to live, endure, and struggle. I had to find an escape, though temporary, but enough to help me keep my sanity. It was this: a narrow escape to oblivion, parties, meeting strangers, taking them home, and passing my judgment on them. So anxiously, I wait for my day to start. Excitement gets the best of me. I was looking forward to this, this moment of escape. It was a caged freedom, but for the time being, that'd do. It was like watching your favorite show on Friday night; you get to be happy and thrilled for just an hour.

I left my prison and was out in the open. I smelled, breathed in, and filled my lungs with fresh air, just what they had been suffocating for. The early morning dew from the crisp air leaves a glistening color of crystal radiating on each leaf. On some, it looked like a teardrop, not of sorrow, but of freedom. For once, it felt as if the world revolves around me. At a distance, not so great and safe, a dog on a leash barks at a dog that is stray. A stray that is spat on, pelted with stones, and cursed upon. But the stray walks, unbothered, happy, and free, while saliva spills out of the mouth of the barking dog as the chains hold him captive. On my left, verdant bushes bloom, holding out to me their rosiest, liveliest flowers, and on which bee sits, and suck their juiciest, sweetest nectar. I envy the bees, for they do it every day, unlike me. But never mind, tonight I am the bee, the free stray, the blissful air. Tonight, I am unchained and beautiful. My plans for today will initiate once the moon glances on our filthy soil. However, the place of my freedom is a bar, where drunk men grope girls. It's not the best place, but I have a good eye.

***

The man from across the room is watching me for the past 10 minutes. He is alone, and with no one to talk to, his eyes do not leave me even for a minute. I feel naked with his creepy glances. The least he could do was walk and introduce himself. But then again, can I really blame him? I did put some extra effort into myself. Last I saw myself, I looked pretty hot. My tight, lustrous silver dress had no straps, and they were capped perfectly to expose my tits. The dress is just below my ass, and God help him if he sees that. I wonder if he has seen my tattoo that runs along my left leg, Psalms 27. Although only 27 can be seen, I will allow him to see only that. My nail polish matches the bright, matte pink lipstick that covers my thick lips. I stay away from the color red as my mother hates that color so much. No eye shadow, just mascara to brighten up my eyelashes, making them seem longer. Everything matches my even brown skin tone with no powder or foundation. One of the things I was blessed with was flawless skin. I licked slowly around the rim of the glass, which was half filled with white wine. He is seated at a VIP table, and his eyes are on me as if I am a gazelle and he a predator, waiting for just the right moment. He is waiting for me to look at him, and so I do. He gets my attention as our eyes meet. He passes me a smile that is wrinkled, creepy, and desperate. I smile back, acting innocent as if I hadn't had my attention set on him for the last 15 minutes.

My smile was enough, a green light for him to make his move on me. He gets up, straightens his blazer, and walks up to me. His steps are impatient as he looks around the bar, making sure no one gets there before him. As he draws near me, he checks me out, my legs especially, and now he finally sees the number 27 and I can see his Adam's apple bubbling. Times have changed. Men were now interested in black women. I suppose it started as a woke culture and men felt that to support, they needed to hook up with black women. After all, that's where their minds always wander off to sex. Once they got the taste of black women, everything changed. They discovered something great, and soon, men threw themselves at any black women they saw.

"Hello beautiful!" he greets me.

"Well, Hello Mr.-"

"Micheal," he introduced himself.

"Ah, Micheal," I act as if I don't already know everything about him. "Like the archangel, Micheal?"

"Yes, straight out of the Bible," he says with a smile as he exposes his cream-colored chipped teeth. So he comes here often and gets drunk. I wonder what racist, demeaning thing he said to get knocked out. Either way, I am always glad when people like him become so empty and alone that they have to cling to bottles. But then again, their drunk actions only harm others.

"You know," he says as he signals the bartender for some wine. "I have been watching for some time now."

"Oh, really?" my act continues. "I am flattered." I can't stand him—his cheap cologne, his bad breath, his idea that he is charming—but I maintain my composure.

"And you are...?"

"Whatever you wish to call me," I gaze at him slyly, giving him a flirtatious smile.

"How about pumpkin?" he grins.

I roll my eyes. I couldn't help it. Pumpkin? What the hell is wrong with this guy? Has he ever been with a woman? I snort and laugh to cover up my disgust. "I have never been called that," I cringed. "Anyways, my name is Alanah, my friends call me Lana."

"That's a pretty name for a pretty lady," he flirts as his pinky finger touches my hand.

He gets close to me, although his gigantic stomach causes him trouble but he manages somehow. "Do you like an archangel, Lana?" he whispers into my ear. I cringe even harder. I look at him with doe eyes and nod. His bad breath, his voice. I think all the wine I just chugged is about to come back up. Well not that I would mind throwing up at him, but not today. Today, I must do what frees me.

I don't like this man at all, but he would never know this, because of that smile I have on my face. I take a deep breath, smile once again, and give him the confidence he needs. "I was wondering..." my hands play with his, "You have this expensive suit on. Do you have somewhere you want to be?"

"I am where I should be."

"But this place is so boring? I hate it when I am bored." I act tipsy. "I wish I was home. I am never bored there," I frown.

"Oh, I have an idea," I jump up. "Why don't the two of us head home? There, I'll keep you busy all night."

"All night?" he gulps. I can see sweat beads forming on his forehead.

I nod with a smile.

"I like the sound of that," he said, almost like a growl. He sips his wine, reaches for his wallet, and leaves a 100-dollar bill. "After you," he says. Men are so predictable. In a place like this, their thoughts are singular: sex. Play along just a little, and you will have a puppet for the night.

We walk to our cars, and I walk slowly. Each step is a tease for him. He followed me from behind, and I could feel his eyes set on my ass. Of course, no less than I would expect from a guy like him. Etiquettes are the last thing he has. I drove very slowly, making sure he was following me all right. He was a little drunk, so I can't have him drive recklessly. I keep puffing from my vape. I hate the smell of cigarettes, but something about the smoke that corrupts my lungs pleases me. The smell of mint and gummy candy! It almost reminds me of Christmas, wanting presents but never receiving any from my family. My only gift, which was wrapped so clumsy with tape and Christmas wrapping, was mint candy and a pack of gummy bears from Mr. Haruki.

I took him to a place that only a few are aware of. I step out of my car, the night air becomes cool, and the stars in the sky mix with the moonlight up the driveway of the parking lot. The house is grand, but yet modest. It took me three years to build. I remember how pleased the architect was with my design; it was basic yet complicated and functional, exactly like my life has been for these past five years. But my landscaping, for some reason, came to me in a dream. I wanted to step out of my car and feel like I lived in a forest, like a sleeping beauty. I have trees and white flowers, and the smell of vanilla is always present. The clear glass surrounded my garage so that I could always see the outside. It's a single-floor home, but I have a basement in which nobody but a few knew existed.

"Wow! Wow! Wow!" I heard loud applause as he screamed with amusement. He was fascinated with how my house looked from the outside. "Ain't that a beauty? It's not much of a surprise your husband or boyfriend is rich. You do dress rich," he laughed at his own joke. Like I'd cheat on my man for a sleazebag like you. "I am kidding. Just FYI, I think women today are capable of earning. I totally support women earning more than men," he defended his crappy humor. *No, you don't. You just wanna have sex with me.*

"Is it rented or do you own this place?"

"Why does it matter? Let's go inside. I have a surprise waiting for you." He follows, but midway, he changes his direction and finds his way to the front porch. "Where are you going?" I asked him.

"Inside. I thought-,"

"The surprise you are anticipating wouldn't be fun there," I interrupt him. "I have a special place, just for the two of us. And it's just there, at the side entrance. It's connected directly to heaven." I pass a cunning smile, one that is full of tease. He asked no further questions and followed me like a dog. We stepped inside and walked the narrow hallway that was decorated with sconces and paintings. With each step, a sconce would light up. Each scene was followed by a painting. The hallway was connected to my basement. I opened the door to my basement and walked down. I looked up and saw him standing by the door. I saw him nervous, as if suspicious of me.

"What's the matter, baby? Afraid of the dark?" I mock him. The lights in the basement aren't turned on yet. I want to see how stupid he is. He shook his head and followed my lead. I clap, and the room lights up. His shoulders, which were tensed just a minute ago, drop as he looks around and is left in awe. A smile creeps up on his face as he looks over at the big, fluffy bed with satin pillows.

"Well, aren't you something, Lana," he applauds me as the gold table in the center of the room catches his attention.

"Help yourself," I signaled him to the table where fine red wine and cigars awaited him. But rather than wine, he reaches for the alcohol and chugs it down to his unholy throat. The alcohol drips from his mouth, and he looks like himself, a no-good slob. I lay on my bed, vape in my hand, revealing my leg, his eyes set on it like prey. He gulps, takes a step towards me, then stops.

"What is it, Marcus?"

"You have protection?"

"It's right there in the dresser," I point it out to him. He rushes towards the dresser, clearing his throat, stops again, coughing, but a shock takes hold of him. "How did you-," he stumbles. He blinks as a terrible headache disrupts his movements.

"How did I what, Marcus?" I soothingly asked.

"Know my… name," he coughs and kneels down to the ground. "What's happening?" I could see him sweating profusely, fear taking hold of him.

"Silly rabbit," I say, watching him cough again and again, both his hands around his neck, scratching it. "That's poison, duh? But don't worry, that won't kill you. Not yet. It's just a sleeping drug. You need that. I bet you haven't slept in a while." He reaches for the alcohol on the table and drinks it again. "Well, aren't you the dumbest? That's the drugged drink, you imbecile." He shook his head rapidly, trying his best to keep his eyes open, but the sleeping drug took over him.

"Perhaps if you had read the bible, you'd know otherwise: 'When thou sittest to eat with a ruler, consider diligently what is before thee.' You, Marcus, are the glutton, and I will be your ruler tonight."

He opens his eyes, afraid and clueless. He darts his eyes from one corner of the room to another, trying to make sense. Then, he sees me staring at him. "What- wait, what's going on?" His speech is dense and slurry, and a sudden realization hits him. He is hanging upside down. His head is dangling to the ground, his ankles chained to the room, and his arms tied behind his back. Fear erupts him as he starts screaming, begging even for mercy, asking for forgiveness for a crime he doesn't even know of. I wait for him to grasp the situation, for him to understand that he is the fly wrapped around my web, and at any moment, I will eat him.

"Marcus Themly, the judgment is upon you. Your fate has been sealed. Comply, and I may just show you mercy." But my words offered him no answer he sought, so he just looked even more confused. However, having him in that state, the one he deserved, brought a smile to my face. At this moment, his only companion was fear. Three lines of wrinkles were mapped on his forehead, the color of his skin turned red, and his veins unveiled themselves on his face as if his head would pop at any given moment. He had been hanging upside down for a little over an hour, and it made him look even uglier. he looked like a blob filled with enormous masses. The poor fellow resisted the chains that held him. he gave his all trying to lift his body, but all efforts were to no avail as his belly got in the way.

I walked up to him, and each step I took made a sound that echoed across the room. I bent down and got closer to his face, just at enough distance to keep me safe from his polluted, bad breath. He looked at me, and then a sudden surge of energy had him jolt anywhere the chains allowed him. It was his moment of realization: who I was and what he had done. After the struggle in vain, he gives up. "Please," he whimpers, saliva drooling from his mouth. "I did no wrong. I had no part in it. As God as my witness, I am innocent."

"Marcus," I said calmly, comforting him. He awaits my response, hope in his eyes. "Shut the fuck up. Speak only when I allow it, understand?" he nods obediently.

I let go of him, and he swung around. "Spoiler alert! Behave well, and I will reward you. Be a bad boy, and you will die. Regardless, the pain will be there."

And like a wild cat, he bucks and screams, "Please! Help me! Somebody Help!" He cried a little more until he ran out of breath. Then, he stops and gives up. "Okay, okay, you have questions, right? So, help me up so we can have a conversation."

I gave Mr. Haruki a nod, who was in the house waiting for us, the man who tied him up. He stood in the corner of the room where no light reached. Mr. Haruki is the man who knew about this place, about me. He loosens the chain on Marcus but offers him no support, and he falls down on the floor ruthlessly. As he falls down, he screams louder than usual, full of agony. The thudding sound made sure that his arms were pulled out of their sockets. "Stupid bitch! You broke my arm." His cries continued, tears rolled down his cheeks, and spits came out of his mouth. But neither I nor Mr. Haruki helped him up. The two of us only stared at his pitiful state.

Frustrated and tormented, he stops and brings himself up, whimpering all the while. He took a deep breath and calmed himself. "I am sorry," he sobbed in a low voice.

"What? I can't hear you," I teased.

"I am sorry, okay?" he screamed. "I-I-I am sorry. I don't know what got into me. But I have changed. Show me some mercy."

"Have you? When? When you looked into my eyes." I stared at him with my ocean-blue eyes. I was no longer wearing my contacts.

This was the usual practice for me. Anytime I went out, I had to wear my brown contacts and black wig and spare myself from the stares. I hate it when I can see through their glimpses, all saying the same thing: I am a fake.

He bends forward like a whimpering animal, gets on his knees, and continues to beg, but I pay him no consolation. I just watched him beg like a dog, as he is. It's all the same: anger, then fear, and then bargaining, but none of it matters as they all die in the end. He began huffing as if the room shrank for him. He gasped heavily. He looked like a pig and squealed like one, too, a fat, disgusting pig. I couldn't stop myself from thinking of him as pig pork all chopped up into pieces.

"Marcus?" I softly call out his name. However, hate was all that he received from me and no matter what he said and offered, would change that. He was that kid in class who was hated by their teacher. No matter how hard they study for their test, they can't score well. No matter how many times they raise their hand with the answer, they don't allow you to have your moment to shine.

"Would you like to play a little game with me?" I say as I puff my vape.

"Please just let me go-," he cried.

"Shush!" I sighed, tired of his useless pleading. You don't beg the executioner not to pull the lever. Well, how'd I know, and I suppose they do. "Forget it, it wasn't even a question. Besides, you still have time. I am not just gonna up and kill you like that. What do you take me for?"

Each minute to him seemed like an hour and his face said it all, the fright on his face, blood dried on his face, but time after time, tears would roll down his cheeks, and they would dampen the blood. He looked as if he had been off to a war. He knew all too well what awaited him: the game, the fate. There was no getting out for him.

Time after time, he would shift his weight from one knee to another, but he moved really slowly because his arm was still hurting. Out of the blue, he started screaming again until Mr. Haruki from behind grabbed his neck and squeezed it until he stopped.

I signal Mr. Haruki, and he drags him along the floor while he snivels. I guess from the crying he now had a stuffy nose. Poor guy, I can't bear a stuffy nose. He must be suffering really badly because of that. I clap, and the room lights up. Mr. Haruki helps him get up on his feet, his hand still tied, and releases his grip, one that holds his arm and the other around his neck. He struggles to maintain his balance, but in an arched position, he manages to stay standing.

"My fingers… they are numb. Too tight."

"Oh, you mean the strap. Yeah, I'm sorry, I like them tight," I rejected his plea, maintaining my sarcasm. "But hey, look at the positives. The strap around your neck isn't tight or you'd be dead by now." It's not the physical pain that I enjoyed on this animal but the mental. I wanted to destroy him mentally. I wanted him to die, losing his mind, the least this animal deserves.

"Huh, huh, huh," he tries to talk, fighting the mucus and blood that covered his face. I wonder if he could even see from his red eyes. What really bothered me was the gut-wrenching, god-awful stench of his urine that filled the room. I was grossed out, nearly passing out. Still, the fear I imposed on him got me going. It excited me. I wondered if I really was another vicious animal. No, I am different than him. My cause is pure, and this is the only way these lunatics should be dealt with.

"The game is called, 'How desperate are you to keep on living?' Remember, no guesses. You must know the answer. Now, like a good dog, nod if you understand." He nods.

"Good boy," I say with a smile. "Question number One. If there are seven women and one man in a room, how many will leave alive?" He looks at me, grinding his teeth hard.

"All you stupid bitches" he said. I smile at him, tilt my head a bit, and smile again. "Oh, you still have it in you. Good for me. I prefer this over your pathetic cries. Looks like this wouldn't be as boring as I thought." The smile I gave him made him shiver. He licked his lips. I can hear his teeth chattering together each time as if he were thrown outside in the snow naked.

"Is tomato a fruit or a vegetable?" I threw another question at him. After all, I needed him to be sane. I needed him to keep thinking and keep his mind busy.

"*You* should know that answer," he chuckled, "A fruit…something that you women have, a fruity apple-filled worm pussy." He moves forward as if to bite my lips. He is mocking me. The audacity of this animal.   He really has lost his mind. I overdid my bit on him, or perhaps he has always been this insanely mad. Not that it is of any surprise. I can't stand this scum mocking me. At the same time, he makes me laugh. His ability to be intolerably annoying keeps on surpassing his limits to be annoying. I pity those who even knew him and had to put up with him talking. Still, I admire his courage, as no man has ever used those words against me. With stern eyes, I look into his. This time, he knew I had ended my playing around with him. With sharpness in my voice because his cockiness had just suffocated my thinking, and I almost forgot the reason why I had brought him here.

"Where is my money, and what have you done with the child?" My eyes turn to Mr. Haruki as I look at his miserable state. His eyes are swollen from lack of sleep, and his shoulder is dropped. In all the years I have known him, never have I seen him in this state. It's been four days since Carmella, his daughter, has gone missing. And the worry was starting to show on his stoic face.

Please, please let her be well, I thought to myself. If anything were to happen to her, all the blame would lie solely on me. I am the one who they hate, the one with all the money, the one who makes the rules people follow, and the only queen of my empire! So, any pain and turmoil must also be my take. I stare into his eyes, and he stares back at me, knowing exactly what is about to happen. I strike him hard right across his face with one fingernail pointed out, and it leaves a trail of red line streaked from his forehead to chin. I slapped him hard enough to the point of dizziness. He blinked and coughed up some blood, probably broken teeth from the fall he took when Mr. Haruki unchained him.

"Look at me," I order him. He tries looking up but cannot stay still and eventually gets back on his knees. I gently lift his chin. He looks at me through his half-opened eyes. "I have places to be, you know that, right?"

"Yes," he faintly whispers with his trembling voice. His lips are now swollen blue because of the leather straps around his neck.

"Every minute I spend in this hellhole causes me to lose money. Unlike you, time is of immense value to me. I am hateful. There are many things I cannot stand, but none drives me crazy, like wasting time. It broods the evil in me. Trust me, Marcus, I haven't been cruel to you. But what you are doing," I take a breath. "Will make me do unspeakable things to you. Do you now understand the seriousness of my business?"

I brush the bottom of his chin softly with my fingers, exactly how I used to rub my little kitten milky when I was a child. Milky had all white fur and was given to me by my Nana, the only person other than Mr. Haruki who gave me love and protected me from the evil stares of others. Not so long ago, Nana passed away from leukemia, and like that, I was stripped of a little of the happiness I had. I was hollow again, running from one place to another to fill it up again.

She was the first person who revealed that I was adopted and did not give me a look of disappointment. She read me stories and would sneak food to me. She always tiptoed to the basement storage where they used to throw me to sleep the night. Her stories were whispers because she didn't want to alert the house of her presence with me.

Most nights, I would lay in the dark, crying. At first, it was because I was scared of it, but soon, things changed. I found my solace in the dark, but my cries continued because of that one little boy, Patrick. Patrick was a friend I had, and he and I, along with my sisters, would play hide and seek. One fateful day, we were playing hide and seek in the woods while I was counting to ten. Patrick was good and would, most of the time, remain uncaught. That day, Patrick had a balloon on him, and rather than putting it inside his pocket, he kept it inside his mouth. We started the game, and one by one, I caught everyone but him. Hours went by, and there was no sign of him, so I gave up. I waited for him to jump in front of me, laughing at me and saying that I had failed to catch him yet again. Soon, the whole town was out looking for him until someone stumbled upon the lifeless body of a kid, the pale blue face of a boy who suffocated from a balloon.

I remember my mother dressed me in a blue skirt with frills and a black blouse for his funeral. It seemed so strange because, just a few weeks prior, we had been playing by the swings. Now, I was just staring at his lifeless body, all dressed up. His thoughts stayed with me for a long time, haunting me. His laughter, his mischievous grin, his front missing teeth. In that dark furnace room, his remembrance would bring light.

I zoned back in the moment, my eyes on Marcus's body which now seemed to relax as if he was ready to talk. At the corner of his eye, a tear dropped, followed by an uncontrollable sob. "Yes, cry. Let it all pour down from your face." Let guilt consume you. I wonder how many children cried while he touched them. Thinking about those children broke, but I remained composed. The last thing I'd want is for him to think I was soft.

"It's ok, baby," I say to him as I calm him through my empty words and eyes. "Just tell me what I need to know," I asked Mr. Haruki for a towel and wiped his bloody and dirty face with it very gently.

"In the garden by the apple tree…" he whispered. I moved my ear closer to his mouth so I could hear clearly. "Garden by the apple tree. I dug a hole and buried your money there." A smile etched across my face. I was pleased.

"See, you're a good boy. Now, the child. What about the child? Where is she?" I desperately waited for him to talk, but I heard nothing for a moment. Then, he began, "Oh man, oh God. What have I done?"

He starts crying. He moves his head frantically.

"No—

"Look, Marcus," I continued in disbelief. "Tell me. Please tell me the kid is safe." Now, I was no longer cool and composed. Nervousness and fear were all over my face. I grabbed him by the strap around his neck, "Nod. Fucking nod if the kid is ok."

He looks at me, a frown on his face, a runny nose, eyes filled with tears. He shook his head. I let go of him in disbelief, took a few steps back and fell on the ground.

"Holy Mother—Holy Mother of God. Holy mother of God. Pray for us, Sinners," he continued as long as he could while my legs gave up and my mind went blank.

III:
The Existence Was Never the Mistake

The mind, to me, is the ultimate guide that leads to my soul. For me, the heart is nothing but a vile organ that leads you to the depths of despair. Those who lead from the heart are weak and pathetic, as it is the heart that gives hope. It is the heart that gives love. It is the heart that forgives. What good has this heart of mine ever done to me but give me pain? It gave me hope for a better life when, each day, I found myself drowning in a pit from which there came no light. It gave me a will to start again, to meet and find love, to love myself and those I am surrounded with. How do you love when you have not known love? How do you find harmony when everything you have made has only rotted away? My efforts, my redemption, and my sacrifices have all gone to a place that no longer exists. What heart, to me, is an organ whose sole purpose is to pump blood into my vessels and make me live another day. No more, no less. The childish dilemmas and poetic charms of the heart no longer fascinate me. I know as long as I cling to that, I will successfully be able to do what is necessary.

I have lived my life of xx years believing that I had not amounted to anything, that my existence has been a mistake. I looked around and saw people who were living, laughing, and then I would come across people, those I would stare at and say, well, at least I am doing better than them. They were the junkies, crumbled to dirt and bones, those who don't even remember their names. Pitying them gave me a little push to go on feeling good about myself and feel that I wasn't a mistake.

It took me some time to learn, or maybe it was something I made up to make myself feel good: Everyone, every single being, from the smallest of insects to a human that changes the course of history, has a story. It starts with a life, a loud cry, and ends with death, a whimpered, dejected sigh. Stories aren't predestined; they are written, shaped, and formed so others can live by them. That junkie covered in only dirt had his chance, but he found solace in where he is now. So be it. I don't know his story, and ultimately, I doubt that he does too. All I know is that people keep secrets because they are afraid to reveal their true selves. The longer they hold on to their secrets and go on to live a pretentious life, the sooner they forget who they truly are. Soon, they are living a life of an idea that someone else had. Me? I couldn't give a fuck. I don't care to know what society likes or dislikes. I don't wish to know what the outfit of choice is for others to consider me a memorable part of society. I do what I like. I do what is right.

For long, I thought there was nothing left of me, and that may be true too, but I am not gonna end up as the junkie I pity. Along the way, I, too, have forgotten who I am but it is because I had no past. Things have changed, I now have a greater purpose. Fate has me put on center stage so I can tell my story. Do I enjoy it, or is it just another duty bestowed upon me? Now, what do I do? Do I jump in the cold water and save a child that is drowning? Do I jump because a child should live on in this cruel world, or do I jump for myself so

I am hailed as a hero and be remembered for once? Is it really worth it to jump and save when, in the process, I can drown and die and headline the news for barely the next 24 hours as 'the local hero?' Who even cares if I am remembered? What do I do with it anyway? What good is love and care when I am being eaten by sharks?

Whether it is the sharks that devour every lifeless bone of mine or the parents of a child who are relieved that their negligence was overshadowed by some girl who thought hard about her purpose, it just doesn't make any difference. Be it sharks or the parents, when they look at me, all they say is: 'I see you. I know you. I smell you. Your eyes, your trembling hands. The taste of your blood does not lie. The pitiful attempt at redeeming yourself is pathetically humorous. You didn't shut your heart off because the world never cared. You did it because it deserved that.'

Who am I but a twig that breaks off when the wind gets strong?

Yes, but who dictates my life? Who gets to tell me that I am strong or I am weak? How long do I yearn for mercy and belongingness? I have a heart and it beats. I was not a mistake, for I was made different. I have a story. And if not, then I will make one. I no longer lie to myself. I am different, so I live accordingly. I am aware that I must take my journey alone.

This is what makes me feel alive: the idea of my purpose and the smell of blood that comes with it. It sends me shivers; my heart trembles every time, and I become complete. I feel as if a mountain that tops the skies, trees with the greenest leaves, flowers that glues bees and hummingbirds, ocean that has never known oil. It's as if the smell of freshly baked cookies, the ones you cannot resist, the ones that were made for you to take a bite. The more I refrained, restrained, and resisted to take what was made for me; the nearer I was drawn to it. As I held him, I felt the eyes of my prize prying on me, passing judgment on me. How dare they? I am their savior, the one that comes to rid the world of impure.

Why do you hide from me? I am teased by you. I run around the trees just to catch a glimpse of you. What a shame that even in my dreams where only you and I exist, I cannot catch you, feel you, know you. Over and over, I see you in my dreams, your beautiful skin, your colorful eyes, the softness of your lips that run behind my back, yet I can't touch you and truly see you. Do I share you with others? It feels too sacred to be shared. You hide as if you are mine alone, in unknown places. I look for you; my desire draws me near to you, but fate takes you away. I can feel you close to me, behind my back, on my tongue, over my shoulders, under my fingers. It is quiet and somber, yet you whisper in my ear about the destruction of the world.

'You are my love, my strength. come and find me, for I am at the end of holding back this temptation for blood.'

I drift back to my fragile reality, which is grim and empty, lonesome and tragic, hateful and forsaken, my arm gripped around a man's throat, whose face is turned red. Daydreaming has me softened up for Marcus as it has done for me. Once again, my heart has drifted from its job of keeping me alive. Here I am, passing my judgments on him when I have done things far worse than this wretched man. Perhaps it is that idea itself that fuels me to pass my judgment, the idea that a man out here commits crimes comparable to mine. All the same, he is only comparable, but still not me. I have only one rule: no children. Seemingly, it's not the same for Marcus.

I had no more questions, and from the looks of Marcus' swollen-red face, he had no answers left to give. I was raged, my eyes widened, and my face tightened. I breathed exhilaratingly. 'Nothing ever good comes out of anger,' I reminded myself, and I closed myself. I shut my eyes, and there I was, in a different pane, with my love. His hand stretched out for me, stroking my cheeks as I slowly leaned on his warmth. 'It's ok. Go ahead. I am with you… always,' he assures me, and with the bare minimum, I am filled with comfort and peace. My thoughts became linear, and any darkness that shrouded my existence became absent. I opened my eyes, and the warmth was gone as if never there, and so was peace, but my thoughts were now clear. I knew what to do, and I hesitated at nothing.

My nails dug into his neck, seamless and slow. I could hear dense blood pouring out of his neck. I opened my mouth and stuck my tongue out slowly, and each drop made its way into my mouth. He struggled but had no strength left to shed a tear so he hopelessly wailed, and soon his toes curled. In his final effort, he breathed in but could not breathe out. I have destroyed his jugular vein, stopping the blood to his brain and heart! I lowered his body down, and as he faced me, I licked the blood with my tongue and moved it around in circular motions, not wanting the taste to end. It was refreshing, like nice peppermint tea soothing my throat. I placed my mouth on his neck and sucked slowly, having the feeling of not being full. As it hit my stomach, I felt a sharp pain and cramping, but yet exciting!

His now frail body turned cold in my hand. His skin turned into a bluish-purple pale. He looked more macabre than before. I let go, and his lifeless body fell to the ground, barely making much sound. He lay there, still, a single tear dropped from his eyes. The taste turned bitter towards the end while the hint of sweetness was still there. It was the aftertaste sensation that burned as if I drank acid. I felt no sympathy from his defeated face, and only a smile crept across my face. I was reminded that he used a made up name of Micheal at the club. It annoyed me that he used an archangel name. A tear ran down my face, unaware of why I felt such a way. No part of me felt sad for him, but I was overwhelmed. I felt a tightness in my throat. What is happening to me? Why am I like this? Why, again, was I fighting the never-ending battle of good vs. evil? I was tired of my pretentious self. I lost control over my body; I could barely stand, so

I stumbled and fell to the ground. I start to pray to my Father to release me from this evil that has taken over my body.

I put my hands together, my eyes closed. "Father, forgive me for my sins, for they are great. Release me from this path of destruction. Have mercy on me and show me, for I am your daughter, and cleanse me of this wickedness." I prayed for the sick and the weak and I prayed for me, the broken. I thanked my Father for the Heavens so we can motivate ourselves for goodness, for stars so we can look up and dream for greatness, for the moon so we can gaze at it and fall in love, water, and land so we can sustain health. I thanked for what I could thank the father for what he has bestowed on this Earth. In my prayers, my tongue became heavy, a warm sensation filled my heart and my body felt weightless and then a language, unknown to me, gushed out of my mouth. It wasn't the first time it had happened; it usually happened whenever I prayed. I grew up in a church and was baptized in the holy spirit. Though alien to me, this language also felt familiar; I couldn't understand but feel what was it that was being said. In these moments, these words would make peace a part of me.

This sensation always took its toll on me: sweating profusely, light-weighted body, trembling hands, and dry throat, and as always, Mr. Haruki would rush to me and give me what I desperately needed: a hug. My head buried on his warm chest, covered by his hardened shoulders, would always make me feel safe. He carried me in his arms, all the while stroking gently my head, which felt like it was about to explode. As he would take care of me, and as my body and soul betrayed, I kept mumbling my trance prayers. What should not go on longer than some seconds went on for an hour. Prayers are sacred; it is a private moment with the Father, always special and powerful, but for me, they took me somewhere that, for many, never existed. During these prayers, I would come across visions, and just as clueless as I was with the words uttered in a foreign language, these visions didn't bother helping me understand them either. Yet, these visions were serene, beautiful enough that words could not explain what it was. His hand would reach out to me, and I, compelled by the gesture, would reach out, and just when we would rid the distance between us, darkness would surround me, pitch black, nothingness as far as the eyes could see, back to my doomed reality.

I call him Mr. Haruki because he never gave me his name. I wonder about his real name, his origin, his true self. He is a wise man who is secretive, and I never inquired much because I respected why a man of such strength would keep secrets. Whatever his history is, he knows his purpose, which is to help me. But curiosity is human nature, and rather than asking, I just assume things like his home. I assumed that he was from Japan because he once told me that the most beautiful place he saw was Mount Fuji. He told me that he'd trail that mountain whenever he felt lonely. He also once spoke about a town called Fujinomiya and was very highly appreciative of the dumplings that his mother would make.

I met Mr. Haruki on my 16th birthday, one of the most dreadful days of my life. I wish it had been some other day, but then again, if it weren't for what I had been through that day, I would not have met him. It was a special birthday because that day, I was out in the open, abandoned. That damned day, my fears did not lie but came up to me and laughed at me. My truest day, that day summed up who I was: a disgraced burden who was never wanted by anyone.

Rather than going out for any celebration, we went to church since it was Sunday, and no one bothered to wish me a happy birthday because they didn't know it was my birthday. The congregation was in the holy spirit, throwing themselves on the ground and running up and down the aisle. Some of the members were holding their stomachs in pain and crying without tears. Pastor told everyone present to repent, or they'd go to hell. I could smell the intense sweat from some members, some of the mothers breastfeeding their children with a cloth thrown over their shoulders, shouting: "Hallelujah" over and over.

Something happened. Maybe I was angry that no one cared that it was my birthday, or I saw how big of a plaster saint these people were. I couldn't stomach their pretentiousness and lies in the Lord's house. I jumped up from my seat and, as loud as a 16-year-old could, yelled: "Stop lying! You are all lying." I said that because I saw glimpses of their lives, something I wasn't used to as I am now. It was too much for me to process. After all, I was a kid who saw visions of these men beating their wives, some drinking at bars, and groping women during the night. I saw those who mocked the sick for a disease they could not even comprehend. Those who wished death on homosexuals. I saw the pastor staring at young girls, giving them a slight soft touch on their backs, a gentle tight squeeze of their bodies when greeting them, and softly rubbing their hair. He made it subtle and look like an innocent fatherly love, so no one complained, nor any parent objected.

I wanted to throw up, and I wish I did, but I chose to yell. It was a moment where anger got the best of me, and it ended with the entire church looking at me with eyes filled with disgust and scorn. I froze at that moment; those piercing gazes were too much for me, and even my own family being embarrassingly pissed at me made me uncomfortable. Among the stares was the stare my mother gave me, which poked through my body. It was a look of disgust and pure hatred. But I didn't care anymore. I felt the intensity, which scared me, but I was on the verge. I cared no more about her or any person in the church. As she realized I felt her gaze turn into a plead. There, I took charge. I gave her a look, which clearly meant that I did not care for her. It was a look that precisely said, 'Sit down' because that is what she did. She gulped and sat down and then wiped the sweat off her forehead from the napkin she usually wipes her inflated tears. I suppose it was my birthday gift because that day, it was solidified that I wasn't like others; I was special. And being that made me an outcast in this church, I was already a one for my family so it wasn't an unfamiliar experience for me.

Between the gazes, the pastor found his perfect moment to cash on his: 'The devil is a liar,' and there it was, the attention of hypocrites in the responses of 'Amen.' Fighting them all was a lost cause, so I cooled myself down and sat down. I closed my eyes and started praying, and that is when everything changed; the tongue took hold of me, and my body lifted itself off the chair and straight to the middle of the church. And I shouted, "The Lord is my light and my salvation of whom shall I be afraid?" I quoted the entire Psalm 27 in front of all of them.

And then the shocker: My skin turned white, and my eyes changed to yellow. My skin changed back to brown and then white. I realized something was wrong when the congregation started moving backward and getting up from their seats. They did not run but left the church slowly, leaving the Bible and their belongings behind. When I turned my head and looked back, the pastor was against the wall behind the pulpit, holding the Bible tightly in his hand.

I felt my body was on ravaging fire. I looked around to see where the fire was coming from and who I would need to help escape this fire, but there was no smell of smoke, just an unbelievable burning feeling inside my body. I hunched over, holding onto my stomach, and there was this intense pain that made it difficult to breathe. I stretched my hand to the pastor: "Pastor, please, I need some water." Pastor gripped the bible and said, "Get thee behind me, Satan." He repeated it over and over as he started to shift his body slowly forward, trying to figure out how fast he could run to the door. In disappointment, I took my eyes off him, and that's when I noticed my arms were white.

My body kept changing form from white to brown. I was frightened and looked around for Mother, but she, not surprisingly, abandoned me like the rest. I was left alone, a strange creature that was possessed by Satan, as they said. Only pain accompanied me, the irrecoverable pain that gripped my insides and twisted them. It caused me such despair that I couldn't even ask for help, but either way, it wouldn't have mattered. I gathered courage and walked as far as my feet could carry me, but with each step, I felt exhausted. The steps were painful. I looked down, and my feet were swollen like I had eaten something that brought on an allergy. With each step, my feet felt as if they would burst like a balloon. I dropped to my knees and fought with myself to lay on the cold ground with my back, and slowly pushed myself using my back, shoulders, and buttocks. My hands were too numb and could not help me carry out this task. It may have taken more than an hour just to get to the exit door of the church. The parking lot was empty, and other than my own whimpered cries, I heard phones ringing that people left behind in the church; after all, a lunatic was let loose. People now felt more than just disgust for me; it was now accompanied by fear. From the blurry vision, I could manage to see cars driving at an unsteady speed, tires screeching, and loud honking.

Unable to move, I melted to the ground. Either I was sweating too much or crying, but I remember being so wet that I could see my face imprinted on the concrete from the moisture. From a distance, I saw a white chihuahua trotting towards me. It had brown spots on the ears, and the tail found its way to me, lying there in pain. It licked at my face and just took a seat right on top of my chest, turning his bum towards my face as if I were his master or family.

I lay there in the parking lot, alone, on my back, with my head looking up at the sky; the sun was hot against my face. All I could think at that moment was: why couldn't they take me to a park for my birthday?

It was 1 pm. A cloud covered the sun, and for just a tiny moment, a cold breeze gushed over my curled-up body. An hour-long gut-wrenching pain against the tiniest moment of peace felt to be worth it all. The serene beauty of nature, the power of solitude, it was as if a moment made only for me by God, as if a parting gift from this life. 'Is this what death feels like?' I thought to myself, I always wanted instant and painless death, so fast that I could not even know I was dying. But this was a blessing. I also remembered I bargained that if I could not have an instant death, I to be awarded a death where my family surrounds me. I was glad I wasn't around them; I didn't want to share this private moment with people who didn't want me to be part of their lives. This was perfect, a beautiful end to a tragic life.

"There you are," I heard an unrecognizable voice filled with conviviality.

'Is this how the angel of death greets you when you stand at the brink of death or, in my case, huddled up as if in the womb?' I thought.

"I have been looking all over you," said the voice pleasantly. It shouldn't be hard to look for me, go to places where there is no human. I opened my eyes to welcome the angel of death, the remnants of tears to be found around my eyes; it was a sign that my sorrows were over. A tall man looked down at me with a warm smile. He had a handsome face, short hair, a straight nose, and slanted eyes. He had a well-shaven beard. All in all, it was nothing I imagined a Grim Reaper to be. He looked at the dog that was still by my side, "I see you have made a new friend," then he looked at my sweat-drenched body, "Well, what do we have here?" I realized that he was not my angel of death; my fate was being burned in hell, and this was not how I imagined someone who was about to be thrown into the fire of hell should be treated.

I woke up in the hospital with IVs pumping fluids into my arm and the stench smell of death surrounding the hospital. I could smell the stench of rotten meat all around me, which brought a sour taste to my mouth. The smell of noodle soup sickened me even more, and I gaged and looked around for something to throw up into; anything would do at this point.

I found a cardboard urinal sitting on the top of the table that was next to the bed and reached for it; nothing came up except bitter-yellow fluids. My stomach was completely empty. I had nothing to eat all day, or was it now night?

I heard a retch nearby done in a manner to gather my attention. The visitor sat upright for me, the same person who saw me dying in the parking lot of the church. He had a concerned look on his face; his eyes were tired as if he had been waiting for me to wake up for a while now. Someone stayed for me; I never knew what it was like. "Thank you," I whispered very faintly, holding back tears. "Thank you…for bringing me here."

"No need to thank me. I did what anyone at my place would have done," he tells me. Little did he know that my family and people who claimed to be the righteous deserted and left me to die. I clenched my eyes to keep the tears from flowing, but my lips frowned, which gave away what was about to come. He reaches for my hand, "Hey, hey, precious one, don't cry." But his words did not work as tears rolled down my temple, disappearing behind my ears.

"You will be my Aisuru Ko. Don't cry, little one." I laughed in my head. I'm 16 years old, full-grown with breasts and a round butt that the boys like, and he is calling me little one. Men only showed me compassion when they wanted me to get in their car. Maybe he means little one with no family or brain. Maybe he's mocking me.

Maybe this is what human kindness is like. Maybe this is how people show love and care for others.

I remember on his way out that day I asked him of his name, he stopped turned around and said, "I have no name, people have given me names but I don't think you will like them. So call me whatever you like."

"Haruki," I said to him. I once read somewhere that Haruki symbolizes new beginnings, and although I didn't know if my life would change, I did know that his act of kindness gave me hope that there was good in this world. He smiled at me and nodded. He hid his face and went his way.

I was admitted to the hospital for five days and lay there, not knowing that this man came every day in the morning, noon, and end of visiting hours to check on me. They had no idea who I was or who my family was. And I had no idea who this man, who did what a family is supposed to do, was. Nobody came to visit or check on me, not even my mother or sisters. The police went back to the church to ask questions if anyone knew who I was and was told that I was just a girl who would visit their church once in a while. Nobody acknowledged that they knew who I was. The police officer who spoke with me informed me that I was not welcome at the church anymore and that they would charge me with trespassing if I went back to the property.

That was the last time I had seen or heard from anyone, and it's been six years now. My earthly mother passed away two years later, in 2023, from having multiple strokes and seizures. I heard they blamed her strokes on the COVID-19 injections. In the end, she became a child, an unwanted child just like me. On her way out, she couldn't help herself. She had to be fed, taken to the bathroom, and changed. My sisters were responsible for looking after her, and they did so half-heartedly. They counted her days so they could receive her insurance money and start their lives.

I would go by once every Sunday just to catch a small glimpse of her. I'd hide behind the neighbors' walls enough to get a view of the house and people who had surrounded my life since birth, but again, I felt no attachment to these people who were family. I would watch as they laughed and hugged each other with joy, probably because I was no longer there intruding on their happiness.

I did so for about a year, then one day, I grew tired of them. I woke up one Sunday and felt that aside from pain and loneliness, it offered me nothing. I was just used to the pain they gave me, and it made me feel a sense of belongingness somewhere. The questions that loomed: who was I? and why did they not love me? What made them dislike me so much but yet kept me around? No longer seemed so important.

It rained on her funeral. It was the end of end of November and already Canada was having freezing rain, along with light snow. In the end, she felt what I had been through because of them, so for her sake, I was there at the funeral, at a distance, paying her a visit. I peeked my head from the tree with my face half-pressed against its trunk. While at the funeral, the cold rain on my umbrella-less self did not affect me however I was sick with cold and flu for the following week. Little ice formed on the ends of my hair from the wet rain mixed with snow. I watched as they buried her casket into the ground while my sisters cried. They pleaded with her not to leave them alone.

The week that I was sick and stayed at home, I rotted on my bed with a headset in my ears, listening to Whitney Houston's song "I Look to You." This was my favorite song. It eased my thoughts and calmed my chills. There was hope for me in this song. It gave me the courage to get up every day and figure out what steps I needed to push forward to find out my destiny and who my destiny would end with.

Mr. Haruki was there with me every step of the way for years. We traveled searching for answers. We went to Israel, Moscow, China, the oldest forest, Fossil Forest, Indonesia, Africa, and Egypt, and found the city of Cush, which led us to Nubia, the place where we learned of our destiny and true being.

IV:
Year 1270

The tides are high, and cold sloshes of ocean slap everywhere. The wind shows no mercy with its powerful gusts that shake the ship violently. The Galleon humbled itself to a mere bark from the fury of the Sea Gods. Amidst the fumes, a man stood on deck, drenched with the blood of the ocean, gasping for air, for steadiness. His once proud, long-spaced braided beard was now shrunken. As the strong winds beat against his face, a leather strap barely holding his beard together slapped with force against his left cheek, missing the corner just below his eye by inches, the tip of the beard touching his eyelashes and leaving a burning feeling right above his eye.

The Voyage was supposed to be a simple one, ready for battle with all his armor and a crew of one hundred and fifty men; there were two vessels, each holding a crew of seventy-five. He stood there and watched as the ship behind him got swallowed into the water, men falling quickly into the dark ocean. He prayed a prayer in his heart for the defeated: *See you in Valhalla.*

Deep down, regret consumed him. His thoughts, once stoic, now wandered how bad this idea was. Bravery seemed foolish now. A dream of a child that should have slept off. Dreams are dreams because they are distanced from reality. Why would a sane human leave the comfort of his home, abandon the pleasure of flesh and warmth, and voyage thousands of miles away into the unknown for some gold coins, land, and good-for-nothing knowledge? The tales of the great Viking warriors who conquered many lands had spread quickly, and because of fable tales, he had to prove that in his old age, he was still the greatest King in Scandinavia, even if it meant leading his men to death.

The Kraken, the strong winds, the fury of the ocean, the sinners on the ship. The fate seems to be sealed. It was time to conclude the journey and prepare for Valhalla, for the Lord of the Seas showed no mercy, no cries were heard, no promises were respected, and no tales of warriors materialized. Death in the north, south, east, and west. The Kraken roared louder; the King of Scandinavia, now just a sailor, could smell the bones of the fallen. 'How unforgiving is the ocean,' he thought to himself. Just a few days ago. Then he wondered why he lived in the mountains when he could have found his peace in the seas. Now, he was reminded why. When he ignored the cognizance, the screams of those already left for Valhalla made sure he knew.

The Vessel rocked with such great power that it brought him to his knees. His sword was embedded in the board of the ship, holding him steadfast with two hands. He held the sword as he looked straight ahead, thinking of his son. 'Oh, how he had grown into such a mighty man of power.'

Norick, his only son with dark hair and piercing green eyes, a handsome boy of eighteen, was to be at this battle, but as strong as he was, the flu got the better of him, and like a little child, he was curled up in bed being pampered by his younger sibling, Jessica. When the King was bidding his farewell, Norick cursed his luck, for he wanted to join the voyage with his father so that he could learn the ways, the true ways of his father. To see, with his own eyes, how a king fights. Now, at the very least, the King smiled at his son's blessed luck, but a sudden surge of being forgotten pierced his heart.

"I cannot. There is so much the boy must learn," the King cried. It was just a wish, a guilt, a jab at the time for being so impatient. But time never promised anything. The purpose of time is far greater than just a King of Scandinavia. Alas, the apathetic Time had come. To remind the King that his life is to be just another tale that now kids in the streets of Scandinavia will tell one another: a once-great King set out on a voyage to conquer the world. Instead, the sea swallowed him.

The king stood up. Old he may be, but he still had the spirit of a king.

"I cannot leave them behind," he firmly declared. "There is so much for them to learn." As he looked ahead, he knew that the time had come; this would be the last story of this great king, and with all his strength, he stood up and cried out.

"Let me live, oh Great Rán," The King bargained, "You are the goddess of all things, the most powerful. You are the ruler of this sea." He awaited an answer, but all he heard were the brutal screeches of the sea. 'How dare God,' the King thought. He felt sick to swallow his pride and beg the Sea Goddess for mercy. The prideful king brings himself down to a bargain, but he is met with nothing. The vessel spun uncontrollably in the Ocean. He felt sick as the food came up from his stomach. He could not hold it in, so he opened his mouth to release the drink and food he had consumed earlier that day. It was a mockery of him, but now was not the time to think of pride and honor. Now, on his knees, he must beg.

During his imploring, he is reminded of a story once told to him by a slave during one of his many voyages about a great king called

Zacula, the mighty dark-skinned king whom he never had the privilege to meet and battle, but only heard his tales. He laughed out loud to himself and, with great laughter, continued. His crewmen looked at him, thinking the mighty king had gone mad. He laughed at the idea that he almost believed that a dark-skinned man could ever be a king.

"Oh, great and powerful, Zacula," he laughed. "Let me live. You are more powerful than I, for sure."

Once again, he laughed, stopped, put on a stolid face, and said, "You have more strength and wisdom than I. If you—If you let me live. I swear on my honor that I will give you the greatest gift of all, my only son."

The king's prayer was sacred, for he knew his honor was what made him accept that he was the true King of Scandinavia. He knew well, and he knew good, that his promises weren't empty. Right now, the king made it clear to himself that he was not to die a miserable death in the sea.

"Oh, Great King Zacula," he exclaimed, his arms spread out. "You must have children and a daughter to that; who would not want to be with such a handsome boy like my son? They say that you exist, yet no one has seen you. What kind of king are you to hide and never show yourself?"

"Show yourself to me," he miffed.

"Show yourself to me!" He raged, but no Zacula answered. In anger, he grabbed the knife from his waist and shouted to the waters. "Is it life you want? You have taken half my crew. Whose life is it that you want? Here, take mine!" and with one movement, cut his right hand straight down the middle. The blood poured onto the floor of the Vessel. With each spill of his blood, the ocean swept in to clean it off the deck.

"There is no King Zacula," defeated, he mumbles. "It is me; I am the only one. I am—was the only King. Norick will take command after me." The Ship was shocked once again. He raises himself, declaring, "I refuse to go down on my knees. In this pitiful state. Here me, O Sea Goddess! I am the King, The King!"

Proud, he stands, his chest puffed, veins popping on his forehead, eyes bloodshot red. The cruel and unforgiving water smacks one of the few remaining crewmates. Desperately, as the sea readies itself to devour him, as he slides along the ship, he grabs the King in an attempt to save himself, and he knocks the King down with him. The King took a hard fall and felt a sharp pain in his body. He cries a scream of pain. A small but sharp knife he once held in his hand out of anger and desperation was now stabbed into the side of his abdomen. Dejected, he fights no more and accepts his end. With a blurry vision, he watches the rest of his mates swallowed by the sea monster, Goddess, as he once knew it. He takes a deep breath and takes out the knife; the warm blood spurts out of his body, mixing with the relentless water. He feels tired, lost, and, above all, embarrassed to meet his end in such a way. He dreams back to the day he was first crowned the King. A 13-year-old King who was meant to rule an eternity, and so he did, but the eternity for the king lasted only for 45 years.

He lay down on the ship, waiting with his eyes closed to be swallowed up by the ocean. Although displeased by his fate, he felt he lived up to his purpose. He led rightfully, loved his wife dearly, and raised Norick to be a just King. He still wished for the Gods to be kind to him and let him live just a little longer so he could make his son even wiser than he was. The water beat against his face as if trying to wake him up, but his body, his breathing, and his spirit said otherwise. If he inhales, he will suck up too much water, which might let him drown. The water pushes to his mouth and nostrils; it feels as if he is suffocating. His body feels weak. The smells that surround his nostrils are not familiar to him; he can hear something but cannot tell what it is. As he moves his head, there is a gushing feeling within his ears, and he feels a warm fluid running down the side of his face. He tries desperately to open his eyes, but the weights of his eyelids are just too heavy.

He lays there sucking in the freshness of the smell, inhaling and exhaling, taking into his nostrils the smallest oxygen from the air that his body will allow. With every breath he takes, a sharp pain hits his chest as if something heavy lay on top of him.

Nothing is familiar to him, not even the sounds that he struggled to hear. He lays there, and he feels a gentle warmness on his hand, stroking his fingers and a soft voice close to his face. The language is not recognizable. It's not English. Is it the language that they speak on the North Shores? He wonders.

"Valhalla," he faintly whispers, "How kindly have you greeted me."

The warm breath against his face is soothing to him, warm hands rubbing against his body, causing his pain to intensify, and as quickly as he felt the pain, it was then gone. Only for it to return shortly after. Wanting desperately to see who was touching him, he tries once again to open his eyes. He felt comfort and warmth, but his body kept giving him pain. It reminded him that he was still among the savage waters. Is his soul still fighting? "Why must you fight?" He tells himself. "Life is fragile, unjust, and miserable. Let peace be my keep now. Time did me no favors; God abandoned me. I am alone, truly alone."

***

He manages to open his just enough to see for the last time, to gaze deep into the pitiful, cursed existence. There, he saw a shadow, dark, leaning close to his face. He tried to raise his hand as if to shield himself from the shadow, but his body wouldn't allow it, and with a small, cracking voice, one that he found from reaching deep within himself.

"Is this a dream?"

The shadow speaks to him, a foreign language, but his mind tells him that he understands what is being said to him, so he closes his eyes and relaxes his body, allowing the shadow to take full control. After all, he gave up. A warmness rubs his cold body, giving him pleasure. A pleasure that he has no control over. At the gate of death, he felt embarrassed about his humanness. He creaks a smile, faint but real, as he acknowledges his awkward manliness.

The taste of warmth against his lips awoke him. He swallowed what was pressed against his mouth, A tasteless drink, warm but thick, sliding down his throat with ease. It reminds him of his mother when, one winter, he fell sick, and his mother, against his wishes, did whatever the Völva told her to. Though he disliked the drink his mother forced him to drink, he found comfort in the arms of his mother. This moment was no different, except he was extremely thirsty, so much so that when he finished drinking, he yearned for more of whatever was fed to him.

In his struggles, he finally manages to open his eyes with ease and see beyond the haziness. He hastily finishes the drink from the hard, round mug placed by his lips. The hand that fed him is steadily holding the mug. With his lips still closed on the mug, he lifts his eyes up slowly, wanting to thank the person who is helping him. As he slowly moves his eyes upward, his vision becomes clearer to him; the blurred figure becomes known to him within a few seconds.

The figure startled him. The hands that fed him were too dark. To see better, he shook his head, with respect, to pay his gratitude. He smacked his head hard enough that he started seeing doubles. He pinched his eyes, took a deep breath, and saw clearly what was before him, now, with his eyes wide open and mouth agape. He tried to speak, but he failed. What he saw, what sat before him, was something that, in his many voyages, he had never come across. "Who—Who are you?" he manages to say.

The face of the figure before him remained motionless; though inhumanely phlegmatic, the figure had the features of a human. A sound came from behind the figure, to which the figure obediently responded by standing up and backing away, his head down.

"No, no—wait," he said crisply, unable to make the sounds any louder. Each word came out with every swallow of saliva. His throat felt raw and burned, along with the saliva he had swallowed; it must be from the salt in the ocean. He thought there was still the taste of salt left in the back of his throat. This sensation made it clear to him that this was not Valhalla, that his heart was still beating, and that his prayers were answered. He laid back, needing rest even though the words seemed to suck all the energy from him. He felt a cool breeze and turned his head slightly to the left. There was an open window with long, deep red curtains that swayed softly back and forth, not with force, just enough to let in a small amount of breeze. The curtains looked grand, with gold trimmings along the edges, giving him just the fire that burned with small stone-like figures, ones he had never seen before, giving him just enough light to know what grand was. After all, he has stolen many curtains on his journeys.

In solitude, a smile came across his burnt lips. 'I'm not dead,' he thought again. However, the smile that crept across his face wasn't about him being alive but the realization that he was in a land that possessed great wealth. He closed his eyes, readying himself for sleep, a nice and quiet sleep that he knew he deserved. BOOM! BOOM! BOOM! The series of loud bangs jolts the poor king awake from his once-soon-to-be slumber. Against his wishes, he raised himself gently from where he lay.

He traces his step to where the annoying sound came from. Since darkness now loomed in the room, and given his alienation from the surroundings, his eyes were rendered useless in this situation. It became rhythmic as if he were at a pub, drinking and dancing with grand celebration from one of his many journeys. The sound led him outside; he knew this as the fresh night air filled his lungs. He opened his eyes now and was left astonished. The stars were now brighter than he remembered them to be, perhaps because he now, for the first time, truly gazed at the sky. The more he stared at the sky, the darker it became, as if changing colors only for him. He lifts his hands, aiming for the stars, hoping to grab a star and treasure it and boast about it to his people. He smiled at the tales the kids would tell their friends about a king who was lost in the sea, the king who fought death with bare hands, the king who brought home with him a star and immeasurable wealth.

BOOM! BOOM! BOOM! The rhythmic sound continued. He slowly gazed out into the distance, trying hard to see where this rhythm-like music was coming from. His eyes remain stubborn and refuse to cooperate with him, and bring with them, as if a gift, a slight blurriness. He tried to squeeze and shut them quite a few times, but all to no avail until tears welled up from excessive rubbing, which cleared some of his vision.

He looked closer and found, to his surprise, tall figures dancing, shaking violently with every beat of the sound. As he approached, sensing his presence, the sound stopped! And there, for the first time, he focused on the figures—human figures—but their skin was as dark as the bark trees that were used to start a fire that warmed the cold air within his castle.

In astonishment, he gazed, not knowing what stood before him, bewildered by their presence of grand nobility. Their stature was tall, slim, and incredibly firm. The King, who was raised among warriors and was himself a warrior, was in awe. For him, what he saw was handsome and beautiful. The color of their skin, the darkness of it, no black color in his land or his dreams ever so came close. He wondered if he were to explain to his people about what he saw, what words would explain in truth. As he is mesmerized by his thoughts, he gathers the attention of the majestic beauties that, for a long time, the universe had held a secret. As they looked at him, he felt his stomach gnaw from the inside. Something from inside of him wanted to come outside. Was it hunger or fright? He didn't know. The king was scared, being in the land of the unknown, surrounded by a race he had never seen before.

It hit him then. "No, this can't be!" he gasped. He paused in worry, recollecting his memory. "Dark people from the legends?"

His mind wandered from one thought to another, everything that had happened so far. Was it really God, or was it all one final dream, a longing a dead person has, the last inclination towards hope? But if this is really true. If the legends are true. Then, it would mean that he was given what he asked for, prayed, and begged for in his dooming ship. The realization set in that he was in a once-considered childish folk. Fear set in, sweat beads formed on his forehead, and his chest became heavy after all; he made a deal with not a God but a devil. For God doesn't do deals, not unless you are Satan, and the King of Scandinavia was a pious man.

In his fear, he held his head high up, chest puffed as he had done a hundred times before when faced with death—pretentious bravery, not for the opponent but courage for himself. "If this be my death, then I say to it: face the King with all its might, for I am the rightful, resilient, and true. And hear me clear, my enemy, I don't deal in cowardice.

Like my father before me and his father before him," he stumbled to make balance. "Like my son after me, and his after him—" he coughed. "I will go down with dignity and grace."

They stared at him in silence. The fire that burned gave way for him to have a clear vision, and as they stood still, the women were quiet. They had slim, firm, jet-black long hair that was wrapped in two with a gold ornament made of string. He was in awe of their grandeur as they swayed, each one in tone with the other, tilting their heads slightly to the left. They opened and closed their eyelids seductively.

Drawing him in slowly to take small steps towards them, it was hypnotic as he approached without recognizing his steps. They turned and looked at him with piercing eyes that were blue—blue as the ocean's mesmerizing quality of pure essence. Their skin sparkled within the light from the flames, and the clothing they each wore was seductively enticing.

The king approached in sequence, each one bit down on the corner of their lips, which caused a drip of blood to slowly slide down the corner of their lower lip. How beautiful those lips seemed—full of life, with a prominent thickness, yet desirable and enticing.

The men, each with a tiny goblet about an inch in diameter, had gold, rubies, and white stones that shone around the rims. They placed the goblets to catch the blood, and as the weakened state king stood and watched. He was clueless as to what his course of action was: to run or speak. Instead, the king froze where he stood, against his will. They moved towards a clear tub that looked like it might be made from glass. It was filled with murky water, white as milk. The men poured the cup of blood into the water.

And slowly from the waters emerged a figure, as the milky water or substance slipped slowly from its body. As he rose slowly, the king could see small hands wrapped around his neck and childlike fingers, and panic took hold of him. The King's body shivered from fright, teeth chattering as he tried to keep calm in order not to bite his tongue.

V:

The Thrones Beneath the Trees

He glowed as the milk dripped on his body; it felt as if the light came out of him. His demeanor, his eyes, and his body did not lie; he was the man in power, and his strength alone dictated their lives. They danced at his tune, at his words, at his eyes. The children wrapped their fingers around his neck tightly as if to suffocate him, but his face said otherwise. It didn't take long for the King to realize that this was a way for these children to show their fondness with him.

Behind his broad figure was something innocently beautiful, something fragile that was not meant to be touched but only admired. Her chestnut skin was much lighter than the others, and her curly hair fell down to her waist as she raised her head from behind his shoulder, finally revealing her delicate features.

She was seven, maybe eight. Her eyes met the King's, and she moved her head, slowly with rhythm, from one side to another. He was captivated by her innocence and the beauty she held. The children swiftly lifted her up as if she were a feather and placed her

51

gently on the man's shoulder. Firmly, with each balanced step, they moved closer to the King. Curiosity was all over their face; they knew not much of the King, and he knew at this moment they wanted nothing more but to know who the stranger in their home was.

It was time for the King to acquaint himself with the people, as he saw no hope of running. He stood against the pain, but as soon as their presence intensified, his legs gave away, and down he found himself, and again, he was left with his consciousness slowly slipping away. He foolishly wished that all this was nothing but a harmless nightmare that would wake him up, and he would have a laugh at his stupid dream. Instead, he felt the discomfort of his hair being grabbed and his body being dragged on his back. The pain he felt was a reminder that this was no mere dream but his accursed reality: a king being dragged by the hair. The violent grip was then released, and his eyes opened wide, and he, on his back, looked at the stars that glimmered through the dark clouds as if a storm was about to greet them.

The King felt tired, as if he had been there for hours, but he knew only a few seconds had passed.

Then, a will within the King sparked, perhaps his honor, and he stood up, greeted only by stares and silence. The strong man, with the beautiful child on his shoulders, stared as a child grabbed onto his finger. The man rubbed her tiny hand with his thumb.

"Greetings," the King, with a croaked-up voice, said, embarrassed, and he cleared his throat. "My name is Newil."

Newil awaited a response, but all he received was silence and the giggling of a child. The man shushed the child and said warmly, "Welcome, Newil." He was taken aback; the alien tribe spoke his language fluently. "Please have a seat," he gestured the king towards a marble seat decorated with gold trimmings, with eight tall candles placed on the table.

Everything they used and wore did not shy away from revealing the immense wealth it held. An island that was part of a fairy tale with gigantic trees that soared in the skies; they were so huge that the newbie had to bend his head to see them in their beauty. The incredibly thick trunks with their dense green leaves were bigger than his face. The beauty, seen from his eyes, was serene. It was a world on a different plane. But beneath its beauty, there was something sinister. Surrounded by the ocean, the King smelled a strong stench of decomposed blood.

The King, who has slain thousands of his enemies, knew all too well the smell of blood, especially rebellious blood. The blood of those who want nothing but the world, who want to sit on a throne made of gold, who want to make love with women of the finest skin and flesh, who want to breed the strongest offspring, who want to feast on the juiciest meat and drink the oldest wine. The smell of their rotten blood is haunting with doomed dreams. That smell and that blood surrounded the very corners of the island where light doesn't reach. Now, the King, who is no different than the slain, thought: Who kills whom? Who is King now? Who is barbaric? Who sits on the throne of gold and whose blood reeks the corner of the island? Fear takes hold. For all the king knew, for all the king had learned was never to show his weakness, and that was all he did: he donned a brave face.

Newil looked at the leader of the darkest color, who sat beside him, and commanded him to do the same. Up close, Newil admired his sharp cheekbones and his large nose. He was old, but his body was young, metallic, and strong. Among the other shirtless men, he was the only one who wore an emerald magnificence robe with perfect gold threading. His fingernails were oddly long but well-cut and polished. He was calm, and every muscle of his body was in control as he tapped, with a rhythm, from the index finger of his right hand.

He stood up, turned around, and looked down at Newil and, without even the faintest warning, screeched at him. A scream was loud enough that it forced him to cover his ears. He felt the intense pain in his ears as if his eardrums had been exploded. His head was spinning, and it was then that he saw what he did not believe; he realized that he should have remained a mortal king, meant to be forgotten, rather than voyaging across the sea for honor and glory. The guests were lifted slowly up in the air towards the trees with their bodies crouched until they reached the branches of the humongous trees. Their relaxed nature made it evident that they were awaiting something like a predator waiting to close the distance with the prey. Their prey, however, seemed to be coming from the ocean, as all their heads remained fixated on the ocean.

Newil was confused and no longer hid how agitated he was. He cluelessly looked at the ocean for answers until a small gray cloud filled the air coming from the sea. The smell of blood was replaced with that of seaweed; a pungent, musty smell of dead sea creatures also accompanied the scent. From the clouds came a lady, unclothed, with black curly hair with streaks of gray around the ends of her hair, reaching almost to her knees. Her hair, however, was not naked. Each strand of her hair was accompanied by tiny trinkets of gold and red emeralds.

The King was bewildered; was this his end? He kept on wondering. In his entire life, never was he ever this sure of his end. The strangeness of this place, the wealth, and the beauty were the dreams he had when he was a naïve child. He was awake; it was a dreamless sequence. He saw it with his very eyes and comprehended the inconceivable ghost.

She was the reflection of the moon; her image was clear enough that the lines on her forehead could be seen. She looked starved, with big, wide eyes, cheekbones sucked in, and her lower lip sunk in her mouth. Her naked body bore stiff breasts with no nipples and a long, slender waist with wide hips. Aside from her being malnutrition, she looked to be in her early 30s.

Including Newil, everyone silently watched her, including him; everyone gulped at her. Her presence was striking, as if even by blinking, you could miss it. Swiftly, she stepped on the warm sand, and in an instant, her lower body, from the hip down to her feet, changed to an elongated snake-like black body with silver scales. "What am I seeing?" a desperate whisper escaped Newil's tongue. She was different from the others. She could move like a snake, slithering away from one place to another and not leaving any trace. Every movement she made from disappearing into the sand and reappearing, she did so without any sound and in a harmonious way. She was welcomed and embraced by them as if they were her own. She made her way beside him and appeared in front of the man who commanded everything. She bowed and softly chanted, "King."

Newil was no longer a king. He was but a Fisherman whose fate was overturned when the big fish that was supposed to be his prize destroyed his dory boat and now awaited to devour the defeated fisherman. There was only the King in this land, and he was listened to when he talked and bowed when demanded. The snake-like woman had a pleasant voice that, for the tiniest of moments, gave Newil the peace he desperately sought. He forgot where he was and who he was. No longer a king, no longer in the land of the unknown, just a mortal being in awe of God's creation.

The chants began, all calling out 'King' until the King raised his hand, and everyone fell quiet out of respect, but what Newil suspected was fear.

"The promise cannot be broken," the snake-women said, looking up at the King. "With this union, our ancestors shall find their freedom from the curse."

Those who surrounded them nodded. The woman turns her gaze on Newil. "As promised, he must drink the blood for 500 days and 500 nights. He must be placed in the ground of snakes with a seal of blood placed on his chest." Slowly, the people began chanting in a humming tune alien to Newil. Scared, he just looked from one place to another, trying to make sense of the punishments awarded to him for a crime he could not recall.

"We shall drown his soul with our blood," she violently proclaimed. "No light shall touch his face." They began screaming cries of pain and covered their faces. Their cries were in tune; they hummed, then screamed, and they continued as long as the snake women pelted Newil with punishments.

She got up and closed the distance between Newil until only thin air remained. The cries came to a halt, and with a low voice, she said, "This man is weak. He barely hides his fear. Time will only make him weaker. But there will be one... who will love her, and our bodies will be carried to a place of splendor." She traces her steps back to a place from where she can gaze upon the moon. Her eyes gazed out while her thoughts wandered to the day she had dreamed of miserably, a smile of amazement on her face. "They shall cast her aside as if a stray. But for her, I will pluck my eyes out so she can see," her eyes filled up with tears, but they didn't flow down. She looks back at Newil, "Your breath shall be placed within her lungs."

She turns to her people, "We must shield her from the light, for they will search and try to find her." She looks at the child who holds the King's finger tightly and passes a warm smile; she replies with a shy giggle. Her eyes then stare into Newil's soul, frightening him. There, he wished nothing more than to escape, to wake up from the nightmare. Like a child, he prayed to be taken away, but all he could do was to stay, listen, and speak nothing. He thought of running, but everywhere he looked, death greeted him. He was in the middle of nowhere. Hope was now a stranger. She stretched her hands and reached for his face; he shivered but didn't move. Gently, her fingers with long nails ran across his face, shutting his eyes. All Newil felt was fear and something wet on his face. Newil, frightened, forgot to breathe; the wet substance ran down his face. Only after he touched his face and saw it under the pale moonlight did he realize that it was blood.

"Oh, Father," Newil prayed, about to throw up, "they are about to eat me." The once-proud king was now reduced to child-like behavior, on the verge of tears. The hollowness of his chest traumatized him until he felt something soft holding onto his hand. He looked down to see the joyous child of no more than seven looking up at him with a shy smile. Her smile drew him back from the folds of insanity in which he was cruelly slipping.

When the woman stopped talking about prophecies, things calmed down, the king took his seat, and those at the top of the trees descended. The sound of drums resumed, and the fresh air that Newil desperately desired returned.

As things turned serene once again, a wooden plate was offered to him, the sight and aroma of which growled his stomach. The plate had all kinds of meat, followed by two additional plates made of silver, each containing fruits and vegetables. The King was no stranger to poisoned food, so he remained hesitant until the True King ordered, "Eat. The journey ahead will not offer you such luxury." That's all it took: an order and a terrible hunger. While he dug into the food, Newil wondered about his son, his life back home, and a newfound will to escape.

VI:
The Roots I have Not Known

I have not known money; I did not come from a wealthy background. Life, as I felt and knew, was more grand than the thirst for money. This was my belief. Ever since I was a kid, I found myself to be a wise person, a child who thought like an adult, a responsible individual who knew the value of happiness. A kid who knows the thirst for money leads you to bad places. Soon, I became the kid who would worry not about what I'd be getting for Christmas but whether a turkey was affordable. If only I knew that it was not my problem. If only. Then maybe, just maybe, I would have known the mystery, which was happiness. I remained confined to my beliefs and paid less attention to money. I lived by the dreadful quote, 'Money does not buy happiness.' I would repeat it like a mantra until my stomach would growl, and I would feel the emptiness so intense that it would hurt my stomach, or I would pass by a shop, and the pretty white dress would blind my eyes. It was only then that things would become much simpler, and philosophical thoughts invented by bored and broke people about happiness and love started to sound ridiculously funny. I was in between these two: happiness and comfort. Strangely, I had none. I needed both, but I knew fate hadn't ever been kind to me, so I settled for one. Money or happiness, I would ask myself, and I would answer myself instantly: Does it matter?

As if preordained, I knew it. I knew it like I knew my name. I knew my end. I always felt a strong sensation that no greater purpose could ever fill the void in me. That no matter what I do, I would, in my last breath, drown in regret. What a loss to do so much, to get so much, only to feel empty all over again. There will always be something missing, and with that, now, I have made my peace.

Sense knocked into me, and I told myself: If I am to be alone and regretful, I'd rather be rich. After all, happiness is often depicted as fiction in books and movies. I made money, and it gave me confidence that I was right about my end, so I made some more. Then I found I was different, and I made sure I played my role, and for that, I made even more money. It was as if I invented my own happiness. Money had nothing to do with it but me. Giving meaning to meaningless things to make myself feel good was something only a human could do, not money.

Mr. Haruki was an adroit man. He was good at what he did; he always saw a step ahead. I shared my fortune with him; the trust that I had in him was itself ironically bought with money. I saved ten thousand dollars, and the rest was done with the magic of Mr. Haruki, who took them and invested in aerospace and animal farms. I started at ten grand and ended up with millions. Things were changing; it was a new beginning, the past was now distant, and I was forgetful. I dreamt it all, a world of change. This new place in my dream was a horizon, a clear and welcoming one that did not shake its hands with the goners but buried them. It was a place where everyone was equal, a place that did not promise only a certain believer a paradise and rest an eternal flame. In that new horizon, the sun drew itself closer to the earth but did not burn life; instead, it bestowed a shining light that gave them the courage to start again. The moon brimmed its warm embrace to comfort, and there, up on that cliff, I rested, overlooking the neverending bluest of a calm ocean. There, with the world made just for me, I felt desolate, yet I found calm.

I looked over at the clouds, the magnificent clouds with the whitest of white color, not even a spot on them, quiet and motionless, serene. Ah! to be a cloud, I wondered as I flew across them. Appear and disappear whenever they want. They were waiting for the rain so they could disappear again. But it would probably take a few more hours till it would rain. I was fine with the rain as long it happened after my meeting. The tropical flash flood hit the South of Florida a week ago, and people were still in distress. It was raining almost every day, which became the reason the meeting was delayed so many times. Today, at all costs, I had to acquire the land in Kemet. Many had eyes on this place, and everyone was ready to pay any price for it. This meant my position was not favorable, and Mr. Haruki's charm could only work till today. Any further delay, and even Mr. H will be unable to convince him to wait.

I wasn't in the mood for a movie, as I needed to keep my head clear, so I chose to watch the News. It was a terrible idea. The world was in shambles, and Florida was in some post-apocalyptic world. The streets were flooded three days after the flood. Many houses were now disintegrated into piles of plywood. Cars were on the sidewalks and, in some places, still drowned. The report stated that some parts of the state, especially the southern part, which was affected gravely by the flood, were without power, and people were now left in the dark. 'People will do anything to survive,' I mumbled when I saw a man with a raft paddling through what once were streets.

I hate watching the news. It forces me to sympathize with people; I want to deal with only my own problems, and worrying about others doesn't make sense. I wish no harm to them, but the more I know of their trouble, the more my need to help them arises. Now, all I thought about was how I could help accommodate these people through my company. An image zipped across the screen, and I felt a sharp pain in my chest. It happened so fast that if I were to blink, I'd have missed it. I had a yearning to see that man again; if he made me feel such a way for just a blinking moment, then this man was capable of things I am not. I felt drawn to him; it was more than just the flesh; it was something beyond that that called me. I jot down the name of the news podcast: EMN Entertainment Monologue News.

"I need the footage of that," I said, passing him the piece of paper on which I had written the name.

Mr. H, who was not watching anything on the IFE, looked at the piece of paper and took out his phone. "You know someone from this place?" I asked him.

"A few," he answered and began scrolling his contact list. He stated his name to the person on the phone and requested the footage, and the call ended with 'I'll be waiting.' Mr. Haruki knew people, lots of them, from every place. He shook hands with everyone, including those from the entertainment industry, real estate, and politics.

Five minutes in, Mr. Haruki played the video to me from his phone. "There," I said when I saw a glimpse of him. He rewinded. Pause. Play. Pause. Play. "It's him," I said, restless.

Worried, he asked me. "Who is he?"

"The man from my dreams." I had a smile on my face, I am sure. I was blushing, I know. Mr. Haruki looked at me, making something out of it, but he knew himself that butterflies danced in my head. My heart ached with pleasure. He looked majestic, beautiful. I couldn't tell if he was the prince of the Middle East or a gladiator from Spain. I couldn't care about it; all I knew was that he was the man from my dreams. I was so desperately drawn to him that his being anything did not matter to me; if he was a serial killer, it still wouldn't change a thing. No one was worse than me.

He had long dark brown hair, like that of a stallion, touching his neck. His face donned a stubble; it wasn't short nor trimmed. I zoomed in and saw a hint of gray, like calm, thin waves in the magnificent ocean. He had a long Greek nose, which stretched on his face and looked steely. He had naturally pointy, natural, winy lips, every curve of which was vivid. This was the man who had known the sun, who walked truly under it, and befriended the great ball of fire. He carried it on his face with great pride, his tanned skin glowing. I looked closely, and I saw the art of the Sun on his face. The specks of brown surrounded his long nose.

He was beautiful. He was a creation of a supreme being, and I could smell him. His scent was engraved in my brain; it was a garden with no end, filled with every imaginable flower. My eyes gazed at him, and his hazel ones, too, searched for something; they looked into mine. His eyelashes, how beautiful they were, long and thick. On his forehead, he had a few lines. I wonder what he worried so much about. I could see a tattoo visible from the white button-down shirt he wore, just below his collarbone. I could see the ink but not the words.

"The stars and moon are the ambiance;

of the love I so desire,

as they perfectly entwine,

for your presence stays hidden behind the moon in the daylight,

I shall cover you with my love,

so that you may shine brightly at night,

I recite as my thoughts swirl over him. I look breathlessly into this nameless man's eyes. Then, he was off the frame, the color left, and greyness took hold. There was silence, and that confirmed that this was the man I so dearly longed for. He was in my dreams, becoming a part of me. I knew it like an omen that he was the one person my thirsty soul quenched for, to be released from this entity of darkness that took root inside me, the one I battled with every day.

In the corners of my heart, I craved love, a sense of belonging. I wanted to be loved, to be held. Being free of worries was, to me, a myth. And a glimpse of him now gave me a disease called hope. Now, I was dreaming, believing there was something worth living for. It was his arms I wanted to be held in, his words I wanted to be comforted by; with him, I wanted to feel what I once found to be bizarrely dramatic.

But time is running out for me, and the pack needs to be sealed. I shook my head to relieve myself from these distracted thoughts and bring myself back to reality. Is he married? Does he have children? What does he do? Again, what, where, when, how? Every single thing a person could imagine or think about in a short window of time ran through my head.

The phone rang, but I did not answer. I don't want to. I know what the other end of the phone will sound like. I am tired, and I do not have patience for this. But I have to answer. I have no choice. I have put too much into this. I think of nothing else and answer the phone.

"Ola," I say cheerfully.

All I hear from the other end is the screams of a vile person. a loud tone with an unbearable accent. He speaks Portuguese but poorly, very poorly. If I weren't so tired, I would have laughed first.

An African man speaking Portuguese is a rare occurrence. Rare because he doesn't speak that language. I suppose he knows a few words, and now he has massacred that language.

It is considered my misfortune that I do my business with such a dandy imbecile who is just a lap dog for the underground. A dirty profession that gives him the idea that he can speak to me in such a tone.

"We were supposed to meet at 10," he spat over the phone. "Not only are you an hour late, but your receptionist won't let me up to see you."

This wasn't news to me, his tone. It happens every time Mr. H isn't around. It hurts a man's prestigious ego to talk to a woman with respect. They'd be careful with how they talk to a man beneath me, the man who worked for me, but with me, rage takes over. The only time a woman can have respect is when they opens their legs for them. For these dogs, I wouldn't even let them think such filth, hence their frustration. Poor guy.

I reply with silence. I am wondering where Mr. H has been. He said it'd take him some minutes, but it's been an hour, and I haven't heard a word from him. For such a punctual man to be late is bothersome. "Is there something you're not telling me, Iyah?" he interrupted my thoughts.

I sigh. He rubbed me the wrong way. I wait a little while, he annoyingly asks me if I am there. "Yanni," I say. "How long have we been working together?"

"What?" he asked, confused.

"I said How long have we been working together?"

He takes a pause, and stammering, he replies, "Two—maybe three years?"

"Two and a half years," I reminded him. "And in these years we have worked, have I ever given you any notion that confirmed that you and I were equal in this business?"

He remained quiet until he broke the awkwardly unforgiving silence. "No."

"So what gives you the idea you can now talk to me in that manner?"

"My apologies. I got carried away."

This is Mr. H's job. He is good at disciplining these misbehaving kids who forget their place. "Have you heard from Mr. Haruki?"

He said no, which infuriated me. I knew he was lying. He knew what was going on in this city. His being gone without saying much was a problem. In all these years, this had never been the case.

"I'll call you when I want you. In the meantime, behave and wait," I said as I ended the call with Yanni. The office overlooked the flooded, wrecked city. On any other day, the 20th floor would have been nice. Today was not that day. The grey clouds loomed over the city, and I was surrounded by tall skyscrapers. I swirled in my office leather chair while thoughts remained on Mr. Haruki. He is a man who knows how to take care of himself and is good when it comes to a fight. Still, I feared. Something felt wrong, and my intuitions were dangerously true.

When he gets back, I need to tell him that my body is changing. And with that, my thoughts. I feel nauseating; just the night before, I was overwhelmed by the thirst, and trying to take just a sip, I slipped, and now I am too far into the ocean.

The nights are chilly, and something painfully grips my spine and drags me down the horrifying soil where only fire resides. That fire is now calling my name, and I fear it. I don't fear its ravishing heat that will melt my bones, my soul. I fear what it brings: isolation and a painful one. I would assume that, in the end, the place I rest will feel like home. The thought alone makes me curl up and leaves me with an intense, childish desire, almost a murmur of my heart, to be in the warmth of someone. Someone who knows who I am, what scares me, and what irritates me. Someone with whom I won't have to talk constantly to fill the awkward silence. But here I am, alone inside the four walls, wondering why I, of all people, am chosen for a burden so unnecessary, so cruel. Well, it is, after all, a childish desire. No wonder I am left disappointed.

My body is changing, and that transmogrification, I suppose, is what I should call it; it has an optimistic sound to it: a change. Indeed, I am to achieve peace through my demise. My body has been changing so rapidly; it's like being evacuated from the house you have been trying to build after a week's notice. And then, one day, a guy shows up at the door, gives you notice, and demolishes what you have been fighting so hard to build. I guess, in one way or another, I shouldn't complain. I will be free of this marathon that has no end, no prize, and no other racers. I run it alone. It was a useless race. One I shouldn't have been on anyway. I hope death is an end to all; I pray to God for it.

Mr. Haruki is absent, and I wonder if he knows that I have been bedridden for seven days, and it feels as if I have been glued to my bed forever, and every time I, against the pain and a numbing body, push myself to get up, I feel as if my back has been infested with larvae. I check my back in my bathroom mirror to see if it's true and am relieved every time. I conclude it to be just another bad dream, but when I cough up golf-sized blood every day, I am reminded this grueling occurrence is no nightmare but my reality. I called the doctor that Mr. Haruki hired to look after me and take care of the momentary pain I receive every once in a while, but the looks he gives me and false assurances that I'll be good in no time tell me that I am alone and doomed to follow my fate. I hate it, but I forget everything for a while when he delivers blood to me; the warm blood gives me, for just a timeless moment, relief. Then I forget what pains me; then there is no Iyah, no prophecies, no fate, no past, and no future.

The doctor would leave enough blood for me to be fed twice daily, though I found pleasure in my consumption, but my body took no advantage of that. Not anymore. Instead, my condition declined. My body grew weak, and my pain intensified. I would sleep for the whole day and would wake up tired, drenched in sweat, as if I had been running. My throat was always dry, and I was left with this insatiable hunger. My stomach would growl, and there was nothing I could eat to shut it up. Not because there was nothing to be fed, but because anything I ate, I ended up puking it all out. And with it came blood, as if an excuse for it came out every time I ate.

The blood that I vomited had a fresh yet stale smell that clogged my entire bedroom with the pungent smell of death. The intoxicating smell drowned me; how ironic was this end? I laughed at the thought, and every time I did, I cried a little for the pain it caused in my stomach. How rude not to joke at your own miserable fate. The doctor usually paid me visits once every month, but this week, he visited me almost every day. I suppose the more I saw him, the more I grew firm that I was nearing my end. I was getting closer to the fact that my fate was sealed like those before me. Here I thought I was different and that I would be the one to end this suffering, this damned lineage that was bound by some promise which never lived beyond 25. And all for the incapability to find love and have one. To die for love. How pathetic is the idea? I was supposed to live for it, and now I am dying for it. Time mocked me, and love ridiculed me with its alienation. To save myself, I must find love, said Mr. Haruki to me one day. He said as if it were impossible. The look on his face was as if he had revealed a job too difficult to do. I think I laughed, too. How come they never found love? How ugly they had to be to be loveless? Many of me had been reborn centuries after centuries and failed. Embarrassing that I will soon join them and take my seat of shame next to them, and hope the one after me will succeed. But it won't, as the next will also laugh as I did.

Love was easy, or so I thought. I saw it happen in the movies. A glance, a very short second where eyes meet, and the world just stops or maybe collapses. Mountains burst open, the ocean violently crashes at the shore, the wind tears down the trees, and predator catch their prey. It just happens, and you remain unaware; you just don't care for a moment. Worries let go, lost in space. A moment when only two heartbeats and faster than ever, nothing else matters: the climate, the animals, humans, stars, the mountains, nothing. You are reborn and filled with a purpose. It just gets easier.

So would my love, if I am ever to get one, break my curse. Would he, the gentleman who gave me the glimmer of hope, be my savior? Save me from the wrath of the Gods? Or will he be the destruction? If he were to be, then all hope is lost, and I will, for the last time, put him down like I have others.

It is quiet now. I am alone in my office, and no sound disturbs me. Time seems to be still and ignorant of me. I think of nothing as I stare out the window, and the golden rays of the sun embrace me.

VII:
The Whispers that Smother

A month has gone by, and I haven't heard anything from Mr. Haruki. Not a word. He felt silent. Alone, during my sleepless nights, I'd call his name out. I contacted private investigators. But so far, nothing. They gave me nothing but false promises. It was like he disappeared from the face of the Earth, and soon the question would chill me, 'Is he alive?' Deep down, I knew well that he was. It felt weird for me to accept that he was gone. He had a purpose which was far greater than his life and mine. He was well-versed in the prophecies; he understood my visions and dreams thoroughly. He withheld information from me, and despite my pressing him time after time, he'd hold onto it, saying, 'In time.' So I trusted him and his 'in time.' So, accepting he was dead was unbelievable. The man possessed the skills and mind to sense trouble and stay away from it. He knew how important it was for him to live.

In the meantime, through some miracle, or maybe the magic of my pre-ordained life, I got better. I still felt weak, but I was not frequently coughing up blood. I was healing. I wasn't thinking of death anymore. Death'll have me whenever it deems fit. I knew now this well, very well indeed, that despite the purpose I had, despite the wealth I had, despite the prophecy I carried, I, for one, was not in control over anything. I simply stopped worrying about the end. I was merely a pawn controlled by some entity no longer here. And I found it best not to protest as I knew how futile it was. Only the fools fight fate and bend the wind where they want to; I was that fool once. I felt proud of being that fool as I felt the world was at my feet when money began flowing in. I felt deep into my bones the pride of a fool when I saw the fear in those eyes, when I devoured them as they begged for mercy. But then, when I coughed balls of blood, I wondered, is this a payback? Is this my blood or that of those I robbed of their lives? When on some cold nights I could barely move a muscle or feel my consciousness slipping, it was then that I humbled down to settle for a pawn to be the prey of some vicious predator that hides in shadows staring at me with its golden eyes, and all I hear are his growls, hungry ones, mocking ones, that talk to me. Tell me that fool I am, I have been, and a fool is all I ever will be.

Days went on, and miserably, I got better, but I felt even worse. The hole inside me grew bigger, and I grew tired of myself, this never-ending torture and moroseness. I was that annoying baby who cried all night, begging for attention. That's all I ever did: complained and whined with no one to pick me up and sing me lullabies.

I induced myself into business meetings. I attended meetings at Mr. Haruki's place, and as much as I hated them and their conniving smiles and loud laughs, and their overcomplicating jargon to make me look stupid, their repetitious 'I'll take care of it, don't worry about it.' Unbearable it was. I sat in the office, attending to them in groups and individually, their never-ending ramblings, boasting about how they had saved my assets and stocks, and their lousy pitches. During the day, they'd be self-centered, talk about themselves, tell me about their wives and gifts they bought them, and during the night, they'd get flirty; some try to move around in the room, talk slowly, get a bit personal, and inquire what I do in my free time. I hate them, those narcissists standing by the window-glass overlooking the city, sipping on whiskey.

They'd talk and talk and talk until all I would hear would be them mumbling while my mind would dance around about the prince who enchanted me. Most times, I'd just think of Haruki; sometimes, out of worry about him, and sometimes, I would curse him for leaving me to attend to his job. As much as I despised them, I still found myself agreeing to attend these arduous meetings. It took my mind off things. The man of my dreams and Mr. Haruki were still on my mind, but I was grateful I was thinking less of those odd dreams. I was sleeping just fine. That was how tired I'd be talking to them.

Days went on when, one day, I was delivered an invitation to an exhibition accompanied by a grand bouquet of the freshest, reddest roses. It was a private exhibition, very well-known around the world, by Mildred Krasinski, a business tycoon. She had her hands deep into automobiles, but behind the curtains, we all were aware that her billions in fortune did not simply come from shipping cars. She was well known for smuggling arms all around the world. She was loved, hated, feared, and, most importantly, respected by everyone in the country. I never saw her alone, always encircled by politicians. Important, powerful people. Crossing her was inviting death. None crossed, and those who had tensions with her, even suspicions, were either found dead one morning or never found.

Mr. Haruki warned me about her; he told me, 'Greed is what brings down empires, emperors, warriors. Greed is a curse, and Mildred is the personification of that sin.' He stressed that if I ended up doing business with her, that'd be the moment to know that I was corrupted and would soon meet my end, lying unconscious in my bed with a bottle of pills or be found on a shore. Death. Death.

Death. Why does everything point me to death? Why was I born if every waking moment, every word slipped out of the tongue, reminds me of my end?

Mildred had a hobby of collecting paintings from all around the world and time; painting alone wasn't her thing; she loved cars. She owned cars as old as time, pieces that were the rarest and the most beautiful cars that could not be made again. She teased the world; only the most powerful, influential, and luckiest were invited. I was one of those privileged ones, and I knew good missing this opportunity would go down in history as the worst decision ever made.

I still wondered who had invited me; I knew well it wasn't an invitation from Mildred. It was an anonymous letter asking me to join them. I suspected trouble, but for some reason, I was drawn to it, the pleasing way I was asked to join, and how desperately I wanted to attend the exhibition.

I smelled the roses, and my stiffened body decomposed into a mellow. I melted in its warmth. I read the letter.

Dearest Lady Iyah,

Though the ink of my name shall never grace this parchment, I cannot restrain my hand from writing to you. Anonymity is the veil I must wear, yet my admiration for you, radiant as the sun's first light, shines through unbidden. For a time longer than words may capture, I have observed you from a distance, marveling at the way you command your affairs with such elegance, strength, and unfaltering grace. Your presence carries a majesty that renders even the grandest of moments small beside thee. You're an art, a muse of incomparable charm, and your poise is a song unsung by even the finest poets.

There has been no occasion until now where I might respectfully present my desire to meet you to bask in the pleasure of your company. I have often pondered when that moment would arrive, and lo, it appears fate now offers its hand.

On the night when the stars conspire to dance and time itself holds its breath, the distinguished exhibition, *The Grand Visions of Steel and Canvas*, hosted by the indomitable Lady Mildred Krasinski, shall unfold in its annual splendor. A gathering of resplendent art and masterful cars, where the elegance of form and the power of creation meet under the gaze of discerning eyes. It is a night meant for the finest souls, and I, daring to dream, wonder if you would honor me with your presence and accompany me at this most exquisite of affairs.

There is no grander night than New Year's Eve and no worthier companion than you, Lady Iyah, whose every movement seems to carry the grace of the world's most delicate masterpiece. To see you amongst such magnificence would be a vision to imagine. It would be a moment when my heart would be fulfilled. Might this be the moment we meet, where the stars align, and I may, at last, gaze upon you not from afar but at your side?

Should my request stir your interest, know that the night awaits, and I, humbled by the mere thought of you, shall be honored beyond measure by your acceptance.

If you would care, please accept my humble offer. A car will await you at your hotel at 7 pm. I have advised my trusted chauffeur to wait by your hotel till 8. If you care, please join me. I would, with desperation, hide under my guise of patience, wait for you.

In admiration and mystery,
A Devoted Admirer.

On the invitation letter was the date: *31ˢᵗ December*

I wondered what Mr. Haruki would advise me. Given his caution for Mildred, he would for sure tell me against such a thing. And I, for sure, would fight him. I'd tell him that I would not draw any attention. I'd go there with the intention of admiring art and not business. This would be my true intention. To witness the rarest of luxury.

I was going. What could be worse than Mr. Haruki's absence and attending to the ungrateful people I had my business with? I was already at rock bottom. There was also this feeling of longing by this unnamed admirer of mine. He sounded royal and gentlemanly. I was now curious to know who he was.

I had 15 days, and I needed a haircut and some shopping.

VIII:
An Uninvited Guest

Two days from now, I would be in the presence of my mystery admirer, not that I was looking forward to it or anything — actually, I was, and that was what made me anxious. I hadn't decided on the dress I would be wearing, and I couldn't bear to look just average in an event as grand as the exhibition, the host of which was a woman of strength and dominance. She was the epitome of Virago, surrounded by vultures, ready to devour what she had built, but too afraid to make a move because if there was someone more dangerous than Mildred in the country, then it was Mildred herself. Although the art exhibition was not her main focus, this was an event more significant for her for the sake of keeping up appearances, and she did quite well. So, I needed a dress, and I was growing insane because I just couldn't find the right one. It had to be perfect.

My day began with pretty much the same routine that I had been following for the past couple of months, ever since Haruki went missing. I had a lot on my hands that day already pertaining to my business, while not having bought the right outfit for the night that was to come in exactly two days from now was on my mind, nagging me and not letting me be present in the moment. Usually, I would not be reacting in this manner. After all, I didn't need to worry about how I would look because my looks were both a blessing and a curse, and one thing I could do the best, among a plethora of things, was to look irresistibly enticing. But there was something different about that evening. Even though I knew I could wear anything and the men would not be able to resist it, that evening was not about other men. It was about him.

Who he was, I knew not. It was unlike me to get this excited about meeting someone, but something about this person made it impossible for me not to care. The mystery that lurked around this man was not just about his anonymity — it was far beyond that. The moment I laid my eyes on the letter, I felt a connection, an instant one at that. It was so strong that I couldn't keep my hands off of it, and the moment I held it in my hand, I wanted to read it all at once — curious as to what the contents of that letter held for me. It was as if another quest, another wall to break down and see past it. And when I did satiate my curiosity by swallowing every word that was forged on that piece of paper, I could not help but feel an urgency brewing inside me to see the one whose hands have articulated a letter, the words of which seemed to have been coming directly from a place of passion and yearning to see me, to be with me even if it meant for that evening.

Still in my bed, I held the letter in my hand, but my eyes were not on that piece of paper so delicately prepared. My eyes were rather surveying the ceiling of my room. Something about the man who wrote that letter made me think of the man I would see in my dreams almost every day. Could it be him, I wondered, but dismissed the thought right away, scoffing at my own far-fetched imagination. Turning on my side, my eyes fell on the old table clock, which made my eyes shoot! It was already 7:19 am. I was running late — again! I rushed to the bathroom, got ready as fast as I could, grabbed my car keys, and rushed to my workplace. Well, Mr. Haruki's place.

The rest of the day unfolded like any other day would. And when it came to an end, I had no energy to shop around for the dress, so I decided to leave it for the next day. When I reached home, I made my way to my bedroom, hoping to crash into my bed as soon as I was inside. As I reached for the doorknob, I heard the bell ring. Exasperated, I made my way downstairs, wondering who it might be at this hour of the night. Given that another entity presided over me, I felt slightly bad for the one who rang the bell, for I knew it wouldn't be safe for anyone to visit me after midnight. As much as I enjoyed tearing apart the skin of my prey, I was too tired to get excited about it, so with heavy footsteps, I made my way toward the entrance.

Before I could reach the entrance, the doorbell rang one more time. This was more than enough to make my guard go up. Every step that I took after that was carefully curated as if it would allow me to anticipate who might be on the other side. Once I reached the entrance, I swung open the door in order to catch the other person off guard. To my surprise, there was nobody outside. I was a little annoyed. I didn't come all the way from my bedroom door to deal with a stupid prank, but as I turned to close the door behind me, my eyes fell on the basket that lay on the threshold of my place. I looked from left to right to see who had left it like that on my doorstep, but there was nobody to be seen. I could have just left that basket there and returned to my room, but something that lay on top of the basket caught my attention. It was a note!

It was a note that looked exactly like the one I had received earlier, inviting me to the art exhibition. I knew instantly that it was placed on my doorstep by the same person who had sent the invitation, and how could it not be by him when the note had the same envelope and was wrapped in a bow in exactly the same way as the invitation note? I immediately reached out for the basket, grabbed it by its handle, and brought it inside, closing the door behind me. Such a present — or whatever it was- was going to keep me awake, not that I slept regularly. But all my exhaustion was now gone, and in place of it, anticipation and exhilaration had taken over.

Placing the basket on the countertop of the kitchen, I sat by the dining table with the note in my hand. The note was written in the same handwriting as the invitation, but the note did not have as many words as the invitation. All it said was that the dress was from my admirer and that I should wear the one sent to me by him to the gallery. Did he know I was going berserk about not having the right outfit for the evening? Was I being stalked? I chuckled at my own thoughts, and just like that, I slipped into the thoughts of him, the man who had dared to invite me to a gallery that he wasn't even a host of. Who could he be? Could he be someone rather detrimental to me, to the cause? Could it be a trap laid out for me, woven perfectly based on my vulnerabilities? Whatever it was, I could find out on my own, and I was more than willing to do that without much reservation. Of course, Mr. Haruki's presence must have made a difference. A huge difference at that, but now that he was not around and nowhere to be found, I had to deal with this uncertainty and many more that were to follow after it.

The man had gone above and beyond to save me from the trouble of finding the right dress for the exhibition. I couldn't thank him enough for that, but then he was privileged to have his present accepted by me. It was a privilege not everyone could enjoy.

Grabbing the basket, I ascended the stairs to my bedroom. Closing the door behind me, I walked over to my bed and placed the basket on it as gently as I could, as if it weren't a basket of a dress, but a basket of kittens.

As I reached for the dress that lay neatly folded in the basket, gorgeously adorned, my heart began racing, and adrenaline coursed through my veins. Taking it out as gently and carefully as I could, I held it in my hands; the fabric felt soft and smooth in my hands. Every inch of it was made of satin silk, making it slip right through my hands and drop to its full length. My jaw dropped in awe of the beauty. I needed to see for myself how the dress would look on me, a part of me feeling nervous in front of the elegance of that beautifully crafted crimson-red gown.

Once I slipped into it, I found myself flabbergasted at the sight of my own reflection. Its fitted bodice wrapped around my curves as gracefully as it was woven. What was more mesmerizing was how the delicate straps and the neckline accentuated my collarbone, providing an exquisite contrast to the flowing hem of the gown. While it was covered in silk that embraced my entire front, what I loved the most about that gown was the back of the gown that dipped low, reaching down to my waist, providing an alluring yet tasteful reveal. I couldn't wait to see myself dance in this dress on the floor of the gallery where Mildred's exhibition was to take place, but of course, I would do so with grace and allure in the arms of the man I was so mysteriously invited by.

The night I had been so earnestly looking forward to had finally arrived. I was not the kind to feel out of place when it came to attending events and parties. In fact, such places were where I tended to lure in my prey. However, the uncertainty of the night, the possibility of seeing the man behind that letter so mysteriously sent to me and written so adroitly, had me on my toes. I had worn the satin silk evening dress, every inch of which was a blood-red hue. It fit me perfectly, accentuating my figure, as if it were made just for me and not a dress that was picked from a store. He had seen me before, and it was doubtless, but how had he picked up a dress for me that seemed to have been made, keeping my silhouette in mind as if I was present in front of the person who made that dress throughout the process?

Slipping my bathrobe down my shoulders, I stepped into the shower, quietly feeling every droplet of water fall on my skin. I could have stayed in there for hours had my phone not rung. It was as if my trance was broken, and I was brought back to my reality — a reality that I would otherwise avoid, for I did not have my guardian with me. Who was Mr. Haruki after all, if not a guardian for me? Had he been around, I would have felt a little more confident than I already was. He would have given me the validation and the approval I needed to attend the art exhibition. Of course, Mr. Haruki would have had his reservations about having to be in the presence of a woman like Mildred. But then I would have felt much safer, knowing Mr. Haruki was watching over me, even if I went without his approval.

Nonetheless, breaking out of my thoughts, I stepped out of the bathroom, hair wrapped in a towel, body drenched in water, my feet leaving wet footmarks as I made my way towards the mirror that stood tall in the far-left corner of my room. I peered deep into the mirror, as if I was digging a hole into my own reflection. What I was trying to see in my own eyes, I couldn't be sure of that myself. It felt like I was trying to summon the image of the man who had invited me to the exhibition. Perhaps the entity who presided over me could show me his face. Could he be the man of my dreams? But then again, how would I know when I never saw his face, but just his silhouette?

Standing there in the cold breeze that made its way into my room through the window left ajar, I felt my body shiver as the wind brushed against my skin. I glanced at the clock on the wall, and it was already half past seven. I knew the chauffeur would wait only until 8 and would be on his way if I didn't get downstairs and get in the vehicle. I walked over to the window to see the car that the man had sent. There it was parked outside my place, waiting for me to get inside and get on the move for the night that awaited me with many mysteries woven in the very bosom of it. I couldn't take the tension anymore, too, so turning away from the window, I walked over to my bed, on which lay my dress for the night. Slipping into it, I did my makeup, wearing the most alluring shade of classic red that complemented my outfit. And before I knew it, I was standing in front of the matte black Rolls-Royce Phantom.

The chauffeur was waiting outside the car when he saw me make my way toward the vehicle, ready to be escorted to the exhibition. As I neared the car, he nodded his head in an attempt to greet me and then went to the other side of the car, holding its door open for me to get inside. Once he closed the door behind me, he stepped behind the wheel, ready to drive away into the darkness that engulfed the streets. Then, after a drive of 20 minutes, the moment came when the chauffeur pulled over, and there I was, sitting in the car right in front of the gates of the gallery where the exhibition was to take place. Like a roller coaster, thoughts began rushing through my mind, and what appeared to be an eternity was, in actuality, a fraction of a second.

I waited for the man to step out of the vehicle and hold the door for me, but to my surprise, he remained composed in his driving seat. I found it strange how the driver had come and gently ensured my safe arrival at the gallery, but dropped his gentlemanly act when I was finally at the gates of the gallery, and the man may not be pleased with the chauffeur not seeing his responsibility to the end. But when he didn't move a muscle, I figured I was on my own from here and onwards. My curiosity wouldn't let me sit and wait for anyone to come and escort me — at least, those were the etiquettes of that place, so I decided to step out of it on my own. However, before I could reach for the lock, the door flew open from the outside. There stood a man in front of me, stretching his left hand towards me and quietly asking for my hand, while holding the door with his right.

As I placed my hand in his, his face, which was already carved into a smile like it was a crescent moon, broke into a smile much bigger and brighter. Stepping out of the car, I followed the man a couple of steps while the chauffeur drove away. When the car was gone and I had stepped on the pathway that led to the gallery, I finally got a chance to take a good look at the man who had probably invited me to the gallery despite him not being the host. Since Mildred was no less of a celebrity, there were people from the media waiting outside to capture the moments of that starry night with their never-ceasing flashes of cameras. Those flashing lights, even though they brightened the dark, ominous night, blinded me for a moment, making it almost impossible for me to take a good look at him. And as if torn from the crowd, in his safe embrace, holding my hand in one hand while his other on my shoulder, he escorted me inside. It was when we were inside that I got a chance to look at him.

The world started spinning the moment my eyes fell on him. The night could not have unfolded in much worse circumstances. It had only begun, yet I could tell the night was headed for anything but calm. I expected a lot from this night, but nothing as close to what I was seeing right in front of my eyes. How could that be even possible? I kept asking myself. But then again, it was not the first time that something from my dream or someone, for that matter, would come to life. They were, after all, already there, existing in some far-off land, but never did I expect what or whom I saw in my dream to come to see me right in my face. How could it be possible for me to see the same person, first in my dream, then in the videotape of my aunt's husband, and now right in front of my eyes, as the man who invited me to this exhibition? I wasn't the kind to get scared easily, no! Nobody could affect me in a way that I would feel my world was crashing down, but the one who stood right in front of me was making me feel all sorts of emotions.

From feeling happy and relieved to see him standing in my presence to feeling a burning rage and wave of sadness, I felt every emotion there was in the book. It was as if I was looking at someone whom I held dearly to me while I hated that person from the deepest core of my heart. My head was indeed spinning, and I felt I would throw up as I felt my stomach churning. I thought I was going to pass out. It was a sight so horrendous that it made me feel that way, but it was the strong connection I felt towards him. Even though I found myself in his presence for the first time ever, well, at least physically, I couldn't help but feel that the connection so magnetic I could feel with him in that moment was a bond created long, long ago. It was as if I had known this person all my life and admired him for no apparent reason, yet hated his guts at the same time. It was a blend of several emotions that I was made to feel even more intensely than someone else would, because of the entity that presided over me. It was only natural for me to want to run away, but then I wasn't the kind who would give up without getting all the answers. And I was about to get the answers that I wanted, no matter how and by whatever means necessary.

Eyes beaming with fire, I fiercely looked at the man standing next to me and turned my torso towards him as if I was about to unleash on him all the storm that was brewing inside of me.

"Iyah, don't you look amazing, young lady?"

The voice came out of nowhere, stopping me dead in my tracks. This was yet another unexpected meeting. How many more surprises await? I wondered.

IX:
What Lies Behind The Face

The words struck like lightning and thunder. All these months, I had been looking everywhere I could to find him. Yet he remained away from my sight. No stone was left unturned. Every natural and unnatural method was employed in order to get my hands on him. However, no matter what I tried, I could not get so much as a hint of him. And there he was, walking towards me, tearing through the crowd, making his way towards me, taking each step in his usual, calculated manner, as if it was not a stride he was taking but a strategic move he was making. I was already struggling to keep the storm under control that was forming deep within me, and now, when he was there right in front of my eyes, I could feel it in my deepest core that I was losing to that storm building within me. It was only a matter of time before everything was going to come crashing down. And I could not help but feel thrilled at the idea of unleashing the beast that dwelled in me. Oh, what fun would it be!

"My, my! Look at you. Aren't you a beauty?" said the voice again. The voice belonged to none other than the man I had been looking all over, but the man who vanished into thin air, not leaving any trace behind.

"Well, well, if it isn't Mr. Haruki," I said, with a smile depicting my displeasure.

"I can see the woman is not pleased to see me," said Mr. Haruki, taking one more step towards me, smiling.

"Freeze where you are, or else there will be consequences."

The moment my eyes fell on Mr. Haruki, I became completely oblivious to the presence of my mystery man. I was not even sure if he really was my mystery man, but he was the only one who acted like I was his guest. Like he knew I was coming, and besides, he didn't seem to be an errand boy. By the looks of it all, he was the man whose hands had meticulously crafted a letter so beautiful and charming that every word dripped with the gallantry that the author possessed. The whole time was spent in anticipation of him being in front of my eyes, and when he was — and ever since he was, there was hardly any moment of intimacy, of exchanging words. It was as though everything was plotting against me getting to know him. Like it was a sign, a warning, or could it be a conspiracy of the curse that I bore for all these years, and may perhaps carry it with me to my grave, that kept me from finally building a connection that was solely woven with unpretentious love with no catch whatsoever?

Whatever it truly was, only time would tell, and right now it wasn't the time. I needed a chance to get closer to this person who had invited me here, a place that I was going to, which would make me bear strong resistance from Mr. Haruki. But he could not stop me, could he? How could he have stopped me from doing so when he was nowhere to be seen? A lot was happening in those brief moments. Before I could take a good look at him, the paparazzi got in the way. And even though he was right by my side, I could not see his face. A word to him, I could not speak. I must admit, I had been patient. It is, nonetheless, not one of my strong suits, yet here I was, waiting unwearyingly for the moment to present itself when I would not only speak with him but would also get a chance to take a good look at him. But who was I kidding? Amidst the chaos of people coming and flooding the hall where, at any moment, the exhibition was to take place, not to mention the unsettling feeling within me — a beast impatiently waiting to be unleashed — my own patience was wearing thin. I needed to know this man, but what more obstacles were there for me to cross in order to get to know this man, or even have a moment of luck to have a good look at him? For even though he stood inches away, I could not give him my attention. For quite some time, I could not even tell what he was doing all this while, when I was struggling to contain my anger towards Mr. Haruki.

Mr. Haruki chuckled at my remark and, taking another step forward, threw his arms around me to take me in his warm embrace. The man knew for sure how to calm the storm that brewed in me, no matter what the reason might be.

"You seem to have done a great job looking after yourself, I must admit," said Mr. Haruki, still having his arm wrapped around my shoulders.

I could not stop my lips from transforming into a crescent moon, and Mr. Haruki found the crack in the wall he was looking for.

"There, there, it is! Don't pretend to be mad at me when you can't keep up with the appearances, Lady Iyah!"

And there was yet another chuckle by Mr. Haruki. The tension in the atmosphere did lighten up a bit. It was enough to get my attention to come back to the hall we were standing in. While the horizon of my attention broadened, the man whose invitation had brought me here disappeared.

When I saw Mr. Haruki, I almost forgot all about him. Almost abruptly, my entire attention shifted from the man standing next to me to the man who was taking his strides toward me from another corner of the hall. Seeing Mr. Haruki made my head go spinning around. I was like, what the fuck?! He had been missing, for only God knew when and where he had been—nobody had any clue. Hell, I could not even use my instincts and the "special" powers I had because of the entity residing in me. And here he was, attending an event he would not let me attend had he been here. As it turned out, he was already here, but I could not see him. Just how he was here and where he had been, I could not understand. I could not find out. Of course, my attention shifted from my secret admirer to Mr. Haruki, who went away somewhere I could not reach. Now he was there, acting as though nothing had happened, and everything was the same as before. No, it was not. I wanted him to explain. There was a lot I wanted to ask him, and I would if he stayed any longer than a couple of minutes and if those minutes were not spent looking for that man, who was now nowhere to be seen.

When he was standing next to me, I could not help but feel anger towards him. It was as if there was an urge to fight with him, punch him, knock him down, but at the same time, hug him, fall in his embrace, and cry my eyes out, letting years of trauma and pain out. Now, he was gone. He may still be somewhere in the hall, but in that moment, he was no longer standing next to me. Could he have felt left out when Mr. Haruki decided to show up? Could he have found it offensive for me to completely disregard his presence and act like he did not exist? Could Mr. Haruki have threatened him in any way? Was he too taken off guard when Mr. Haruki appeared? Several questions were flooding my mind. I was growing agitated, anxious, worried, and restless all at the same time. The tension grew to a point where it started showing on my face. I turned my head from left to right and right to left. There were people, beyond my capability to count. Many men were dressed in black, and I could not even get a good look at him to tell from behind if it was him. I did not know where to look for him, and that uncertainty was driving me crazy.

I wanted to still take my chances and look for him, while my pride made me freeze in my spot. Before I could focus on the dilemma I was in, my thoughts were interrupted by Mr. Haruki. He had always been the man I could count on, despite his recent disappearance. Though I was not sure whether he was going to help me find him or if it was because of him that the man disappeared.

"Mr. Haruki, there is a lot I need you to answer me, but first…"

Before I could finish my sentence, Mr. Haruki, nudging my elbow, caught my attention and, using his eyes to navigate through the room, he signaled me to look at a man standing by the bar, his right hand in his pocket, his left, grabbing onto a round glass of red wine.

"There he is. The one you are looking for, Lady Iyah," said Mr. Haruki, with a smirk on his face. At that time, I could not tell if that was a good smirk or a bad smirk. But now was not the time to focus on Mr. Haruki's lips. I needed to be in the presence of that man — the man who had been no less than a magnet for me. There was a strong urge to find him and … and do what? Well, back then, I could not tell myself what exactly I wanted to do with him, to him. All I wanted, in that moment, was to find him. And I did.

Shifting my torso in such a way that I was now directly facing him, with his back toward me, I was just about to take my first step toward him when he suddenly paused what he was doing. From where I was standing, I could tell he was pouring himself another glass. Not continuing to pour anymore, leaving his glass half-filled, he looked to his side, and that was when I was able to see, for the first time, his jaw, a sharp, clenched jaw that soon twitched a little. Holding his glass and the bottle in his hand, the way he was while he was pouring wine, he turned on his heels. The distance was much between the two of us, but when he turned, his eyes caught mine. It was as though he had already sensed I was looking for him, and now that he found me fully attentive, he was ready to show himself to me.

"Looking for someone, Miss?"

He did not speak those words — at least not from his mouth. We were still standing far enough for the people to pass. He was far enough for me to see him, but not close enough for me to hear a word he'd say, but I could still hear him. The room was noisy. There was a lot of chatter, and of course, people were coming and going. There was a clanking of glasses and utensils. Every sound had grown louder. I could hear someone whispering from a mile away. I could not understand how he knew about this because he was making good use of this ability of mine, and he was communicating with me. There were words. There was just no sound. Did he know about me? Of course, he did. How else would he be able to pull such a stunt without fearing for his life? He sure knew a great deal of things about me. There was no other explanation. There was no possibility other than that the man knew about my… well, my powers. He was brave and bold. I must give him that. It required a massive amount of courage to communicate with me, not through the natural, human ways of communication. If he knew that, he sure as hell knew a lot more. But how much more, that I had to find out for myself.

I must admit, the adrenaline rush of that moment increased the thrill I was feeling before. I wanted to see how far he would take this. He wanted to play a game. I was up for it. I wanted to see how good he could be at this charade. But then I had to be very careful because if he could communicate without uttering a single word, then there was a strong probability of him having the skills to read my thoughts, and that was where it could get tricky. That was where it had the potential to go south and wild.

I was still not fully trained to keep my powers under my thumb. There were a great deal of things I was still learning, and with someone out there, aware of what I was capable of, without us knowing him — the stranger — by us, I meant Mr. Haruki and me, a lot could go wrong. I was drifting away in my thoughts at that moment, and by the look he had on his face, he might not have gotten a hold of the entire thought, but the piece he did get made him talk more.

"So, what have you got on your mind, Miss Iyah?" he ended his question with yet another smirk.

"Who are you? And is this how you plan to spend the evening?" I needed him to see that when it came to flamboyance, I was a better player.

That's it! No more quiet communication. No more silence. No more distance. He placed his glass on the bar counter, and as I turned my back towards him, I could hear his footsteps approaching. I let my mouth form a crescent-like smile, and before I could place my glass of wine, which was courtesy of Mr. Haruki, I felt a hand reach my back, slowly making its way down to my waist. Grabbing my waist with a touch that felt almost like a feathery one, he came closer and whispered in my ear, "Haruki is right. You are indeed a true beauty."

A chilling sensation ran down my spine, making me flinch — only slightly. I was not the kind of target that could come without a fight, but was he there for a fight? I could not make up my mind about it because the closer he got to me, the calmer my inner demon became. It was as if he had an antidote to the poison that was brewing inside. It was as though he was the sight for a sore eye. He was playing a game, and there was no doubt about that. But was he playing that game from the other side of the fence, or was he someone who just made his entrance in my life like a ray of sunshine after a heavy rain?

The night went on, and I found myself in his presence. His presence did not come alone, but it was accompanied by anticipation. There was a surge of emotions. There was a lot that was going on that night. It was undoubtedly chaotic, but amidst that chaos, there was a serenity about the whole debacle. What else could it be if not a debacle when everything that I had learned so far, acquired so far, the walls that I had built, taking years for their thick, concrete structure — it all stood on the verge of collapse. I was not blind! No, don't expect me to be one. Nor was I naïve to fall for just anyone I would find myself in the arms of. I had been with men before. They had been nothing more than prey to me. There existed no bond between a man and me other than a bond that a predator has with its prey. That was what a man was to me — a prey. And I was there for a reason, so how could I have allowed myself to get carried away? I didn't, or did I? It's hard to tell.

What I can tell you is how that night unfolded further, and the person who kept my inner beast, the monster quietly presiding in me on the edge, was the man who invited me there. It was because of him that I was attending an exhibition that I would have otherwise avoided. I may have felt tempted to join, given the hostess was a troublemaker, and nothing would make me thrilled than an encounter with troublemakers. However, Mr. Haruki, in a normal set of circumstances, would have kept me from going, but then he was nowhere to be found. And then he suddenly showed up at the same event he would have fought with me to keep me from attending.

Now, coming back to the events of that night, there isn't much to say because, honestly, nothing much happened. But while I tell you this, know that even when there was nothing happening for the world around me and Caleb — yes, that's what his name was — a lot was happening in our world. Yes, our world! We had in what was no more than a couple of hours, an eternity. At least, that's what it felt like to me. While the night unfolded in the norms of the daily and the usual, I found myself in a world totally beyond my imagination, something way out of anticipation.

He told me his name was Caleb. For the first time in my life, I felt I had found someone I could rely on, but as he continued to tell me more, dig deeper into my soul, I could feel there was something that was not as it seemed or as he was trying to portray. Imagine you meet someone at an event, that person is not hosting, but takes the liberty to not only invite you but also move around the place as if it were his own. That night, he made me drop the wall that I had built around myself. It took years' worth of work to build those walls, and he had some charm about him that, very effortlessly, he was able to make me drop those walls, one by one. In the midst of the comfort that he provided, while I allowed myself to unravel my life in front of him — of course, holding back a few details here and there — he kept his story all to himself. Yes, there were bits and pieces about his life that he shared with me, but the more he told, the more it felt like he was holding back. He did make me feel like he was the one I was looking for, even though there was no one I was looking for. But being in his presence almost instantly made me feel that he was the one I needed.

Whatever it was, Caleb was not showing me who he really was. There was something he was holding back, but what it was, I could not tell at that time. What worried me more was that in just one meeting, he and I had grown a little too close for those who met each other for the first time. Days went by, but there was not much that I heard from him. There were, however, times when his thoughts would cross my mind. There were times when I would naturally start having a conversation with him in my head. It was as if he was communicating with me in the same manner as he was doing that night. Then, one day, while I was standing by my window, enjoying a midsummer night wind, I saw him standing outside my place. Things were about to take a turn. For good or for bad, I could not tell.

X:

I Know You

That night, as he stood on the lawn, I just watched him from afar. Was it too early for me to invite him inside? But then… was he someone who needed my permission? I stood by the window for what seemed like an eternity; he adhered to the same spot where I first found him. He did not take his eyes off me. Not even for a brief moment. It was as though his gaze froze on me, and as the night grew colder, the gaze became more and more intense, the ice having no chance of melting anytime soon. At some point in the night, one of us had to move from whence we stood. I did not know who'd give in first. I continued to stay in the focal point of his gaze. I stayed there, not moving an inch, watching him as he watched me. There was something about the way he looked at me that did not want me to look away. What was it? I could not tell. But something about it made me feel… different. Did I enjoy it? This was yet another thing I was not sure of.

I had always relished the feeling of being someone with an upper hand, someone who had the power to call the shots. I loved how my prey — which was mostly the case unless I was in Mr. Haruki's presence or one of my close people — would feel a tense sense of uncertainty. But this time, it felt different. Who was the hunter and who was being hunted, I could not tell. Besides, there was some other reason why it was peculiarly satisfying to be watched by him. His eyes were lingering over me, his gaze burning my skin. It was the thrill of the chase that made me feel a heightened sense of exhilaration, but this… what this really was, I could not put my finger on, and then suddenly, I was hit — hit by a realization.

Did I not believe until now that I had complete control over this entire fiasco? Yeah, well, I could not have been more wrong. I stayed there for how long, I cannot remember, but while I stayed there, not even a muscle was moved. It felt like I was in a trance. Now, I do know there were many superstitious things happening, and many a creature was lurking in the dark, some in my favor, most against me, but what I was experiencing at that moment was something I had never felt before. Was I intoxicated? No, it did not feel like I was intoxicated. My head was still clear, but it was focused solely on one thing and not on anything other than that. That thing being Caleb. What seemed to be an eternity must have been no more than a couple of hours because even though I was not looking, I could still tell that it had been no more than three hours since midnight struck.

This encounter with him was strange in ways unimaginable. Every single thing about it defied reality, rationale, and reason. But then, what was there in my life that ever aligned with reality or scientific reasoning when I was, after all, living a life that people read about in books in the face of fiction? Nobody could have believed the things I had been experiencing ever since I opened my eyes to the world — the human world. I was standing there, free seemingly, but I was no less than a prisoner, his eyes being the bars in which I was captivated. What did he hope to get out of this, I could not tell. Why did he make me freeze like that? At first, I thought I did not move because I was so deeply held by his gaze that I could not muster enough energy to even flinch. Soon, it dawned on me that I could not make a move even if I wanted to. I stood frozen in my state, and in that particular state, I was hit by the realization that I did, in fact, want to move from the spot I was standing in. However, I could not.

The moment he saw that I was beginning to realize what was happening to me, he felt exhilarated, as though he was finally achieving what he had been planning. From the distance that was there between us, it was not humanly possible to make out clearly what expressions the other person had on their face. However, it was different for me — and for him as well. I could see his face gleaming in the dark, though there was no glow. His face, which had been straight for all this while, now suddenly began to shape into a curve. He was smiling — a smirk, it was. Was it something evil he wished to gain from all this, or was it my attention that made him smile, I could not tell for sure. I was not sure. And that scared me. This man had already been someone difficult to read. Never, in his presence, did my instincts work appropriately. My heart would skip a beat, sure, but with the racing of my heart, there came no other feeling, making it impossible for me to understand whether I felt excited and thrilled in his presence or if it was a response from my body, trying its best to alert me.

Suddenly, the distance between me and him was reduced to none at all. How did he do that? He was standing too close to me. When did he come here? I did not take my eyes off of him even for a second not even a split second at that. Then how come I did not see him coming into my room, standing face-to-face, right across from me? It was all very confusing, and I must admit I was beginning to feel adrenaline rush through my veins. Was I losing control? No way! I could not let that happen. I must not lose control over this situation, no matter what it takes for me to regain control.

Now that he was standing in my room, I wanted answers. And a lot of them, for that matter. As I took a breath in, I noticed the little distance that was there between us after he came into my room; it was now reducing even more. He was closing in on me. He came so close to me that I could feel his breath on me. However, that did not stop him from coming even closer than that. Was there any space left for him to cover? I was surprised how I did not even flinch, and there it was — the realization of it all. I could not move, not because I was captivated by his gaze, enjoying the warmth of it falling on my cold body. I could not move because I was captivated by him — quite literally.

He did something. Was it a spell that he'd cast on me, making me unable to move? Was it an effect of something I ate? Wait a minute! Was it the apple? No, there was no apple, nor was it an effect of something I ate. It was him. He had imprisoned me without even putting on me shackles that had physical existence and the shackles the naked eye could see. It was the shackles he had put on me through his gaze. For the first time in a while, I could see the places shifting, the tables turning. The one who had been hunting for all this while, it felt like now that was being hunted. Had I got myself into trouble — yet again?

The atmosphere in the room grew tense, and I could feel fear creeping into my head. Oh! My head! I could not let him sneak a peek into my head. As I was preoccupied with my thoughts, I heard a chuckle. And it came from him.

"I see I have frightened you, have I not?" said Caleb with a smirk so cunning that it made me shift, but only in my head, for I could not move, not even for an inch.

Then, as though continuing to read my thought, he began, "You want me out of your head, don't you?"

It was said so softly that I could barely make out his words. But then, ever since he showed up, when did we ever need words said out loud for us to communicate? Even though I did not want him intruding on my thoughts, I needed to talk to him, and now that he was already in my head, I might as well use that to my advantage.

"What do you think you are doing?" I did not really say these words, but by now, you already know how he and I had been conversing all this time. There came no response but a chuckle.

"I am a great teacher, Iyah. Am I not?"

Deep down, I knew what he was talking about. He knew for sure I struggled to control my powers. A lot of them, I was still learning how to navigate through, communicating telepathically being one of them. However, there was no way I was going to let him take the credit for it. According to him, he was "teaching" me how to make use of my abilities for my own advantage. No, he was not! he had no idea what I was capable of. Hell, even I was not, but I was not going to let him use that for his own benefit. Now that he was already in my head, I decided to make use of this chance to talk to him and ask him questions that had been building up inside me for a very long time.

"What questions might those be, Iyah?" said Caleb, laughing again, only this time it was a sinister one. "There is no escape from here. There is no way to go," he continued. His words did not say it all. There was more to it than he told me, and I knew what it was. That's when fear — sheer fear took over me. That's when it dawned on me that he was right. He was right when he said that there was no escape.

"I am right about one more thing, Iyah," he said, looking deep into my eyes, his gaze piercing through mine. "Tonight will be the end of it all. It will be the end of you."

As the last words escaped his mouth, his eyes turned black. His pupil had grown to a size thrice its original with no hue in it — no nerves whatsoever. Just the hollowness of it all. The hollowness of the night, the hollowness of his… soul. While I still remained unable to move, my body began to shiver as chills ran down my spine. The room that had moonlight peering through the windows had now gone completely dark. There was smoke all over the place. When did the fire take place? It never did. It was not fire. It was not the smoke that would be produced by a fire. In fact, there was no smoke. It was the darkness of his soul that had engulfed the room in its entirety.

"Tonight, will be the end of you, Iyah," said Caleb as he took a step back and slid his hand in his jacket. He reached out for something. When he took his hand out, what he held in his hand instantly made me believe his words. Yeah, it was definitely going to be the end of me.

Caleb held in his hand a blade that matched no other. It was so sharp that a feather would split into two halves if it were dropped on it. The length of the blade was no less than the length of a palm, and the handle of it was equally long. Sleek and sharp, it was no ordinary blade, for it was a knife that the world first saw its glimpse three centuries ago. As far as its capabilities are concerned, the dagger could slit through your soul, be it human or a creature of another realm. And if the blade was struck in your neck or your heart, your soul would shatter, and there would be absolutely zero chances of you getting another chance at life. This meant no resurrection.

"There it is. There it is, the horror you have been seeing all your life in others as you stand between them and death, only to remove yourself in the most painful of all manners. How does it feel to be on the other side of the blade?"

His words cut deeper than a knife would. But now was not the time to think about the emotional pain. I needed to figure something out — and quick! "Do you think you have any chance of escaping?" He asked. It was rather rhetorical.

Raising his hand in the air, in which he held the knife, he threw his hand at me in order to strike. Just as the blade was about to land on me, a hand came from nowhere, grabbing Caleb's. I was rescued. Needless to say, I was still under the influence, whatever it was that made me unable to move a muscle. I was relieved, and suddenly, I felt I could move again. I surely owed my life to the one who saved me, but then who was he? When the person did show his face, not even in my wildest imagination could I have expected him to be my rescuer. And for all the right reasons.

Coming back to my senses, the first thing I saw was Caleb struggling to get his hand free from the grip of my rescuer. As they were struggling with each other and since the room was dark, I struggled to see who it was who came to save me. In the midst of the chaos, Caleb somehow managed to get his hand free from the grip of the other person. Then, pushing that person away, Caleb made his way to the window in an attempt to get out of there. I did not see Caleb jumping or leaving or even flying, for that matter, so how he left my room was something I could not tell. There was no way I could. Relieved that he was gone, it was now time for me to thank the one who came to my rescue. Meanwhile, the room had come back to life. Even though the lights were off, the moonlight resumed to peer through, making the room light up, providing it with enough illumination for me to see things around in my room.

Thinking that I owe my gratitude to the one who saved me moments ago, I turned around to see the man's face. What my eyes saw was something I could not believe. Standing in front of me was not a creature from some other realm, nor was it Mr. Haruki who had saved me a thousand times before. It was not one of my minions whom I had retained over the course of time in order to save myself from any surprises — not that I needed any rescuing from surprises of any sort until tonight. It was a man in his mid-twenties, someone whose face I could not have recognized under any circumstances, given that that person never got a chance to live up to the age of mid-twenties. Then how was it even possible that it was him? How was I seeing my childhood friend, whom I lost in the embrace of death when he was still a kid, in his adulthood? He never made it to that age, then how?

Several questions began flooding my head; my relief was taken over by a sense of doubt. Tears began flooding my eyes, but then I had to pull myself together, for there was no possibility it was Patrick. He died when he was still a child, and the man standing in front of me was no younger than the age of 27 or 29. I didn't know what to do or how to make sense out of this entire commotion. Why was everybody leaving me with a thousand questions without being courteous enough to answer a single one of them? Why??

"Who are you?" I asked, my voice trembling as it left my throat.

"You know who I am. You know it, Iyah."

With the response came the realization. It was more than enough to make me lose my sanity. My head was spinning. I felt I was either going to throw up or I was going to collapse. But before any of that could happen, came the voice of that man again.

"It's me, Iyah. It's Pattie."

Pattie? No way! That was what I used to call him. But how was that even possible?

"Iyah, it's me, Patrick," the man said again.

But this time, when he spoke, I felt my head spinning so fast that I could barely keep myself on my feet, and in a matter of seconds, I collapsed.

Gasping for air, I woke up, panting hysterically. For a moment there, I was dazed. Where I was, I could not tell. After a few seconds, looking around, scanning the room, I came to realize that it was my room. Something still did not add up. I was in my bed, but then how did I end up there? I was growing anxious, and the more nervous I got, the more confusing it all became for me. Running my eyes across the room, I noticed that the window of my room was open, and it was still dark. As I continued to look around, I could feel my throat had run dry. I needed water.

I turned to my left, where the bedside table was, to see if there was a jug lying on it. Thankfully, it was half-filled, enough to quench my thirst. Nevertheless, as I extended my hand in the direction of the jug, my eyes fell on the clock that was sitting on the same table. It was 5:15 in the morning. That's when I came to my senses, only it realize that it was a dream. Or was it?

XI:
In the Shadows

Was it easy for me to put an end to all this long before things could take a turn for the worse? And... even if I could, did I want to *actually* be sensible about it and make the right choice? I don't think so. But could you blame me? Would you not want to be loved by someone so passionately that the fire born out of that passion would burn everything that came in the way of that shared love, that shared bond? All my life — before he came in it — there was lust but no love. There was tension, but not the kind I felt with him. No man could make me feel that way before we crossed paths, him and I. Could it actually be love, or was it just physical attraction? And even if it was nothing more than physical attraction — a hunger for another body, then what was it? My head would spin every time I would try to find the answer to this one question: what was it that we shared between us, him and I? It sure wasn't just our lustful desires, the burning fire of which would inflame us both, and oddly enough, he and I both could see it — feel it.

I could have easily forgotten him. I had done that before, and I could have very well done it this time, but no, he was not meant to be forgotten. He wasn't meant to be let go. In fact, he was meant for so much more, and not just in isolation. No, he was meant for a lot of things, and all those things were meant to be with me — my involvement with him and his involvement with me. Do you know what the most bizarre quality of love is? Yes, you read it right. It's love, I am talking about it — it was indeed love that came into my life in the most unexpected way. I could not have imagined a better way or even a worse way of falling in love with someone, let alone with him. Oh, wait! Did I say I was in love? Indeed, I was because of what I felt for him. It was something I had never felt for anyone before. And the way he would make my heart skip a beat in his presence, nobody else could. Nobody was even capable — and that's what surprised me, took me aback, when he could actually pierce through the wall I had built around my heart and made his way right through it.

Coming back to the bizarre yet amazing attribute of love, it comes into your life in the most unexpected of ways and in ways unimaginable. Never underestimate the strength of love, for your mind cannot even fathom how far love can make you go for the sake of your love. Imagine someone like me, within the very core of whom resided another entity, a being of another world *or* underworld — who knew — nonetheless, fell for someone so ordinary yet so extraordinary. Yes, that's what the dilemma was all about. He was like just another guy, but to me, he felt like he was a man of sheer significance —a man so charming that every inch of his body screamed of the chivalry that was deeply instilled in him. It was rare. It was something I had never seen in anybody else. To tell you the truth, there was no way I could have fallen in love with anyone, let alone with a *human*.

That's what scared me the most. It began scaring me to the deepest core of my being long before I admitted to myself that I was indeed in love with him. He was a human being, and I … well, do I need to spell it out for you? I tried, you know? I tried not to fall prey to a feeling as absurd as love, which later felt like a feeling so beautiful that nothing in my life before or ever felt like it. I tried not to fall for his eyes — the eyes that I would catch lingering around all over the room as though those beautiful eyes were searching for someone, and that someone who turned out to be no one else but me. and I tried not to fall for his eyes, the eyes that would leave every sight and land on me the moment I'd enter the room as though the only purpose of those eyes was to find me, look at me and follow me wherever I'd go. I tried, and I tried hard not to fall for the eyes, the eyes that, when I looked at them, when I looked deep into them, they were deeper than the ocean — so deep that I would drown in them long before I would even know that I was falling for him and that I was falling for his eyes, his eyes that allowed me to look deeper into his soul, making me fall for him all over again. And it was not just his eyes, no. It was more than that. And no, it was not just me and my fantasies or my yearning to be loved by someone, to be held dear by someone. It was not my desire that got to me, but it was him. It was all of him who made me feel like I was falling in love with him with every moment that passed by and every moment that I found myself in his presence.

I tried not to fall for his words, too, you know. Those playful remarks he'd throw my way, the way he would flirt with me like it was just another thing in his day, so casual, so effortless, yet it felt like every word wrapped itself around my heart. I wanted to believe that it was just him being kind, just him being... Caleb. But then he'd catch my eye with that grin, and I'd feel this flutter deep in my chest, as though my heart had a mind of its own, pushing me closer, whispering that maybe this wasn't just a passing moment.

I tried not to fall for his personality, either. You know, the way he could make anyone feel comfortable, like you were the only person in the world when he was talking to you. He had this natural charm, this effortless ability to pull you in, like gravity. It wasn't just about his looks, though they certainly didn't help my situation. No, it was the way he laughed, the way he spoke with this quiet confidence, like he knew exactly who he was and wasn't afraid to be that person, no matter who was watching. And that drew me in, piece by piece.

And so, I fell. Slowly, at first. Little pieces of myself are giving in. His laughter pulled at the strings of my emotions, his touch—oh, how it sent shivers through me, lingering longer than it should have. And I tried to be cautious. I really did. But you can only hold back for so long when someone looks at you like you're the only person in the room.

It was intoxicating, the way he made me feel like I was someone worth loving, someone special. I felt alive in ways I hadn't before; my mind constantly drifted back to him, replaying our conversations, his smile, and the way his eyes darkened with something unsaid when he was close to me. My heart was no longer mine to control, and it scared me how quickly it had become his.

It was only after I realized I had fallen for him—completely, helplessly fallen—that the fear crept in. Not just the fear of how much I cared, but also the fear of what I wasn't seeing. The parts of him that my love had blinded me to. I could feel it sometimes, this quiet warning deep in my gut, whispering that there was something I wasn't looking at closely enough, but the pull of his presence, the weight of his touch—it kept pulling me back to him.

A part of me felt something—like something was still missing, like he wasn't telling me everything. Even though he had so much to say, even though he could talk to me for hours on end, there was this feeling deep inside that something was being held back, something important. It was like a veil over his words, as though what he shared with me was just the surface, and beneath that surface was a whole world he wasn't ready to show.

The worst part of it all was that I couldn't put my finger on it. I didn't know what it was that he was hiding, or if he was hiding anything at all. Maybe it was just my overactive mind, my fear of being too vulnerable, too exposed. But I couldn't shake the feeling that there was more to him, something deeper, something he didn't want me to see. Was it something dangerous? Was he protecting me from something that could hurt me? Or worse, was he hiding something so significant that it would change everything between us—whatever it was that we shared?

I couldn't stop thinking about it. Every time we were together, every time he would laugh or lean in just a little closer, I'd feel that unease creeping in, just for a second. Like a whisper in the back of my mind, warning me that something wasn't right, that there was a piece of him I wasn't seeing. And I wanted to ignore it. I wanted to push it aside and just be in the moment with him, to let myself believe that what we had was real, that I wasn't missing anything. But that feeling lingered, and no matter how hard I tried, it wouldn't go away.

It was maddening, the way he could be so open and yet still feel so distant. There were times when I'd look into his eyes and see that familiar warmth, that connection that drew me to him in the first place, but then there were other times—moments when his gaze would drift just slightly, when his smile didn't quite reach his eyes— that made me wonder what was going on inside his head.

I didn't know whether I should ask, push for more, or if doing so would ruin everything. I didn't want to lose him, but I also didn't want to be blindsided by whatever it was he was keeping from me. And maybe that was the real fear—that whatever he was hiding would destroy what we had, that it would shatter the fragile connection we were building, leaving me with nothing but questions and regrets.

And then there was Patrick. Always there, even when he wasn't. I don't know if it was guilt or something else, but Patrick's face started appearing more frequently in my dreams. It was like he was trying to remind me of something, trying to pull me back to a reality I was running from. At first, it was just in my sleep. His voice would echo in the recesses of my mind, his familiar face calm, always watching, as though he was waiting for me to acknowledge him.

But then it got worse. He started appearing in flashes during the day, too—just out of the corner of my eye. I'd be with Caleb, maybe sitting too close or laughing too freely, and suddenly, I'd see Patrick standing in the corner of the room, just watching. Always watching. And for a moment, it was like everything would stop, like the air around me got colder, heavier, suffocating me. I'd blink, and he'd be gone, but the feeling would linger, that unease.

I couldn't shake it. I tried to convince myself it was nothing. Just my mind playing tricks on me. Maybe it was the guilt of loving Caleb when Patrick's memory still lingered. But each time I saw him—dream or vision—it felt more real, like he was really there, reaching for me from someplace I couldn't see, couldn't touch. Why was he reaching out to me? I could not understand. What was even worse was the fact that Patrick and I were kids when he died— or so I thought. Then why did I feel guilty for being in love with Caleb when there was nothing between me and him? Perhaps it was the guilt of being in a situation so vulnerable that I was constantly at a threat of being harmed, and my friend Patrick would have wanted me to do better, to know better than this.

There was one night, after a particularly long day with Caleb, when I couldn't sleep. I had stayed at his place later than usual, our conversation turning soft, intimate, as though we were sharing parts of ourselves we hadn't before. His hand had brushed against mine more than once, his fingers curling slightly as though they wanted to intertwine with mine, but he never did. He never crossed that line, but it was so close. I could feel it. And I wanted it—I wanted him.

That night, when I finally drifted off into a restless sleep, Patrick was there again, standing at the foot of my bed. I remember every detail so clearly—his expression, the sadness in his eyes. He didn't speak this time. He just stood there, staring at me, like he knew what was happening, like he was disappointed in me. And that's when I started to wonder. Was it Patrick trying to warn me about Caleb? Was there something I wasn't seeing, something I should have noticed but didn't because I was too wrapped up in how Caleb made me feel?

Or was it just me, my guilt manifesting in these strange, haunting visions?

I started paying more attention after that, to Caleb, to his words, to the way he interacted with me. I began to wonder if maybe I had missed something—some sign, some clue that he wasn't who I thought he was. But every time I looked into those deep, ocean-like eyes, every time he smiled at me, that fear, that doubt, it would slip away, and I'd fall all over again.

It was a cycle. One that I couldn't seem to break. I wanted to trust him, wanted to believe that what we had was real, that I wasn't just another girl he flirted with, but that quiet voice in the back of my mind—it wouldn't let me rest. And then, when I wasn't thinking about Caleb, I was thinking about Patrick. His face, his voice, his presence—it was always there, lurking in the shadows of my mind, making me question everything.

I didn't know what to believe anymore. It was all driving me insane.

But then maybe things could change. They could change such that I could actually decide whom I could trust and whom *or what* I could not.

I was losing myself in Caleb's eyes again. It was easier to do than admit that something was wrong. His warmth, his charm, it all felt so real, so intoxicating, as if he could pull me away from everything that frightened me, everything that lingered just beneath the surface. But lately, Patrick had been showing up more—his presence slipping into my dreams, his voice soft yet persistent, calling me back to some truth I couldn't grasp. Every time I tried to make sense of it, Caleb was there, with his soft words and gentle touch, pulling me back into his orbit.

I tried talking to Mr. Haruki. He had always been a source of comfort and wisdom, someone who had been in my life for as long as I could remember. If anyone could help me sort through the mess of my feelings, it would be him. But lately, he had grown distant. Whenever I brought up Caleb or mentioned how I felt something was off, he would only offer vague, cryptic advice.

"Be careful of what you don't see," he told me once, his eyes narrowing as though he was watching something only he could see. "Sometimes, the shadows hide more than the light reveals."

I didn't know what he meant by that. Shadows. Light. What was I supposed to be careful of? Was he talking about Caleb? Or was it Patrick? The more I tried to press him, the more distant he became. It was like he knew something but wouldn't—or couldn't—say it out loud. The last time I tried to talk to him, he simply sighed and muttered something about time revealing all truths. It left me more confused than before.

Caleb, on the other hand, seemed more attentive than ever. He noticed everything. He picked up on the smallest details—the way my shoulders tensed when I thought about Patrick, the way my mind seemed to wander when we were together. He never let me drift too far, always pulling me back with a touch or a soft word. And yet, that nagging feeling—that something was wrong, that I wasn't seeing the whole picture—only grew stronger.

Then, one night, something happened that I still can't fully explain.

I had been having another dream about Patrick, but this one was different. It wasn't like the soft, comforting presence he had once been. This time, his figure was darker, more distorted, like he was struggling to reach me. His voice, once calm, sounded urgent, almost frantic, as though he was trying to warn me about something. I woke up in a cold sweat, my heart racing, my skin prickling with the sensation that someone—or something—was in the room with me.

I sat up in bed, my eyes scanning the darkness, and that's when I saw it—a shadowy figure standing at the foot of my bed. At first, I thought it was just my imagination, the remnants of my dream playing tricks on me. But as I blinked, trying to clear the sleep from my eyes, the figure remained. It was tall and formless, shifting in the shadows like smoke, its presence heavy, oppressive.

I couldn't move. I couldn't scream. My body was frozen, paralyzed with fear as the figure seemed to inch closer. My mind raced, trying to make sense of what I was seeing, but nothing seemed to make sense. This wasn't Patrick. It didn't feel like him. Whatever this was, it felt... wrong. Dangerous.

Just when I thought the figure was going to reach me, there was a knock at my door. A soft, familiar knock that immediately broke through the fog of terror. Caleb.

He called my name quietly before stepping inside. The moment he entered the room, the shadowy figure seemed to dissipate, vanishing into the darkness like it had never been there at all. I gasped, my breath coming out in shallow, ragged bursts as Caleb rushed to my side.

"Are you okay?" he asked, his voice filled with concern as he gently placed his hand on my arm. His touch was warm, grounding me, pulling me out of the fear that had gripped me moments ago.

I nodded, but my hands were still shaking. "There was... There was something in the room," I whispered, my voice barely audible as I struggled to find the words. "I saw something..."

Caleb's expression darkened, his jaw tightening as he looked around the room. "What did you see?" he asked, his voice low, serious in a way that sent a chill down my spine.

"I don't know," I stammered, my mind still trying to process what had just happened. "It wasn't Patrick. It didn't feel like him. It felt... wrong."

Caleb's eyes softened as he looked back at me, and he gently pulled me into his arms. "I believe you," he whispered, his breath warm against my ear. "It's Patrick. He's trying to get to you, to control you."

I pulled back slightly, confusion flooding my mind. "But... Patrick wouldn't—he wouldn't hurt me."

Caleb sighed, his expression pained as though it hurt him to say the words. "I know you don't want to believe it, Iyah. But Patrick isn't the same anymore. His spirit... It's dangerous now. He's not at peace. And he's trying to use you to stay connected to this world."

I stared at him, my mind reeling. Patrick, dangerous? It didn't make sense. Patrick had always been a calming presence, someone I could trust, even after he was gone. But the shadow I had seen, the feeling it had given me... it hadn't felt like Patrick at all.

"You have to trust me," Caleb said, his voice gentle but firm. "I don't want to see you get hurt. Whatever that thing was... It's connected to Patrick. And the more he appears to you, the more you're in danger."

I swallowed hard, my throat dry. I wanted to believe him. Caleb had always been there for me, always protecting me, caring for me. But this? Could Patrick really be dangerous? Could the presence I had felt in my dreams be something darker than I'd imagined?

I nodded slowly, letting Caleb's words sink in. He was right. I had to trust him. I had to believe that he was looking out for me, that he knew more about this than I did. After all, I had been seeing Patrick more and more, feeling his presence in ways that weren't normal. Maybe Caleb was right. Maybe I was in danger, and I hadn't even realized it.

As Caleb held me close, I felt a strange sense of comfort wash over me, like everything would be okay as long as he was there. He was my anchor in all of this, my guide through the confusion and fear. And as much as I wanted to hold on to the memories of Patrick, I couldn't deny the growing unease that his presence was bringing into my life.

Maybe Caleb was the only one I could trust now.

But wait a minute! What was Caleb doing in my house at this hour of the night? At that time, it didn't matter to me. I just didn't think about it. And why would I have thought about it when I was getting what I wanted? I was finally getting the love, the genuine care I had been looking for all my life. It was right there now, in the presence of Caleb.

XII:
A Deadly Kiss

Part I

That night stayed with me, lingering like a shadow, refusing to fade away. Caleb's words echoed in my mind, convincing me more and more that Patrick's spirit wasn't just some ghostly memory. No, Caleb had planted the seed in my thoughts — Patrick wasn't just present, he was dangerous. I found myself clinging to Caleb's warnings, like they were a lifeline in a world that was slowly becoming stranger every day.

I couldn't ignore the growing presence of Patrick. It was no longer just in my dreams, though those haunted my nights like never before. I felt him in the daytime too. It was in those still, quiet moments that everything felt off, too still, as if the air held its breath, waiting for something to happen. And every time I turned to see if he was there, there was nothing. Just the empty, eerie quiet and my growing sense of unease.

Caleb, on the other hand, was always around. He felt like a constant, like a warm presence I could rely on. When I felt the world closing in or when Patrick's ghostly figure seemed too close, Caleb would be there, steady and sure. I leaned on him more than I realized, letting his calm, soothing voice anchor me in reality. I trusted him, or at least I tried to. But deep down, something in me stirred, something that didn't fully understand the situation.

At first, it was little things. Objects in my room didn't feel right. Sometimes, I'd walk into the kitchen and feel the air shift, like it was alive somehow, reacting to me, sensing my presence. It was subtle, almost too subtle to notice, but it was there. And then, one afternoon, it became impossible to ignore.

I had been thinking about Patrick again, about how his presence had started to take over my life, haunting my dreams and creeping into my waking hours. My emotions were all over the place. My head ached from trying to make sense of it all, and then, as I sat there, something moved beside me. The vase on the table shifted, just a little. I blinked, wondering if I imagined it. But before I could dismiss it as a trick of my tired mind, it moved again — more obvious this time.

Then the book on the shelf tipped over. My heart jumped, and I stood up, backing away from the table like I had just touched something hot. It wasn't my imagination. Something was happening.

It didn't stop there. The shadows in the room began to move too, not like normal shadows that just sit there, minding their business, but like they were alive, curling and stretching in the corners of the room. It was like they were reacting to me, feeding off my fear. And the more afraid I became, the more they moved. My heart raced, my breathing quickened, and I had no idea how to stop it.

Then there was a knock at the door, and I nearly jumped out of my skin. My pulse was pounding in my ears as I turned toward the door, knowing exactly who it was before I even opened it. Caleb had this uncanny way of showing up exactly when I needed him, like he could sense my fear. I rushed to the door, opening it to find him standing there, concern etched on his face.

"Iyah," he said, his voice soft as he stepped inside. He didn't even wait for me to speak. "What happened?"

I wanted to tell him, to explain everything, but the words stuck in my throat. The room still felt charged, like the air was buzzing with energy. The shadows hadn't completely settled either, still lingering in the corners of the room. Caleb seemed to understand, though. He always did.

"It's Patrick," he said quietly, his tone firm but gentle. "He's getting stronger."

I shook my head, feeling the lump in my throat grow tighter. "Why? Why would he do this to me?"

Caleb stepped closer, his hand resting on my arm as he looked into my eyes. "Because he doesn't want to let go. Spirits like Patrick — they're desperate to stay in this world, especially if they were close to someone. He's not the same as he was when he was alive, Iyah. He's lost, and the more he tries to stay connected, the more dangerous he becomes."

I wanted to believe Caleb. I really did. He had been right about so many things, and he was always there when I needed him. But I couldn't shake the feeling that maybe Patrick wasn't trying to hurt me. Maybe there was more to this than Caleb was letting on.

Despite my doubts, I couldn't argue with what I had seen. The objects moving on their own, the shadows stretching and twisting like they were alive — it was all too real. Perhaps Patrick had truly changed; perhaps Caleb was right. But the part of me that still remembered Patrick as he had been, the kind friend I once knew, couldn't accept it completely.

Caleb must have sensed my hesitation. He always seemed to know what I was thinking. He stepped even closer, his hand moving from my arm to my shoulder, his gaze locking onto mine. "You have to trust me, Iyah," he said softly, but there was an intensity in his voice. "I'm here to protect you. I'm the only one who can."

His words wrapped around me like a blanket, comforting in their certainty. And as much as the doubt tugged at the back of my mind, I found myself nodding, even though I wasn't sure if I fully believed him. Caleb had always been there for me, showing up when no one else had. Maybe that was enough.

He led me to the couch, guiding me to sit down as if I were fragile, as if I might break. His arm stayed around my shoulders, anchoring me as I tried to steady my breathing. "You're scared," he said softly, his voice soothing like a lullaby. "And that's exactly what Patrick is feeding off. Spirits like his, they thrive on fear. The more scared you are, the stronger he becomes."

I nodded, trying to calm the storm of emotions inside me. I focused on Caleb's voice, on his steady presence, and the way the room seemed to settle with him nearby. The shadows were still there, but they no longer moved. The air no longer buzzed with that strange energy. It was like Caleb had brought everything back to normal just by being there.

"You have to stay calm," he continued, his voice gentle but firm. "Don't let Patrick get into your head. Don't let him in."

I swallowed hard, nodding again as I tried to follow his advice. But no matter how hard I tried, I couldn't shake the feeling that something was off. "What if he's not trying to hurt me?" I asked quietly, barely able to get the words out. "What if... what if he's trying to tell me something?"

For a moment, Caleb's expression flickered, just for a second, and I thought I saw something dark in his eyes. Something possessive, almost. But it was gone before I could be sure, replaced by the same look of concern he always wore. "That's exactly what he wants you to think," Caleb said, his voice low and serious. "He's trying to confuse you, to make you doubt yourself. That's how spirits like him operate. They twist things, make you second-guess everything."

I didn't know what to say. A part of me wanted to believe him, to trust that Caleb knew what was going on, but the nagging doubt in the back of my mind wouldn't go away. Patrick had been my friend, and the idea that he would try to hurt me didn't sit right. But what could I do? Caleb was the only one who seemed to understand what I was going through. The only one who had been there when things got truly terrifying.

The room felt calmer now, like whatever strange energy had been there was fading away. The objects were still, and the shadows had retreated to their rightful places. Caleb always had that effect — when he was around, the world seemed to go back to normal. And I couldn't deny how much comfort that brought me.

"Iyah," Caleb said softly, turning my face toward him with a gentle hand. "I'm not going to let anything happen to you. You know that, right?"

I nodded, my heart beating fast as his eyes held mine. There was something in his gaze that made me feel safe, even when my instincts whispered for me to be cautious. But I ignored that small voice inside me, choosing instead to lean into Caleb's warmth. He had never let me down before.

"I know," I whispered, my voice barely audible. "I trust you."

His smile was soft, almost triumphant, as he pulled me closer. "Good. Because we're going to get through this together, but you have to trust me completely."

The weight of his words settled over me like a heavy blanket. I wasn't sure if I could give him what he was asking for, not fully. But for now, it was enough to have him here, beside me, making the world feel safe again. The shadows danced at the edges of the room, but with Caleb there, I could almost pretend they didn't exist.

Perhaps if I trusted him enough, everything would turn out all right.

At least, that's what I kept telling myself.

The next couple of days passed in a blur, with Caleb always by my side. I tried to go back to some kind of normal routine, but everything felt off-kilter. The small, subtle signs that something wasn't right kept piling up — the way objects would shift when I wasn't looking, the way the air seemed to hum with tension when I was alone. And Patrick, or his presence, seemed to be everywhere.

He was in the shadows of my room at night, in the quiet moments when I thought I was alone, in my dreams. Always there, just out of reach, watching. Caleb told me it was Patrick trying to break through, trying to get inside my head, and I believed him. But a part of me still couldn't let go of the idea that Patrick wasn't trying to hurt me. What if he was trying to warn me? What if there was something else going on?

But Caleb was convincing. He had answers to every question I asked, explanations for every strange occurrence. "It's the nature of spirits like Patrick," he would say. "They don't know how to let go. They latch on to the people they were closest to, and they can't see that they're causing harm."

I wanted to trust him. After all, he had been the one to help me through all of this. But the more time I spent with Caleb, the more a nagging feeling crept into my mind. It was small at first, just a whisper in the back of my thoughts, but it grew louder with each passing day.

I couldn't deny the comfort I felt around Caleb, the way his presence seemed to calm the storm inside me. But there was something else too, something I couldn't quite put my finger on. It was like the more I leaned on him, the more I felt... trapped.

It came to a head one night, when the strange happenings escalated in a way I couldn't ignore. I had been in my room, trying to sleep, when I felt it — a presence, stronger than anything I had felt before. It wasn't just a shadow or a whisper at the edge of my vision. It was Patrick, unmistakable, standing at the foot of my bed.

I shot upright, my heart pounding in my chest. "Patrick?" I whispered, not even sure if he could hear me.

The figure didn't move, didn't say anything, but I knew it was him. There was a familiar energy to him, something that felt like the Patrick I had known. He wasn't trying to scare me, I could feel that now. He was trying to reach me.

But before I could even process what was happening, there was a knock at the door. Caleb. Of course, it was Caleb. He always seemed to know when I was on the edge of something, always showed up at the exact right moment. At this point, I was beginning to question his sudden appearances every time I would find myself in need of something — or *someone.* I knew he had something special in him, like I did. Like I would use my unexplained powers, which Mr. Haruki never explained to me. That was how he was always able to read my mind. We had been communicating using our minds. But him showing up precisely at the right moment, it just would not sit right.

I threw on a robe and rushed to the door, yanking it open to find Caleb standing there, his face filled with concern. "Iyah, what's going on?" he asked, stepping inside without waiting for an invitation. "I felt something was wrong."

I didn't know what to say. Patrick's presence still lingered in the room, and I felt torn between the two of them. Caleb, who had been there for me every step of the way, and Patrick, who was just trying to reach me, to tell me something.

"I... I saw him," I finally said, my voice shaking. "I saw Patrick. He was here."

Caleb's expression darkened. "You can't let him in, Iyah," he said, his voice more forceful than I had ever heard it before. "You have to block him out. Every time you acknowledge him, you give him more power."

I shook my head, feeling the weight of his words pressing down on me. "But... what if he's not trying to hurt me? What if he's trying to warn me about something?"

Caleb's eyes flashed with something I couldn't quite place — anger, maybe? Fear? "He's not the Patrick you remember," he said, stepping closer, his hand gripping my arm tightly. "He's dangerous, Iyah. You have to stop questioning it. You have to trust me."

His grip on my arm tightened, and for the first time, I felt a flicker of fear, not of Patrick, but of Caleb. Something about the way he was acting didn't sit right with me. But I couldn't pull away, couldn't let myself believe that Caleb wasn't on my side. He had been there for me, always.

"I do trust you," I said quietly, but the words felt hollow.

Caleb's grip loosened, and he sighed, running a hand through his hair. "I'm just trying to protect you," he said, his voice softer now. "I don't want anything to happen to you."

I nodded, but the doubt was still there, gnawing at the edges of my mind. Patrick wasn't trying to scare me. He was trying to reach me. And maybe, just maybe, there was more to this than Caleb was telling me.

That night, as I lay in bed, the shadows shifted again, but this time I wasn't afraid. Patrick's presence was there, but it didn't feel threatening. It felt... familiar. Safe, even. And for the first time, I let myself wonder if I had been trusting the wrong person all along.

The days following that night were filled with uncertainty. I found myself walking a tightrope between Caleb's warnings and the quiet, persistent feeling that Patrick was trying to communicate something important. My instincts kept pushing me to listen, but Caleb's words echoed louder, constantly reminding me that spirits like Patrick were dangerous.

I tried to keep everything inside, pretending like I wasn't torn in two. Caleb noticed my restlessness, though. He was more attentive than ever, checking in on me constantly, making sure I wasn't alone for too long. It felt comforting at first, having someone who cared that much, but soon it started to feel a little... controlling.

I could have been wrong. Perhaps the life I had had made me someone who would question even the most authentic form of love, care, and affection. Had my past shaped me into a person incapable of accepting love in its purest, most innocent form? Could I ever place my undivided trust in someone who was nothing but gentle and kind to me? Had I been so devoured by the unknown demons lurking in the dark and the entity residing in me that I could not see Caleb's love for what it was? I abhorred how my head would be filled with more questions and no answers every time something out of the ordinary happened. And then there was Mr. Haruki.

What had gone into him, I could not understand. All my life, he had been the one person who would go to the moon and back just to keep me safe, and there was no question coming from me that he would not answer. He was my walking encyclopedia, as I would call him teasingly, but I just could not understand him anymore. If he wanted me to be safe, then why the hell was he being cryptic about all that had been happening to me? He did tell me a lot more than I could have taken when I first came in contact with him. I mean, how else would I have known about the curse that made every single moment of my life miserable had it not been for Mr. Haruki? Then why stay quiet now? Wait… the curse! All that had been happening to me lately had to be connected to that deadly curse!

I could hardly catch my breath. The weight of everything pressed down on me, suffocating, pulling me into a whirlwind of confusion and fear. I knew something was inside me—some presence that lingered beneath my skin, something ancient, something cursed. But what it was and why it was there… that was the part I couldn't wrap my mind around. I needed to know. I *deserved* to know. And now, with Caleb's puzzling words and Patrick haunting my dreams, it was impossible to ignore. I had to get answers. And this time, I wasn't going to let Mr. Haruki hide behind his usual evasions.

I was done with the riddles. Done with the half-truths. Done with chasing shadows and trying to piece together fragments of a story that seemed to be slipping through my fingers like sand.

As I walked toward Mr. Haruki's house, the moonlight barely reached the path, leaving the trail drenched in shadows that stretched like long, twisted fingers. The trees around me were massive, towering and dark, as if they were watching, waiting for me to make a move. The air was thick with mist, a cold dampness that stuck to my skin, but I barely noticed it. My mind was spinning, racing faster than my footsteps, every thought colliding with the next. Fear. Frustration. Confusion. I couldn't settle on any of them, but they were all there, clouding my thoughts.

I had never been to Mr. Haruki's house before. It wasn't that I hadn't wanted to—no, that wasn't it. I just hadn't felt the need to. We had always met in other places. But tonight… tonight, there was something different in the air. Something about the way things had been unraveling around me had pushed me to this moment. I was standing at his doorstep, at a threshold I'd never crossed before. The silence around me felt like it was pressing in, waiting to see what would happen next.

XII:
A Deadly Kiss

Part II

When I finally reached his front door, my heart felt like it was pounding in my throat. I stood there for a second, staring at the door, feeling that familiar weight of dread settle on my shoulders. Every time I visited Mr. Haruki, I left feeling even more lost than when I arrived. It always felt like I was chasing answers, but they kept slipping through my fingers. But tonight—this night—something had to change. I couldn't go on feeling this way. I couldn't leave without some kind of clarity.

I knocked as loudly as I could — trying not to, but I couldn't help it, could I? I knocked again—quick raps that didn't care if it was too late or if he was ready for me. I wasn't here for his politeness. I needed answers. I needed them now.

The door creaked open slowly, and there he was. Mr. Haruki stood in the dim light of the hallway, his face a picture of calm, as always—so calm it was unsettling. He wore the same old-fashioned shirt with the sleeves rolled up, his gray hair tied back in its usual neat style. His eyes were tired, but there was something sharp about them, like they could see straight through me. As if he already knew why I was standing there.

"Iyah," he said, his voice low and smooth. It sounded almost like he was expecting me. "Come in."

I swallowed hard, and for a moment, I didn't know if I could step through that door. Every part of me was screaming to run, but I didn't. I couldn't. I stepped inside.

The air inside his house smelled heavy—incense, something herbal, and faintly earthy. It was a smell I had come to associate with him. The room was small and cluttered with old books, scrolls, and strange trinkets that seemed to hold stories of their own, things that didn't quite belong in this time or place. It felt like stepping into a different world. A world where things that didn't make sense were the norm.

He gestured to the small wooden table in the center of the room. But tonight, sitting didn't seem right. I didn't want to sit. I wanted to scream, to demand answers. I wanted to shake him and force the truth out of him. But instead, I sat. It wasn't because I was calm or at peace. It was because I was too tired to do anything else. I was worn out, emotionally drained from everything that had been happening.

"I can see you're troubled," Mr. Haruki said, settling into the chair across from me. His eyes never left mine, studying me like he was searching for something deeper, something I couldn't hide. His gaze felt like it could see through to my very soul.

I clenched my fists on the table, my nails digging into my palms. "I'm done with being troubled. I'm done with the fear. I'm done with not knowing what the hell is going on. You know, don't you? You've always known. And I'm not leaving until you tell me everything. I don't care what it takes."

Mr. Haruki sighed, a sound that seemed too deep for just a breath. He leaned back in his chair, his fingers tapping lightly on the table, his eyes never breaking from mine. "Iyah," he said softly, his voice taking on a tone I couldn't quite place. "The truth is not something I can reveal lightly. It's more dangerous than you realize."

"Dangerous?" I scoffed, my voice trembling with a mix of anger and desperation. "You think I don't know danger? You think I haven't been living in danger every day of my life? Don't protect me, Mr. Haruki. I've been through too much to turn back now."

Mr. Haruki's gaze softened for a moment, and he leaned forward, his elbows resting on the table, his fingers steepled together. He didn't say anything for a long while. The silence was thick, heavy with something I couldn't place. The air around us felt charged, like everything in the room was holding its breath, waiting.

"Iyah," he said finally, his voice quiet but firm. "The truth you seek... It's not easy to hear. And it may not be what you want."

"I don't care," I snapped. "I don't care what I want anymore. I just need to know what's going on. I need to know why I feel like I'm losing my mind. Why am I seeing things? Why does it feel like something's inside me, taking control?"

He regarded me carefully, like he was deciding how much to say, how much I was truly ready to hear.

"I wish I could say that the answers would set you free," he said slowly. "But sometimes, the truth is more burden than release."

I stared at him, a part of me feeling that deep pit in my stomach widen. It was a feeling I couldn't shake, no matter how much I wanted to. I had always suspected that Mr. Haruki knew more than he was letting on, but now it seemed like I had just walked into something far darker than I had ever imagined.

He leaned back in his chair, the creaking of the wood filling the silence between us. His eyes never wavered from mine.

"You asked for the truth," he said quietly. "And now, you will have it."

I held my breath, the words hanging in the air like a storm that had yet to break. I felt like I was standing at the edge of something deep, something I couldn't even comprehend.

"You are cursed, Iyah," he said, his voice steady but laden with gravity. "But not in the way you think. This curse... it is not a simple one. It is bound to your very soul."

I couldn't breathe. The room seemed to spin as his words settled in my chest. My mind went blank, and for a moment, I couldn't move. "A curse?" I whispered, barely able to form the words. "How... how is that even possible?"

"You were born with it," Mr. Haruki continued, his voice as calm as ever. "It's been with you since the moment you drew your first breath. The entity you feel, the presence inside you, it's not something separate. It's a part of you, a part of your heritage. A curse that's been passed down through your bloodline, stretching back to the time of your ancestors."

I tried to make sense of his words, but nothing clicked. My heart was pounding now, my hands trembling as I gripped the edge of the table. "What do you mean, my ancestors? What does this have to do with me?"

"Everything," he said quietly, his gaze hardening. "The curse was born with your ancestor, King Newil. In his desperation, he made a bargain with forces beyond his understanding—forces that were never meant to be bargained with. And now, that promise has come to rest on your shoulders. It's been passed down through the generations, each of your ancestors carrying the weight of the same pact, and now… now it's your turn."

I shook my head in disbelief, trying to wrap my mind around what he was saying. A curse? A bargain made centuries ago? It felt like some twisted story I'd heard only in folklore, a myth I had never thought would be real. I mean, I did know I had a curse and that some superstitious thing always accompanied me wherever I went. Wasn't it the curse that had been giving me these unexplained powers to lure in my prey? Like always, I found myself more lost than found. My head was spinning, and nothing made sense to me anymore. Everything just shattered in front of me, into pieces that were impossible to place in their right spots. The night was going to be long. It was far from over.

"What do you mean, my turn?" I asked, the words slipping out before I could stop them. "Why me? Why is it happening now?"

"Because the curse is awakening," Mr. Haruki answered. "The forces that have been dormant for so long are stirring. And you are the key. Your bloodline was never meant to live in peace. Not as long as the ancient promise remains unfulfilled."

I felt like the ground had shifted beneath me. My head was spinning with the weight of what he was saying, and my heart was racing as if it might burst from my chest.

"You are the key, Iyah," he said again, his voice low and steady. "You can break the curse—or you can choose to let it continue. But either way, the consequences will be great. The decision will change everything."

"I don't—" I began, but my voice faltered. "I don't understand. I don't understand any of this."

Mr. Haruki's gaze softened for a brief moment, as if he was seeing the full weight of my fear and confusion. "You will," he said gently. "In time, you will understand. But for now, you must make a choice."

I blinked, the words crashing into me. Choice? What choice? I had no idea what was happening; I had no idea how I was supposed to handle something like this. I could feel my chest tightening, the pressure building up in my lungs.

"There is no going back, Iyah," he warned. "Once you choose, there is no turning away. But you must decide—will you embrace your heritage, the curse that binds you, or will you seek a way to break it?"

I couldn't respond. My mind was a blur of thoughts, none of them making sense. I felt like I was drowning, the room closing in around me. My hands were shaking, and I wanted to scream, to run, to escape the weight of his words. But instead, I just sat there, frozen.

"You don't have to decide now," Mr. Haruki said, his voice softer now. "But when the time comes, you will know what to do. The choice is yours, but be warned—each path comes with its own consequences."

I couldn't speak. I didn't know what to say. The room felt too small, too suffocating. How could I make a decision when I didn't even understand what was happening to me? How could I decide what to do with something I didn't even believe was real?

And yet, deep down, I knew that somehow, I had already begun the journey. Whatever path I chose, whatever truth I would have to face—it had already started.

I sat there, still as a stone, my thoughts tangled like knots in my mind. The weight of everything Mr. Haruki had told me was too much to grasp, like trying to catch smoke in my hands. A curse? A centuries-old promise? It all felt unreal, like a story that didn't belong to me, yet here I was, trapped in it.

Mr. Haruki's eyes never left mine, and I could feel the intensity of his gaze, the expectation hanging between us like an invisible thread. I wanted to look away, to break free from the pressure of his words, but I couldn't.

"What if…" I whispered, my voice barely audible, "What if I don't want to choose?"

Mr. Haruki sighed softly, leaning back in his chair. The creak of the wood echoed in the stillness of the room. "Not choosing is still a choice, Iyah. You cannot avoid what is already in motion. The curse is awakening, and whether you choose to face it or not, it will find you. It always does."

My chest tightened, and I felt a lump forming in my throat. I had come here for answers, and now that I had them, I wished I hadn't. I wished I could go back to the way things were, back to the confusion and uncertainty that seemed far easier to handle than this crushing reality. But there was no going back.

The curse had found me.

"I've never been to your house before," I said quietly, my voice shaking a little as I tried to grasp at anything that felt solid, anything that could anchor me in the chaos of my thoughts. "I never imagined it would come to this… that I'd be sitting here, hearing these things. I thought… I don't even know what I thought."

Mr. Haruki nodded, a faint, knowing smile playing at the corners of his lips. "It was never about the place, Iyah. It was about when you would be ready to hear the truth. You had to come to me when you were ready—not when you thought you needed answers, but when your spirit was prepared to understand the depth of what you carry."

I shuddered, his words sinking deep into me like a cold wind brushing against my skin. Ready? I didn't feel ready. I felt terrified, confused, and so small compared to the magnitude of what he was saying. How could I be ready for something like this?

I looked around his small, cluttered room, filled with books and trinkets that seemed older than time itself. The smell of incense was still heavy in the air, and I wondered if he had known this moment would come. Had he always known that one day I would walk through his door, seeking the truth?

"Why didn't you tell me sooner?" I asked, my voice barely above a whisper. "Why didn't you prepare me for this?"

"Because some truths cannot be given before their time," he said softly, his eyes filled with a kind of sadness that tugged at something deep within me. "If I had told you before, you wouldn't have understood. You would have rejected it, just as you are tempted to do now. But now, you are on the cusp of something greater, and the time has come for you to decide your path."

I felt my heart sink. He was right, a part of me wanted to reject everything he was saying, to push it away and deny it. But another part of me—the part that had felt the strange presence inside me for so long, that had sensed the dark, looming shadow I could never explain—knew he was telling the truth.

"I don't know what to do," I admitted, my voice trembling. "I don't know how to make a decision like this. How can I choose something I don't understand?"

"You will learn, in time," he said gently. "But you must be patient with yourself. The path is not easy, and it is not without sacrifice. But you are stronger than you know, Iyah. Your ancestors carried this burden, and now it has come to you. But you are not alone in this."

I stared at him, my heart pounding in my chest. Not alone? It didn't feel that way. I had been living with this haunting presence for so long, feeling more and more isolated as it grew stronger. I felt like I was trapped in a nightmare, and no one could pull me out.

"What do you mean, not alone?" I asked, my voice cracking slightly.

"There are others," Mr. Haruki said, his voice low. "Others who have walked this path before you, who have faced the same choices. And there are those who will help you, if you allow them to. But you must be willing to accept their guidance."

I swallowed hard, trying to process what he was saying. Others? I had always felt so alone, so cut off from everyone around me, like no one could possibly understand what I was going through. But now, he was telling me that there were others out there—people who knew what it was like to carry this curse, to feel the weight of it pressing down on their souls.

"Who are they?" I asked, my curiosity piqued despite the overwhelming fear that still gripped me. "Where are these people?"

Mr. Haruki smiled faintly, a glimmer of something like hope in his eyes. "They are not far, Iyah. But you must seek them out. They will not come to you unless you are ready to embrace the truth of your heritage."

I felt a flicker of something inside me—a spark of determination, maybe, or the faintest hint of courage. I didn't know what the future held, and I didn't know if I could bear the weight of this curse, but I knew one thing: I couldn't keep living in fear and confusion.

I had to find a way to break free from this darkness, even if it meant facing the hardest truths of my life.

Mr. Haruki's words hung in the air, heavy with the weight of ancient history and personal responsibility. I shifted in my seat, my hands trembling slightly as I rested them in my lap. The fear was still there, gnawing at me, but alongside it, something new stirred—a flicker of determination. For the first time, I felt like I was no longer running from the unknown. I was standing at its doorstep, ready to confront it.

But what did that mean? What was I really supposed to do next?

"You say I have to seek these people out," I began, my voice steadier than I felt. "But where do I start? How do I even know who they are?"

Mr. Haruki's eyes softened. "You will know when the time is right. Trust your instincts, Iyah. The same forces that have guided you here will continue to guide you. But be patient—answers will not come all at once. You must be willing to learn as you go, and more importantly, to listen."

I nodded, though the uncertainty still churned in my gut. Listen to what? To the curse inside me? To the ancient promise I didn't even know I was part of? None of this made sense, but deep down, I felt like I had no other choice but to believe. I had already felt things moving inside me, forces I couldn't explain—things Caleb had warned me about. And now, here was Mr. Haruki, confirming what I had feared all along: that I was different, that something dark and old had taken root in me, waiting to be awakened.

But what if this "truth" he spoke of wasn't the full story? What if there were pieces I was still missing?

"Caleb," I blurted out, suddenly remembering how deeply intertwined he had become in all of this. "What about Caleb? He's been telling me for weeks now that Patrick's presence is dangerous. He says that... that Patrick is feeding off my fear, that he's using me somehow. Could he be right?"

Mr. Haruki's expression shifted slightly, though it was hard to tell if it was concern or something else that flashed across his features. "Caleb is perceptive, but he does not fully understand the nature of your curse, nor the role that Patrick plays in it."

I frowned. "What do you mean? If Patrick is a part of me... if this curse is tied to my soul, then why is Caleb so convinced that he's dangerous? I mean, things have been happening. Strange things. Objects moving on their own, shadows that seem to shift whenever I'm upset. It's real, Mr. Haruki. And Caleb... he says Patrick is trying to harm me."

Mr. Haruki was silent for a long moment, his fingers tapping rhythmically against the edge of the table. When he finally spoke, his voice was measured, careful. "Patrick is not what he appears to be, Iyah. He is both a part of you and apart from you. The spirit that resides within you carries the weight of the ancient curse, yes—but it is also bound by its own will, its own desires. Patrick... Patrick may very well have intentions that are not aligned with yours."

My stomach twisted. "So, Caleb was right?"

"Not entirely," Mr. Haruki said, his voice low. "Patrick is not inherently evil, nor is he a force of pure destruction. He is bound by the same curse that has shaped your life. But spirits, especially those that are tied to ancient promises, can be unpredictable. They are shaped by the circumstances of their binding, by the emotions and desires of those they are connected to. And in your case, Patrick's influence is growing stronger because the curse is awakening."

I felt a cold sweat break out on the back of my neck. "So, what do I do? How do I stop him from... from hurting me?"

"You must understand, Patrick," Mr. Haruki replied, his voice soft but firm. "You must learn who he truly is and what he wants. Only then can you find a way to either control his influence or sever his connection to you. But be warned—such actions come with risks.

The bond between you and Patrick is not easily broken. Attempting to do so may cause unforeseen consequences, both for you and for him."

I took a deep breath, trying to steady myself. "And if I can't... if I can't control him? What happens then?"

Mr. Haruki's gaze darkened slightly, and his voice lowered to a near whisper. "Then you must be prepared to make the hardest decision of your life. To either embrace the curse fully... or find a way to break it. But know this, Iyah—breaking the curse may cost you everything.

The air in the room grew heavier with the weight of Mr. Haruki's final words. The prospect of "costing everything" settled over me like a dark cloud, a chilling reminder that there were no easy answers to the situation I found myself in. I looked into his eyes, searching for some reassurance, some small flicker of hope that this wasn't as impossible as it seemed. But his gaze remained steady and unreadable, offering no comfort.

"Thank you," I said quietly, standing up from the table. My legs felt shaky, but I forced myself to stay upright. "For telling me the truth. I... I needed to hear it."

Mr. Haruki stood as well, his movements slow and deliberate. "You are welcome, Iyah. But remember—this is only the beginning. There is still much you do not know, much that remains hidden. Be cautious, and trust in yourself. You are stronger than you think."

That was all that was said between me and him. It was now time for me to descend into the night and drag myself to a place I called home. It was not a home you'd want to call home. A home is a place where you can feel safe. It is the safest place on earth for you. Unfortunately, for me, it was a little different.

As I stepped out into the night, my mind swirling with the weight of everything Mr. Haruki had told me, I didn't notice Caleb standing just beyond the edge of the path. The mist curled around his figure, and for a moment, it was as if he had appeared out of nowhere, blending with the night itself. His face, normally calm and reassuring, now carried a shadow of concern as he watched me, his brow furrowed.

"Iyah," he called softly, stepping forward. "Are you okay? What happened in there?"

I froze, not expecting to see him here, but somehow, his presence immediately brought a sense of comfort amidst the chaos. The tension that had been knotted tightly in my chest loosened just a little at the sight of him. Without thinking, I closed the distance between us, drawn to the familiar warmth that Caleb always exuded.

Taking I deep sigh as I took a step forward, eradicating all distance between us, I began, "Cale…"

Before I could finish my sentence — hell, before I could take his complete name, he took one step forward, brought his hands to my face, and cupped it in them. My heart raced as I watched him look deeper into my eyes. It was as if his gaze would dig a hole in my eyes. Caleb, giving me no moment to even allow my mind to linger in thoughts, brought his face closer to mine, his breath warm on my lips in the coldness of the night. And there it was, though immediate but gentle — a kiss that we both had been wanting for so long but resisting for one reason or another. The touch was gentle when his lips touched mine, but the moment they collided, there was no gentleness left, and it was rather wild. It was — desperate.

The world seemed to have frozen as we stood there, kissing each other, almost devouring one another's lips. We stayed like that for quite some time. Was it for a minute? I didn't know. Was it longer than that? I couldn't tell. But what I could really tell was that it felt like an eternity, for the world around us seemed to have stopped, and it was us in the night, under the sky, lost in the moment, the heat burning us up.

We were growing breathless as neither of us let go of each other and continued to explore the burning desire that we shared, not just one of us. And then, just like that, came the release. Parting his lips from mine, which were intertwined with mine, he lifted my face, but as soon as he did, I felt a shift in the air. My head started spinning as if the world had suddenly begun to move. He released me from his arms, and there I was, struggling to stand on my feet, my legs trembling as I tried to reach him with my hand stretched. My eyes began fluttering as if to see clearly, but failed, and before I knew it, the world felt dark. I drifted into a darkness unbeknownst. It was in that moment, I was hit by a realization — though everything around me was a blur — I was met with a deadly kiss!

XIII:
A Luminous Darkness

I thought I was going to collapse. It actually did feel like I had fallen because… well, that's what happened. It was not the floor where I landed. That was the unexpected part of it all. In his warm embrace, on a cold winter night, I fell, and it was the kind of fall I would kill to feel again. Little did I know that many more were what I was looking at in the following year. I did not realize in that moment that I was moving towards my own death —digging my own grave. All I could think of was being there, wrapped up in his arms. His kiss was poison or a love potion, I could not tell. But what it did to me certainly made it feel like the former.

Or was it both? When his lips touched mine, I felt in me the surge of emotions readying themselves to unleash and engulf me, make me lose all control, forget the world around me. All I wanted was for that moment to last longer than it did, and when he released me, I could not stand straight on my feet. Was it an effect of his kiss, or was it the painful reaction of being let go when all I wanted was for him to continue drinking from my lips? Was it a big ask? And when the release came, my head could not process it. I wanted more — more of him. It felt like I could consume him from his lips, sucking his soul and letting it enter my body just through that one kiss. But that moment of utmost pleasure was short-lived. He let me out of his arms, and there I was, standing right in front of him.

However, I could not take it. I felt… I felt betrayed! And with the blend of so many emotions, many of which I had just felt like I had never felt before, I could not take it. It was all just too much for me to take in all at once. I thought I was going to drop to the floor as my head spun. My stomach felt like it was churning, and just as the world became a blur, I could feel myself floating in the air. It was all happening too quickly, yet I felt like I had frozen in that moment. And now it was only a matter of seconds before I would find myself on the floor. The fall came. But I did not find myself on the ground. It was his embrace — again, where I found myself.

When I woke up, I found myself on my side — my face facing the window. It was still dark outside, and my head was throbbing from what had happened hours ago. How many hours had gone by? I couldn't tell. As soon as my head started to clear up, whatever had unfolded began to come back to me. With what had occurred at Mr. Haruki's place came back the bitter-sweet memory of the intimate moment I shared with Caleb. And before I knew it, with a sudden pang in my heart, the sadness of not having Caleb by my side began to settle in. I felt my heart was going to explode, for this distance between me and him was something I was finding excruciatingly painful. I thought I was going to pass out again. There was a strong urge in me to reach out to him. Until that night, I always found Caleb waiting for me or even making his way towards me every time I felt I had no place to go, no place to call home, no place to call mine. Now, when I needed him the most, when the urge to have him next to me, with me, was stronger than ever, I lay in my bed alone. Or was I?

Just as I thought I was all alone in my room and the need to cry my heart out began to take over me, I felt a hand sliding into my shirt from the back, making its way up to the front of my body, clasping my belly. With a sudden jerk, I was pulled closer to the person to whom that hand belonged. No words were said, and I didn't have to turn around and see who it was, for I knew very well that it was no one but him. his cold hand, warm against my belly. Now, normally, I would have jumped and made sure that whoever it was did not have their hand on them any longer for pulling such an act of audacity. No one could come closer to me unless I allowed it. It was usually me making the directions and commands, and the rest would follow. This time, I allowed myself to lower my guard and follow Caleb wherever he led me, no matter how blinded I got while following him.

Yes, it was Caleb. I did not need to turn and know for sure, for there was a lot that made it a known fact that Caleb was there — with me — in my bed, under the sheets. The hours that followed made the night last longer than it should have — longer than I could have imagined.

It had been going well between me and him. That would be a lie, of course. Do you remember the kind of person I was before Caleb made his way into my life? I was vicious, wasn't I? Harming people came very easily to me. My curse, though I didn't understand it then, I used it to the best of its ability to find those who'd cross me and teach them a lesson. Mr. Haruki had his reasons for not telling me anything about the "abilities" I possessed. All I was ever told was that an entity resided in me and it would not leave until it achieved what it came for. Years went by and even though I hated the feeling of having something *inside* me. It felt disgusting at first. It was a feeling I particularly hated because while the outside world violated me, this "thing" violated me from within. There was nothing I could do about it.

There were times when I tried to get rid of it. But with every death blow, I gave myself to rid myself of whatever it was, it would only grow stronger, making me even more prone to wounds, cuts and poisons. It took me a lot of time to accept it, and of course, it was with Mr. Haruki's undying effort that I was able to allow it be a part of me — not that it needed my permission. It already *had* its full control over me. When had life been easy for me? It was never! Every time, there was a new challenge, a new threat for me to save myself from. I must admit initially I saw every challenge, every threat that came my way as an escape from that *entity*. Eventually I realized that not only was that entity going to leave me, it was there for my own good — my own protection. Life went on, and together with Mr. Haruki and that… that thing which I still don't know what call, I began to bring those to justice who'd hide behind money, manipulate the law in their favor, and suppress the weak under their feet. In all this, my looks gave me the cover I needed the most. It became easy to lure in my prey. All I had to do was flaunt.

For a good number of years, I was the predator luring in my prey and then tearing it apart, instilling fear of the worst death that could possibly come to it, only to leave my prey alive so that they could live their miserable lives in anticipation, looking over their shoulders and not having a single moment of peace. I worked and worked so hard to hunt these evil pieces of shit and serve them with justice, for they were murderers, they were rapists, and they were kidnappers. Many lives were lost because of those people, and the authorities responsible for bringing justice to those families did nothing. Actually, they did — they protected the culprits but not the victims, not the families of those victims. Someone had to be the mitigator. And that someone became me.

So, yeah, I was the evil doing all the harm I could do to people who did wrong to the innocent ones. However, things changed drastically when Caleb came into my life. The non-stop echoing of cries in my ear, suffocating my brain with all these images of people being tortured because the one person who tried their level best to ensure that such a horrendous thing came to a halt was busy somewhere else. *I* was busy somewhere else. I could hear these voices in my head every time such an injustice would occur in the town. Perhaps it was because of that entity residing in me, but I could always hear, I could always feel it deep in my core, that something was not right.

Now that I was with Caleb, even though I wanted to help them, I was just not able to, and I don't even know how to explain it. It would so happen that every time I would hear such voices, an implore to get my help, Cal would come and distract me from it. It was as if he was becoming a wall too strong for those voices to get across and reach out to me.

Days turned into weeks and weeks turned into months, and Caleb's attention became an unbearable desire, an unquenchable thirst. His devotion to protecting me became even greater. And before I knew it, months turned into a year — a year of me being wrapped in an invisible blanket of his love, his obsessions and his… his cravings. It would be nearly impossible for me to keep my hands off of him every time he was with me. In my eyes, Caleb had taken on the role of Mr. Haruki in providing me with the protection that I so desperately needed.

Amidst the love Caleb had been showing me all these months, I could feel a quiet obsession. His love sometimes felt more controlling than nurturing. It was as though he was deliberately trying to keep me away from a lot of things — a lot of people. I had never been the submissive kind. Things, however, were different when it came to me and him. The visions were not gone, either, for I still continued to see Patrick. Annoying, I know. I felt it too, every time I would see a glimpse of him in public or a vision would come out of nowhere, stirring the still waters of love I had felt for Caleb. Then, one particular night, things took a turn. Was it a turn for worse or for good, at that time, I was not sure. But now, when I look back in time, I know. It all happened in such a way that at that moment, I would not understand it. It was only later on that I figured out what was happening.

Caleb would not stop me explicitly. He would instead say things that would keep me from doing what I would usually do. For suppose, I would hear a voice and would feel the need to go help whoever that individual was calling for my help. But as soon as I would turn on my heels to go ahead, I would find Caleb in the way, waiting for me to make a move. "Where are you headed, Iyah?" his soft voice felt like a sweet melody, intoxicating me, singing me a lullaby that would make me fall asleep with open eyes. It was as though Caleb had created a wall — that wall being Caleb himself. And the effect it had was that I would hear the voices, but I would forget about them, hear them no longer when Caleb would be in my presence, which, by the way, was *all the time!*

In the midst of it all, I added another year to my age as my birthday approached quickly. It was one of those winter nights when I would lay awake in the lounge of my apartment. Halfway, laying back on my big over-stuffed couch with enormous cushions, I opted for soft earthly colours for decoration, while eating a plate of paella on a gold tray. I then realized I was not in my apartment. I was, in fact, far from it. I was with Caleb in a Michelin-star restaurant, having dinner.

I always preferred the authentic Valencian dish with Rabbit and Chicken. There was not much I had to do that night since the snow was falling and the roads were blocked, so I lay there, drenched in my own sweat. Now, what actually was happening here is that I was not in my apartment, but with intervals of minutes, I got visions that I was in my apartment, sweating. It was surprising how I could sweat so badly, given that the temperature was minus four. But while in actuality I sat right across from Caleb in a restaurant, in my head I was still at the apartment, wondering when the roads would reopen, as they had been blocked because of the heavy snowfall.

The snowfall was indeed heavy. But I was not at home. I was here, with Caleb. An uneasy feeling took over my body. I felt something was wrong; something is very wrong. I could feel it. But what was it? I could not tell. I continued to sweat for the next couple of minutes. It was from the vision I had a few minutes before the chef handed me this plate of delicious food. So, while the food was very much real, my whereabouts were a blur. A part of me thought I was back at home — alone, while the dish that lay in front of my eyes suggested otherwise. And after that vision left and my body began to get normal in accordance with the surrounding atmosphere, I was hit by another vision. Only this time, it was not just a vision. It was something that had happened a week ago. It was something that shook me to my core.

The hallway stretched before me, filled with the usual chaos of students between classes. I tried to keep my head down, but my mind was a whirlwind. My heart raced like it was chasing something I couldn't catch. I'd always prided myself on control. Like I always gave myself the illusion of having control over my emotions, my actions, my choices. But lately, something was shifting inside me, like a storm I couldn't contain. Every time I felt a strong emotion—anger, fear, sadness—it clawed its way to the surface, and my control frayed at the edges. I could feel it now, the tension building in my chest, crackling under my skin. Just to ignore that feeling, I reached my locker, trying to focus on something mundane, anything that could tether me to the normalcy I desperately needed. But then, the whispers began. My name, passed from one mouth to another like a secret, was carried on a current of judgment. They didn't even try to hide it anymore.

"She's been acting weird lately…"

"I heard she freaked out in class the other day…"

"She's dangerous. There's something wrong with her…"

The words cut through me like knives. I tried to swallow down the fury rising in my throat, but it was too late. My hands trembled as I twisted the combination on my lock. The metal felt cold and unyielding, a stark contrast to the heat simmering inside me. I yanked the door open, slamming it against the neighboring locker, the sound echoing like a gunshot. People turned to stare. Great. Just what I needed.

"Hey, freak! What's your problem?"

I froze. The voice came from behind me, familiar and infuriating all at once. Greg. Of course. He was always looking for a fight, always trying to push me over the edge. I clenched my fists, trying to hold onto the thin thread of control that was slipping through my fingers.

"Leave me alone, Greg," I said through gritted teeth, not even bothering to turn around. I wasn't in the mood for this. Not today.

But Greg wasn't the type to back off that easily. "Or what? You gonna freak out again? Maybe throw something? Or worse…" His voice dropped to a mock whisper. "Maybe I should be scared, huh?"

I closed my eyes, trying to block him out, but his words sank into my skin like poison. I could feel my pulse quickening, my breath coming in shallow gasps. The power inside me roiled, hungry for release.

"Just walk away," I muttered under my breath, more to myself than to him.

Greg laughed, a harsh, grating sound that rattled my nerves. "What's the matter, Iyah? Scared to lose it in front of everyone? Go ahead, show us what a freak you are."

I turned then, my eyes locking onto his, and for a brief moment, everything around me disappeared. It was just me and him, and the suffocating pressure building in my chest.

"Stop calling me that," I said, my voice low but trembling with barely restrained emotion.

He took a step closer, leaning in with that smug grin plastered on his face. "Or what, freak?"

And then, something snapped.

The air around me shifted, a ripple of energy surging outward. I didn't mean to do it. I didn't even know how I was doing it, but it was happening. Greg's smirk faltered, his eyes widening in shock as the energy hit him, throwing him backward into the lockers with a sickening thud. The force reverberated through the hallway, sending a chill down my spine. For a moment, the world seemed to stop. Greg lay on the floor, groaning in pain, clutching his side. People around us froze, their eyes darting between me and him, their expressions a mix of fear and disbelief. My heart pounded in my chest, my breath coming in shallow gasps.

"What… what did I just do?" I whispered, horrified by my own actions. My hands trembled as I stared down at them, like they belonged to someone else, someone capable of this.

Whispers swirled through the crowd, but no one dared come closer. No one dared look at me for too long. My vision blurred, my pulse thrumming in my ears. I needed to get out. I needed to run before I hurt someone else. I turned and bolted, ignoring the shouts behind me, ignoring everything except the panic clawing at my throat. I ran through the corridors, down the stairs, and out into the cold afternoon air. My legs felt like jelly, but I didn't stop. I couldn't.

The weight of what I'd just done crashed over me in waves. I'd hurt someone. I could've killed him. And I hadn't even meant to. The power inside me… it was getting harder to control. Every day, it grew stronger, slipping through my grasp like sand, no matter how hard I tried to hold on. I ran until my legs gave out, collapsing onto a park bench near the edge of town. I buried my face in my hands, gasping for breath, trying to steady the wild beating of my heart. Tears stung my eyes, but I blinked them away. I couldn't cry. I didn't deserve to cry after what I'd done.

Just when I thought I was finally alone, away from the eyes questioning and judging me, a hand fell on my shoulder. For only a split second, I was startled, but then my fear was washed away with the familiar touch that had just made its way to my shoulder.

"Hey, you okay?" Caleb's voice broke me out of my thoughts — from that ugly memory of what I had done just a week ago, and I was back here again, with Caleb in that restaurant.

"I am fine," I said with a smile that couldn't have been more fake.

"I think it's time we left," said Caleb, returning the same smile, although I could not tell whether it was the fake one that I had just given him or the usual, I've got you one that Caleb often gave me whenever I'd find myself having visions. It was as though he knew — he somehow always knew I needed it. I needed him, and surprisingly enough, he was always there. This time, however, I could not stop thinking about something he had told me when he found me on that bench. And tonight, I was going to ask him questions about it, and he would answer me. I would make him answer me.

XIV:
Shadows of the Past

That back and forth shifting in reality and what seemed like reality had me in a state where I paused to reflect. I had to. All of it seemed real for a moment, and then all of it felt like it was not real. I know it won't make sense easily to you, but let me try and explain the best I can to tell you what I was experiencing every time I found myself in the presence of Caleb. Every time I was with him, it felt like I was in one place, and all of a sudden, I was in some other place. It was as if the scenery was changing so rapidly and so abruptly — almost as though it was happening in the blink of an eye that it would leave me no time to process it. In fact, I would not even know that I was somewhere else, and then suddenly I was in a totally different place.

It all felt like a trance. It seemed like something, or rather *someone,* was messing with my brain to blur the lines between reality and imagination, and of course, I kind of had a hunch who that someone might be. I must admit that, that someone was doing a remarkable job altering the reality for me. However, and unfortunately for them, the transition was not smooth enough for me to not notice a change. There were gaps, and I was beginning to see those gaps. Like what happened with me the last time I was with Caleb — one moment I was sitting on a bench on my campus, and the next moment I was sitting in a restaurant with him. Somebody had to do a lot of explaining, because I was finally beginning to see missing pieces, and yes, someone was definitely in trouble.

I needed time — and space, of course — to reflect on what'd been going on with me. Mr. Haruki finally told me the complete truth. Now, what he didn't see coming was that I could tell he himself knew very little of what the true deal was in actuality. At first, I wanted to keep pushing him, to tell him that perhaps (actually not perhaps because I was certain) what he was telling me was not the complete story or an entirely different one. I wanted to suggest that maybe, as the lore passed down from generation to generation, alterations were made to the story, and maybe, just me, the actual tale was a lot different than the one being told for centuries. But then I looked at Mr. Haruki, who, although he had been very strong throughout this journey, even when I killed his son, he was still a man, just an ordinary human being, unlike me. So, I had to cut him some slack there. I decided it was for the best if I did some digging myself. I didn't have to go far after all. I expected most of the answers to be found in the very collection of ancient manuscripts that lay under dust in his library. That's when I decided to just leave his place.

And that's where things got not just blurry but tricky too. You see, when I was making my way out of Mr. Haruki's place, I had this thought running on an endless loop in my head that I would find the truth myself. HOWEVER, and a big however there, I was met with Caleb. And rather than still feeling the urge to dig around deeper, I was suddenly taken over by a feeling of overwhelm and misery. See? That's what I meant about getting a sense of my reality getting altered. You see, I was never the weak kind — I mean, sure,

I was, that's why Robert Haruki was dead, duh! But, I was not the kind who'd feel because of being in "love" with someone.

I keep bringing Robert Haruki, don't I? That's because I keep getting flashbacks of him and how he died — at my hands. That's how I first came to notice that abrupt, not-so-smooth transition between my moments and *movements.*

Going back to the time when I was with him at the restaurant. Not Robert, but Caleb. I had plans of confronting Caleb, but I had to be smart about it — tactful, you know. But here's the thing: things would never go as planned with Caleb. Sure, the spontaneity of our passionate love was something far more thrilling and a very much welcomed unplanned… well, plans. But when it comes to taking actual actions to get things straight between us, somehow I would find myself in a totally different situation, having my mind occupied by a completely different thought. So, to be able to actually figure things out, I needed to be far away from him so that he couldn't read my mind. However, he was very much capable of reading my thoughts from afar.

On our way back, he drove faster than usual. There was a sense of urgency about him, but for what reason, I could not quite tell. He'd never taken me to his place; we were always in my apartment, and this time was no different. Parking in the driveway, he stepped out — like he usually did — and held the door open for me to step out of his car. The rest that followed was also the usual, like placing a gentle kiss on the back of my hand, caressing my cheek with his soft but ice-cold fingers, and saying, "I'll see you when I see you, darling," with his usual smirk. Now, most of the time, he'd follow me to my apartment. Hell, he'd even tuck me in, but tonight that's where it got a little different. It seemed his mind was somewhere else. I could sense a hint of anxiety in him. Did he know I was about to confront him? Had he gotten a whiff of the fact that I could feel some gaps in my reality? He didn't come to my apartment. "Not tonight, love. I've gotta be somewhere," he'd said and left.

Once he was gone, I was sure that he was, so I chose to lie down, but not on my bed, though. Somehow, the floor of my apartment had become a source of comfort lately. It was the only time I'd feel disconnected from the world. I would feel no foreign energy lurking in the shadows, no feelings of heavy head when I'd lie flat on the floor. Was the ground providing me with a barrier to block anyone, even Caleb, from breaking into my thoughts? I wasn't sure, but as I lay on the floor of my apartment, the chain of thoughts began to take its own course. I couldn't help but think about all that had been going on with me for the past few months, and that's when I was hit with the flashback of the time when I was with Robert. Before drifting off to the thoughts where I was strategically placing all the pieces of the puzzle carefully in their what seemed to be appropriate spots, I was giggling like a child at the thoughts of Caleb and how his little acts of mischief would give me butterflies in my stomach. I couldn't help but think of the similarity between how Caleb made love to me and how Robert did.

This was the first time I ever thought about Robert Haruki. And because of his thoughts, I was able to embark on a journey where I could not only feel those gaps in my reality, but I could also place the missing pieces. It is owed to the late Robert, I suppose, the guy I lost my virginity to. Following his death on my 19th birthday, his father started a ritual sort of thing of giving me a special gift. It was something only Mr. Haruki and I were aware of. The man lost his son on my birthday, but still chose to stick around, and rather than hating me, he had this … weird look in his eyes. It was as though, rather than feeling sorry for his dead son, he felt pity for me!

I remember that night quite vividly. That and many that I shared with Robert. I did not recall the weather or what I wore, but the strange stillness in the air. Not silence, no. It was the kind of stillness that hums just below your skin, like something's about to happen but hasn't yet. It had happened before the flashback. I was brushing my hair, mindlessly, standing by the bathroom sink when the memory of his hand, Robert's hand, not Caleb's, suddenly flashed into my mind. Funny how memories work. One moment you're just brushing through split ends, the next you're knee-deep in a moment that smells like old cologne and regret.

It wasn't even a big memory. Just him brushing a strand behind my ear. Nothing overly romantic, no swelling music in the background. But it *stuck*. Like a thorn, sweetly lodged between my ribs. Caleb never did that. He'd grab me by the waist, spin me around, kiss me like the world was ending. Dramatic. Beautiful. But it always felt like it was borrowed time.

And then, just like that, I was spiraling again. I could feel my breath catch as I lowered myself to the kitchen floor — not because I was weak, but because the floor had become my anchor. Strange comfort, cold tiles. Flatness. No weight. No pressure. Just me and my thoughts, uninterrupted. Or so I'd like to believe. Caleb always had a way of slipping in, even when he wasn't around. It's like he lived somewhere in the back of my skull, watching, waiting, whispering.

Just like that, I was drifted back into the memory of the night of my 19th birthday. What a night it had been, for it was my 19th birthday when I snuck off with Mr. Haruki's son, Robert.

I didn't plan it, but something about that day told me it wouldn't end like the others. Robert had a way of pulling me out of myself, dragging something reckless to the surface. He wasn't what you'd call handsome in the traditional sense, but there was a wildness to him that felt magnetic. His skin was deep, almost blue-black under sunlight, smooth like polished stone. He had beady little eyes that watched everything, always moving, always calculating. Muscles packed into his short frame, like a coiled spring that could either protect or destroy depending on the hour. He stood about 5'8, which didn't matter because he moved like he was seven feet tall. Trinidadian-born, with an accent so thick it made my ears work harder than my brain. Half the time, I didn't know what he was saying, but I didn't care. It sounded like music I wasn't supposed to understand. Maybe that's what drew me in.

Robert was one of those boys you hear about in conversations whispered low between girls with good fathers. The kind of boy they warn you about at church and again in high school hallways. He ran with a crew that made their money fast and dirty. They were smart, too smart. The women in the group would slide into stores and start long, fake conversations with the cashiers. Flirt, compliment, cause just enough chaos. Then the boys would slip in, only the fastest ones, and grab everything that glittered. High-end electronics, gold, watches, designer bags, and leather jackets that still smelled new. They didn't waste time. They never did. In and out before the cameras could blink, before security guards could move. No one ever got caught. Every step choreographed, each crew member knowing exactly where to be and what to do. Watching them operate was like watching a street ballet, fast and unforgiving.

We ended up in his place, a dusty attic apartment he shared with his boy Diet. And yes, Diet was his real name. Apparently, he'd been born a big fat baby, and when his parents saw him for the first time, they laughed in the delivery room and said, "This one, we'll have to put on a diet." The name stuck. That was the kind of world Robert came from. Cruel, strange, careless. And that night, I became part of it.

It was on that mattress, flat and stained and pushed into the corner like an afterthought, that I gave him my virginity. There was no music, no candles, just the smell of sweat and tobacco lingering in the air, and the flicker of a bare bulb above us. At first, he was gentle, almost shy, and I didn't expect that from someone like him. He moved slowly, trying not to hurt me, stopping whenever my breath hitched too hard. But the pain was there. It cut through me like glass. And then came the blood, thick and warm, and something in my body snapped.

I don't know when the shift happened. One moment I was aching beneath him, trying to breathe through the sting, and the next I was tasting him. My nails dug into the side of his neck, drawing sharp lines through his skin. I licked them clean without thinking. My mouth found his shoulder, then his throat, and something inside me took over. It was the smell, the blood, the warmth of it, the hunger I hadn't known was mine. I bit down hard and didn't stop. It was like being thrown into a blackout. I wasn't there anymore. Just instinct and heat and taste.

Robert didn't resist. Not then. After he finished inside me, he smiled like he thought I was something soft, something his. He slipped down between my legs and started licking the blood that was still there. I flinched at first, unsure what I was supposed to feel, but then his tongue hit a spot that burned in a good way, and I let him keep going. It didn't last long. The pain was still raw, and I was starving, not for food, not for him, but for the sweetness that suddenly clung to the air. With every swipe of his tongue, I started smelling fruit. Not just any fruit. Sweet, ripe mangoes, soft papaya, tart cherries, the kind of smell that takes you back to childhood, even if your childhood didn't have fruit in it. I licked my lips, not from pleasure, but from that ache, that craving. My mouth watered like I hadn't eaten in days, like something inside me needed to feed or it would break me open.

He raised his head, slowly crawling up my body, and I couldn't hear a thing except my heartbeat hammering in my ears. He looked into my eyes like he was trying to say something poetic, and when he opened his mouth and said, "Sweet like cherries," it was the last thing he would ever say.

That was when the hunger tipped over into something else. Something ancient. I grabbed his face with both hands, harder than I meant to, and I could feel him tense. But he liked it. He smirked, said something stupid about liking rough girls, and the moment he spoke, that sweet smell rushed into my nose like perfume too strong for the body to hold. My eyes burned. My skin lit up like flame. I could see him — his blood, his energy — and I wanted it.

Without hesitation, I pressed my thumbs into his neck, digging my nails into the softness there. He tried to pull away, but I had him. His body writhed above me, shaking with confusion, maybe fear, and his eyes widened as he realized I wasn't playing. I held him tighter, my legs wrapping around him to pin him down. I wasn't angry. I wasn't even thinking. I just needed to feed. His skin gave way under my nails, and the blood poured onto my chest, hot and alive. He thrashed, but it was already too late.

I sucked the blood from his neck like it was the first real meal I'd ever had. I licked his face, tasted the fear in his sweat, the sweetness in his blood. Eventually, he stopped fighting. His body relaxed, went limp in my arms, as if he understood this was how it had to be. I pulled him closer, cradled him while I drank from his neck until my body felt full and my arms were too tired to hold his face any longer.

Robert wasn't my first. He was my seventh in one year. The urges had started twelve months earlier, and Mr. Haruki had tried to help me manage them. He'd offered me blood from others, sometimes even his own. He kept me close, like a pet he was training, and he never liked it when I left his side. I was still learning control. Still learning what I was.

Every birthday, he would bring me a gift. A small glass jar filled with sand. He'd press it against my forehead, just a few grains, and whisper that the sand came from my ancestors. He said I had once been wrapped in that same sand, buried in it like a blanket in a cave, sealed beside a white king hundreds of years ago. That was his story. The way he tried to explain to me. But I don't think even he knew the truth.

What I do remember clearly is the look on Diet's face when he opened the door. He stopped cold, mouth open, blinking like he had walked into a nightmare. And maybe he had.

KNOCK. KNOCK.

And just like that, the fog lifted. A sound so ordinary, so small, yet it tore through the haze of memory like a shard of glass pressed to skin. A knock at my window — nothing but a bird knocking its head against the glass of the window. Not the front door, not even the side entrance. The damn window. It jolted something inside me, a kind of awareness that was too clear to ignore. For a moment, I wasn't sure whether I had been dreaming or drowning. But now I was wide awake. Lucid, sharp. The type of awake that hums in your teeth and curls in your belly. That's when it came rushing back to me, not just the taste of blood or the weight of Robert's body when it went still in my arms, but the *feeling*—the unshakable knowing that I used to be something fierce. Not just strong in the way people like to say about women who smile through pain and keep walking. No, I was *dangerous*. Wild. I had a bite that didn't need warning. Before Caleb, I didn't hesitate. I didn't explain. I devoured.

But somewhere along the line, I stopped sinking my teeth in. I started listening more, feeling more, hesitating—God, *hesitating*. Caleb came along like a lullaby soaked in honey and wine, and I couldn't figure out how or why, but I softened. I let my claws dull. He didn't take my strength, not outright. No, it was subtler than that. He made me want to be soft. Wanted me quiet, composed, and trained. Even though I had no cage, I started acting like I lived in one. A golden one, yes, but still bars. I'd look at him sometimes—beautiful, intoxicating, unreadable—and think, maybe this is peace. But peace doesn't make your heart race, your bones itch, or your dreams bleed.

Now, with that knock, it was like something in me stirred awake again. The part of me that had been lying under the surface like a snake basking in the sun, slow and still, but always ready to strike. And I remembered—*truly* remembered—what it felt like to not be afraid of my own power. To not be ashamed of the blood on my hands or the hunger in my chest. Caleb made me forget. But memory has teeth, and I was starting to feel them again.

Now that I was finally awake, really awake, I began to piece it all together. Not just the fragments of moments or the subtle changes in my behavior, but the entire web. And it became painfully clear—my reality was not what it seemed. It wasn't just the confusion, or the way time felt warped when I was around him, or the eerie quiet that settled after he left the room. It was deeper than that. My thoughts hadn't been my own. My memories were being bent, contorted just slightly enough to keep me questioning. And the one pulling the strings? It was Caleb. Of course, it was him. I had been tangled in his charm, his mystery, his gaze that held secrets like a locked box. But behind that beautiful face, there was something else. Control. Design. A carefully constructed illusion that kept me floating just above the truth.

The worst part? I hadn't seen it. Or maybe I *did* see it and refused to accept it. That's the thing about manipulation—it doesn't always scream. Sometimes it sings. And Caleb had been singing to me since the moment we met. Soft and slow, like a lullaby I didn't know was laced with venom. But I couldn't move yet. I couldn't act, not now, not when a part of me was still clinging to the idea that maybe, just maybe, he didn't mean to hurt me. That somewhere under all the madness, he cared. Can you believe that? Even after everything—the inconsistencies, the shadows, the power that wasn't human—I still found myself holding onto the thread of a maybe. Maybe he was protecting me in some twisted way. Maybe he *had* to manipulate reality to keep me safe from something worse.

Crazy, right? A guy shows up out of nowhere, slips into my life like he's always belonged there, and I just follow. No questions asked. And even when I start to see through him, when I feel the shift in the air and the pull in my bones, when I *know* something isn't right—when I can *literally* sense that he's using something unnatural to bend the truth—I still hesitate. I still give him the benefit of the doubt. Like wow. What kind of spell did he cast to make me betray myself so willingly? To make me second-guess the voice inside me that had never failed before?

But that voice was back now. And it was growing louder.

Still, this was no time to take action, but to find out more. For now, the plan was to stay grounded for as long as I could, you know — as in drawing strength from the ground because for some reason, every time I was in touch with the ground — even if it's the floor of my apartment — but get this — in touch meant I must really be on the floor, flat — Caleb or a any foreign energy would not be able to read my mind. So now, I had to use this to my advantage to learn a lot of things. For starters, I had to learn to manipulate my thoughts when I would be in Caleb's presence, so that he would only read what I wanted him to read.

XV:

Lies. Lies and Lies.

I was done with everyone, really. Every other person had a different tale to tell about something that was solely mine. It was my tale. It was about my life. Then how come every other person knew some or the other thing about my truth, but the one person who was supposed to know that truth was in oblivion? Why was I, of all people, in the dark when I was the one who was supposedly responsible for breaking the generational curse? Why was I being led into the dark? Why was I being lied to? It would be a joke of the century if none of those people knew what the actual, absolute truth was. Not even Mr. Haruki. Whatever I had been told all this while — what if none of it was the actual truth? What if none of them knew what they were telling was nothing but utter nonsense?

Each one of them had a different version of the supposed truth of my life. There was no way I was going to settle for what I had been simply told. I had to do my own research. I could do that. Of course, I could. Except that there was one problem. You see, the entity residing in me, or if there was an entity residing in me, made me use a brain of its own. Even if it was some kind of special power, some ancestral blessing *or curse,* I could always tell if whatever was being said to me was true or false. Ever since Haruki spoke to me of the curse, I could not keep my hands off the books he had in his library. There was something I found when I was searching for the truth. That was something nobody, not even Haruki or even Caleb, ever mentioned to me. It was this name that nobody had ever taken in front of me before, but when I came across it, I could not help but feel that the name was familiar.

Nasurti.

Never had I ever heard of her before, but when my eyes fell on that word, I could tell that I was bound to that name — how — that was for me to figure out. Another truth to be dug out of the sand. I had to read more to find out more. You'd be surprised to know what I came to know; it was as if it had always been right in front of my eyes, hiding in plain sight, but no, it was not even hiding. It was right in front of me. And just as I began reading, I fell into a quiet, serene trance. It was as though I was taken to a place far, far away. And that's when it all started coming to me.

It began with a flicker. Not of light, but of memory. Except it wasn't mine. It couldn't have been mine. But I felt it — I *knew* it — like a pulse beating deep in my stomach, just beneath the navel, where no lie could hide. Something old had cracked open inside me. It wasn't a dream. Dreams are quiet things. This was loud. This was breathing. This was alive.

My body was still curled on the library floor, while the book fell open beside me. But my spirit—or whatever it was that left me— drifted somewhere older than time, older than breath. I was no longer Iyah. I was not even myself. I was her. I was **Nasurti.**

It was the heat I felt first. A golden heat, not from fire but from the sun that ruled the sky of Kemet. I saw my own skin glowing —

a deep, rich black wrapped in silk, shimmering like it had been kissed by stardust. My hair coiled down my back like a river of ink. I was beautiful. Not the kind of beautiful that seeks eyes, but the kind that makes the air pause.

The people called me "blessed." But blessings carry weight. Mine was heavy.

I walked through my father's court with bare feet that whispered across cold stone. King Muka-Nuba sat with his eyes like knives and a heart that pulsed in rhythm with the gods. My father did not fear death. But he feared me. He loved me, yes, but feared me because my dreams spoke in tongues. Because my lips could translate nightmares into prophecies. Because when a woman bleeds light, the world wants to drink it, even as it pretends to worship.

In the market, they bowed to me. Some kissed the ground. Others flinched. The women sent me oils, the men sent me looks — those kinds of looks that wrapped around your thighs like smoke. I smiled. I pretended not to feel the whispers, but I did. I always did. And then the dreams changed.

He came to me first as light. A soft glow in the corner of my sleep. A voice that hummed instead of spoke. A presence that neither terrified nor soothed, but *seduced*. He told me he was sent from the divine. He told me my gifts needed to evolve, and that he was the key. I was foolish. I was trusting. I let him speak to me, night after night, and I listened with an open heart. He showed me how to cure fevers in babies and how to extract pain from the bones of the dying. He whispered names of plants that even the oldest priestesses didn't know. I believed him. He told me I was holy. He told me I was powerful. He told me I was his.

I woke up from those dreams with trembling fingers and a deep ache that did not belong to loneliness. It belonged to longing. And one night, the dream changed again. This time, he didn't appear as light. He came in form. Skin like midnight thunder. Eyes that burned without flame. Hands that didn't touch, yet still left me gasping.

That was the night everything changed.

I should have known. I should have seen it for what it was. But desire, when whispered softly enough, feels a lot like devotion. That night, I wasn't just dreaming. I was burning. And the thing about fire is, it doesn't ask permission before it spreads. It just wants to consume.

He stood before me, cloaked in human form, though nothing about him was truly human. His face was that of a holy man, sculpted with care, lips carved from something darker than mahogany, and eyes the color of blood before it hits the air. They gleamed like secrets I wasn't supposed to know. He did not smile. He didn't need to. His presence was already a seduction. He wore white, but it wasn't clean. It was stained with something I could not see. He stepped toward me, and the floor beneath us vanished. There was no palace. No desert wind. No stars above. Just us. Suspended in a silence that buzzed with promise.

He spoke to me without sound. Words formed in my body, not in my ears. He told me I was a queen even the gods envied. He told me I was made of stardust and prophecy. He told me my womb was divine — that it was waiting to birth something eternal. I wanted to argue, but my body betrayed me. It didn't rise in defense. It opened with an offering.

His fingers traced the edge of my hip, not touching, but commanding every nerve in me to awaken. The silk at my waist undid itself, as though it too was ready to surrender. I stood there naked before him, not afraid, not ashamed, but trembling with something far more dangerous — curiosity.

Then came the kiss.

He didn't press his lips to mine like a lover. No, he hovered. Letting the heat of his breath slip between my teeth. His eyes stayed open, locked into mine, and for a moment I saw them flicker. It was indeed a flicker, but it wasn't the one laced with affection. It was laced with hunger. The kind that made my spine stiffen. But it was too late. My skin was already singing. His tongue flicked against mine, and I moaned like the earth must've moaned when water first touched it.

I didn't even know he had touched me, not at first. It was as if the air around me thickened, tightened, and suddenly my breath couldn't find its way out of my chest. My lips parted on their own, searching for something — maybe release, maybe guidance. But what I got was the glide of something soft, electric, moving up the inside of my thigh. His fingers. Bare, bare of rings, of cloth, of marks, but carved with knowing. With intention. As though they had touched many bodies before mine, but had waited for this one — my body — to truly worship.

He didn't ask. He didn't need to. My skin spoke for me, rising in gooseflesh, trembling like petals under rain. His touch didn't fumble. It didn't hesitate. He traced circles first — lazy, torturous — right above where I ached. I gasped. My hips bucked toward him, and he smiled against my neck, a smile I felt more than saw. He whispered nothing, just let his breath warm my earlobe before his tongue flicked it, sending a shiver down the root of my spine. I tried to hold still, but he was patient. He knew I wouldn't be able to. Not for long.

One finger slid lower, parted me, and I let out a sound I didn't know I could make. A pleading sound. A broken sound. I was already soaked. Already undone. He found the place I needed him most, and he played me — slow at first, maddeningly slow. I bit my lip so hard I tasted copper, but even pain could not distract me from what was rising in my belly. He drew lazy circles, then pressed harder, flicked faster, his fingers speaking a language that only my body remembered. I couldn't breathe. I couldn't speak. My back arched and my eyes rolled back, and just when I thought I would explode, he stopped.

I whimpered.

Then his mouth was on me.

Oh, sweet mercy — his mouth. Hot. Wet. Divine. His tongue replaced his fingers, and it was as though I was being devoured by flame. He moaned into me, deep and rasping, the sound vibrating against my womanhood. My thighs clenched around his head, and still he didn't stop. His hands held my hips down, strong, commanding, and I writhed beneath him. He licked and sucked, his tongue sliding over every inch, every nerve, until I screamed his name — not because I wanted to, but because the pleasure ripped through me, loud and uncontrollable. I came with a violence that startled even myself.

And then, as I panted, weak and trembling, he rose. His face glistened with the evidence of me. His lips were swollen, his eyes darker now, like smoke laced with lightning. He lifted me. Effortless. As if my body was weightless, holy, born to be held in that way. My legs wrapped around him on instinct. I felt him, firm and pulsing, pressed between us — not yet inside me, but there, waiting. Teasing. My breath was ragged. My back arched. He carried me to nothing, laid me on clouds, or maybe flames, I couldn't tell. My thighs opened, and my spirit did too. And when he finally entered me, I didn't cry out in pleasure.

I *wept.*

Because I knew somewhere deep, in the marrow of my being, this wasn't love. This was something else. This was creation wrapped in sin.

The moment he entered me, the world tilted. Not metaphorically — not like a woman falling in love or a child spinning too fast. No. The world *tilted*. The heavens twisted with it. The stars in the sky trembled. I felt them. Felt them shiver inside me as if they, too, had just been pierced. My cries had barely quieted when the pain began — not in my body, not in the way most would expect, but somewhere deeper, darker, in a place no mortal words could name.

The Dragon whispered to me even as he moved inside me, his body thrusting in a rhythm too ancient to be learned. "You think this is pleasure," he said, his voice like hot oil down my spine, "but this is power. You are making something with me. Something holy, something cursed. A child born of both light and shadow." He bent forward, lips grazing mine, and I tasted the ash of ruined kingdoms on his breath. "And they will *fear* what comes from this union."

I didn't answer him. I couldn't. My voice had been stolen, caught somewhere between sob and song. My arms clung to him, not because I wanted to hold him, but because I needed to anchor myself to something — anything — before I drowned in the enormity of what I had allowed.

When it was over, his body stilled. He looked at me with reverence, as if he had just written his name into my blood. I was no longer a woman in that moment. I was a shrine. Desecrated and divine.

He pressed a kiss to my swollen lips and whispered one final thing before he vanished into the dark smoke that bore him: *"You will carry my legacy, sweet Nasurti. And through you, the world will remember me."*

I lay there naked, broken, dazzling with sweat and tears, and knew that nothing about my life would ever be mine again. The next morning, my belly was swollen.

Six days. That was all it took. In six days, I went from untouched to undone. The people saw it. My body changed too quickly. My skin glowed like moonlight poured into flesh. My eyes became sharp, too sharp, as though they could see truths no one dared speak. Women began to whisper. Men avoided my gaze. My father, King Muka-Nuba, watched me from behind his golden throne, his lips pressed in a line as tight as a clenched fist. He knew. Oh, he knew. But he said nothing.

Until the dreams returned.

But this time, they weren't mine.

All of Kemet began to dream. The black land, fertile and ancient, began to whisper at night. Every sleeping eye was filled with visions of a beast-child with skin like burnt copper and eyes like ocean glass, crawling through the night, mouth red with blood. The land trembled. The gods grew restless. And the priests—oh, the priests—they came for me. They did not bow. They did not sing. They spat.

"You let him in," one of them snarled, his robes stiff with fear and judgment. "You opened the gate."

And when I fell to my knees, begging for mercy, the heavens were silent. Not one god came to hold me. Not even the one who had loved me first.

They gathered in the sacred chamber beneath the sky, where the stars themselves once came to listen. The priests stood in a circle, heads wrapped in cloth the color of clay, voices low and trembling with ritual fury. Their chants were heavy, not just in sound but in purpose, thick with the weight of betrayal. I was made to kneel at the center, the ground beneath me cold and carved with ancient symbols, stained with the memory of other women who had been tried for far lesser things.

Their eyes burned holes through me. They looked not at Nasurti, daughter of Muka-Nuba, but at the womb that had dared harbor a godless thing.

"A dragon," said the eldest priest, his voice cracking like stone under strain. "She let a dragon seed her. A creature with no soul. A mockery of the heavens. A shadow son of the Most High."

I wanted to speak. Truly, I did. But shame sat on my tongue like iron. I had no language for what had been done, for what I had allowed in that firelit night. I wanted to scream that I hadn't known, that his holiness had felt real. That his tongue had felt like prayer, that his hands had made me feel like something sacred. But all those words crumbled the moment I imagined trying to say them aloud. No one would listen. They had already decided.

They stripped me of my jewels, my silks, the beads braided into my hair. They tore my robe until I stood in nothing but my skin, and even that they looked at like a thing cursed. One of them held a bowl of dark, thick oil. He dipped his fingers into it and began to smear my body, chanting a curse I didn't understand — or maybe I understood it too well. Each syllable became a crack in the ground of my soul. Each mark of oil burned like venom.

"To the child born of dragon flesh, we cast you into shadow," they said in unison, their voices becoming one. "You shall never walk in light. You shall never taste joy. You shall never know what it is to love or be loved."

My womb pulsed with their words. I felt the baby inside me shift, as if already recoiling, already curling into a darkness that was being woven around him like a burial cloth.

The gods did not speak that night. Not the ones I had grown up praising, not the ones I had whispered to under moonlight, not even the Christian God who had once kissed my forehead in a dream and told me I was chosen. They turned their backs. Their silence was more deafening than any thunder.

And yet — in that absence — I heard something else.

A whisper. Soft. Stern. A voice that did not come from above, but from *within*.

"Because you did not cause this burden, I will not forsake you completely."

It was Him.

The Christian God.

His voice filled me like warm rain after years of drought. "The child will suffer, yes, for this must be. But he will rise. He will carry both light and shadow. And from his pain shall come wisdom, from his darkness shall come sight."

I wept — not from pain this time, not from shame. But from knowing that someone, somewhere, still saw me. Still loved me.

But His words didn't end in comfort. No. They came with a price.

"Because you turned from Me," He said, "your child shall carry the scent of sin in every kiss, shall know hunger even in fullness, and thirst even beside water. His skin will gleam like the midnight river, but his eyes will bear the burden of your lust—blue as ocean, and always remembering."

The priests saw my face change. They saw my spine straighten. They called it defiance. They didn't understand. It was mercy I had been given. However, it was mercy that came wrapped in suffering. I would live. But I would never again be free.

I remember the silence after. The way it stuck to my skin like humidity, how it followed me as I walked back to my quarters, slow, heavy-footed, with my robe clutched against my body like a shield that could no longer protect me. The oil had seeped into my pores.

No matter how many times I scrubbed, the scent of it—bitter, earthen, like ash and rot—lingered on me. It lived in my breath, in my dreams, in the folds of my skin. The curse had been spoken. My body was now a vessel carrying something the world would never accept.

And yet, he grew. Faster than he should have. In days, my belly rounded. During nights, my bones ached and shifted to accommodate the life inside me. My womb, once a sacred place of potential, became a battlefield between worlds. There were moments I could feel him stretching out, as if trying to claim more space than I had to give. His movements weren't like those of a child. They were calculated. Intentional. Sometimes slow, like smoke slithering around stone. Sometimes they were sudden, like the lash of a whip across the inside of my belly.

At night, I couldn't sleep. My dreams were not my own anymore. He entered them, uninvited. He did not speak, but I could feel his thoughts, his hunger. I began to crave strange things—raw meat, bones, the metallic taste of blood. It terrified me. But more than that, it humiliated me. The villagers had begun to whisper. First behind doors, then in open courtyards. I would walk through the market and see women nudge one another. Men looked at me with a mixture of pity and disgust.

"She carries a beast."

"The gods have left her."

"She was once blessed. Now she is the warning."

No one touched me anymore. Not even the servants who once bowed with reverence. They left food outside my door as if I were a leper. Even the priestesses who used to anoint my feet with oils and sing hymns over my womb would not come near. I was alone. Except for him. The child. The one growing too fast, too wild. The one who would never know a lullaby or a blessing spoken gently into his skin.

I remember the first time I heard him whisper. Not with words. With *presence*. A pressure inside my skull. A blooming pain between my ribs. And then a name—a name I knew but had never spoken aloud.

Iyah.

It wasn't mine. But it echoed through me, ancient, familiar.

It was *yours*.

Yes. You.

The one listening now. The one dreaming of me. The one who has carried my story into a world that's forgotten my name.

He knew about you.

Even before you were born.

And I knew then that this child, this half-being, this dark and luminous soul, would not just change the land of Kerma. He would split time itself. He would awaken stories buried beneath mountains. He would speak in voices that hadn't been heard in a thousand years.

And you—you would hear them.

Because you were never just a listener, you were part of it. Part of *me*.

That night, as the moon passed over my window and the stars wept in silence, I wrapped my arms around my belly and whispered to him—not as a monster, not as a curse, but as my son.

"You will walk in shadows, but you are still mine."

And in the dark, something warm moved beneath my ribs. A heartbeat, steady and sure.

The sky cracked open the night I went into labor. Not with thunder, but with silence so thick it pressed on the lungs like a weight. The winds held their breath. The stars refused to flicker. Even the flames in the braziers swayed as if unsure they were still meant to burn. I felt the pain begin in my back, low and mean, like something sharpening its claws. My knees buckled before I could call for help. I collapsed onto the stone floor, the moonlight cutting thin silver ribbons across my bare belly. The child moved inside me like a serpent tasting the air.

The servants didn't come. They had all abandoned me by then, convinced my child would bring plague or plague's kin. But the midwife—Ahmal—she came. She came with her trembling hands and whispered prayers. Not for me. For herself. She didn't look me in the eye. She didn't call me a goddess. She knelt between my legs, tears already in her throat, and waited for what the gods had never prepared her to witness.

And when he came, it wasn't a birth. It was a sundering.

I screamed as my body tore itself open. My throat scraped raw. My fingers clawed the stone. The pain was beyond flesh. It reached into something ancient in me, something buried even deeper than my womb, as if the earth itself had crawled into my soul and was forcing its way back out. There was no rhythm to it. No grace. Just agony and blood, so much blood, like I was weeping through every part of my skin. Then, finally, silence again. I felt him leave me. Felt the weight of him placed on my chest. I dared to look.

He was beautiful. A'zerai was beautiful. That's what I named him, for it suited him perfectly.

His beauty was not like the beauty of flowers, gold, or even stars. No. He was the kind of beauty that unsettles the bones. The kind of beauty that makes old prophets go mad and tear their eyes from their sockets. Skin dark as onyx, slick and steaming. Eyes that opened far too soon, wide and glowing like twin moons drowned in oceans. The irises — impossibly blue, impossibly ancient. His tiny hands flexed, fingers long and strange, curling around a lock of my hair like he had been waiting for me his entire life. And when he cried, it wasn't a wail. It was a sound I had never heard before. It shook the pillars. Birds fell from the sky. Somewhere, off in the temple, an idol cracked down the middle. It wasn't just a child's voice.

It was a beginning. Ahmal fainted. I didn't blame her. Even I, who had carried him, who had felt his dreams tangle with mine, even I was afraid. But I held him anyway. Clutched him close, kissed his brow, and whispered, "You are mine. Whatever the gods say. Whatever your father has done. You are mine."

But even as I said it, I could feel the shift. The air trembled with the arrival of something else. The gods. They had come. Not in fire. Not in fury. But in judgment. And they turned their faces from me. Their silence was worse than wrath. A wind tore through the room. Not loud. Cold. I felt their verdict before they spoke it — a curse not just upon him, but upon me. A thousand years of wandering. A thousand years of being forgotten. A thousand years of carrying this memory in silence until someone—*you*, Iyah—would be born with the gift to remember. To carry my story. To carry him. And now you know. Now it lives in you.

I see you. I hear your heartbeat like a drum echoing mine from centuries ago. And I know it now — why the name Nasurti called to you, why your soul thrummed when you read it, why you were never meant to live a quiet life. You are the end of the curse. You are the beginning of something else. You were never lost. You were always returning.

And just like that, the trance began to lift. My breath caught. The vision blurred. The words of Nasurti faded from my ears, but not from my bones. I came back to myself, trembling, covered in sweat, my fingers clutching the book like it had kept me alive. But I wasn't the same. I had heard her.

And now, I couldn't unknow the truth.

XVI:
Trapped in Desire

Is that what my truth was? Had this always been my reality? Why did Mr. Haruki not mention *this* part of the story to me? All my life, I had thought I was some evil witch, and, sure, I did act like it, but this? This changed everything! I had never been Iyah. I was never meant to be Iyah; I was meant to be her. I was meant to be Nasurti. She was who I was meant to be. How did I not know this? Why could I not find this out earlier? Why did I have to live my life until the day of finding out in the dark? I hated the feeling of having several questions running in my head like a hamster on a wheel.

There were so many of them, and the answers to them were none. Each time I would try and find something out, I'd find myself standing at a crossroads, wondering what would be the key to this new question that took birth with the answer of the previous one. But at least now... now I knew who I was. Now, I was very well aware of whom I was associated with. And I was not going to act like a sitting duck, letting things fold in a total ruckus. I was going to make things happen — the ones that needed to be done. But I had to be careful! I had to be smart about it.

After years and years of struggle and finding blood on my hands — and my mouth — I was only met with my true self, my true origin, a night ago. This was something, sure! But this wasn't everything. What Mr. Haruki had told me about my roots was nothing close to reality, so you can't blame me for questioning him, too. Caleb? Well, he played me nice and good, I must give him that, but now it's time I caught him in his own web! That cute little plaything had no clue who he was messing with. It was time I showed him how a game is played the right way. My wrath was this close to erupting on him, no less than a lava flow. But as I said, I had to be smart about it.

The mere thought of catching him, then tangling him and eventually strangling him in the web that was woven with his very own hands amused me. A slight, playful — and vengeful smirk found its spot on my lips, making them curl. And getting a hold of my bearings after being lost for so long, I was now ready to set things right. And hell, I was going to do it my way now. No more relying on Mr. Haruki for seeking the light in the dark, for I was now going to create a fire of my own to light my way. No more leaning on Caleb for emotional support. They wanted to play me around. I was very well ready now to give them the game. In fact, I was ready to show them how the game is played. But before I got anything started — before I actually put my plan in motion, I had to figure out a lot of things.

I didn't know why Mr. Haruki told me what he told me. So, in order to begin with my own plot, I had to determine which side he was on. Could it be that he was as in the dark as I was? I could not be sure of it. A part of me wanted to believe that he was telling me what he had been told and what generations of generations in his family had been told. There was a fair chance that he was only relaying what he was told. Once I figured out where Mr. Haruki stood in all this, I was going to shift my focus to Caleb.

That particular individual was subjected to some special kind of wrath. My vulnerabilities allowed him to enter my life, and that person ensured he manipulated me in the worst way possible. But that was okay. I had snapped out of the illusion he had me entrapped. Now that I was no longer in the dark about who I was, to whom I truly belonged, I needed to find out what purpose I served as someone associated with Nasurti and… A'zerai. But first, I had some digging to do.

I wish you were here… with me… right now. In my room… me in your warm embrace.

I did exactly what he had been doing with me. It was, after all, never the words spoken from the poisonous tongue of his, but his mind through which he'd quietly creep into my mind and speak to me, making me feel like he was right here, with me. There I lay in the center of my room, on the cold floor that was barely concealed with a rug that served as the only source of warmth in the coldness of the night. I had walked from Mr. Haruki's place to mine, but had no recollection of the way from there to my apartment. Only when I came back did I take the battle to my bathroom, where I defeated the serpent. And besides the current feat, all I could think of was what Nasurti spoke to me of. And now, it was time for me to set a plan of my own into motion. It needed him. It could not be set in motion without him. *I* needed him. Whether it was coming from a place of emotions that he had over the past year, instilled deeply in me, or a place of vengeance, I could not tell. But I was sure about one thing: he *had* to be a part of it. It just wouldn't work without him.

To lure him in, I needed his master to be a part of this play. So, when I got back from Mr. Haruki, I mindlessly made my way into the bathroom and under the shower. I didn't bother to undress. I didn't think I needed to. I was beginning to feel a sensation of burning up in my skin, and I needed to cool off that heat, but oh, cold water was not what I was looking for. And the water… well, the water wasn't warm enough to soothe, nor cold enough to jolt me back. It just… was. Falling. Beating against my body like a soft warning. My clothes clung to me almost immediately. My dress was turning heavier by the second, plastered to my skin as though even it refused to let me go now that I had come this far. The straps slipped slightly off one shoulder as the wetness made everything shift, tighten, mold against me like a second skin. I didn't adjust them. I didn't care.

I didn't care for the world in that moment. I knew he'd come, and for him, I had to allow myself to get wrapped in the moment — and the moment required heat. And so, just like that, the world outside the bathroom blurred.

In the bathroom, as I leaned into the stream, I allowed it to soak me through, my curls growing heavier until water dripped from the tips like melted pieces of thought. My breathing slowed. My eyes closed. And the silence around me folded in. I could hear her. I could hear her again. It was her, and I wasn't mistaken. It was Nasurti. I heard her, but not in words this time. I heard her in my memory. In breath. In moan. The kind of moan that wasn't born of pain but of sweet ruin—the kind that slithered into you when your mind was trying to keep still and your body… wasn't.

She spoke to me in my dreams. She spoke to me in a language I didn't speak, but I understood each word that came out of her mouth. It was as though I knew how she felt when the Dragon showed up. I could tell the temptations she felt when the Dragon made his way to the most vulnerable parts of her soul, exploring the desires of the skin buried deep under. It was as though I was feeling the same heat now, crawling under my skin, burning each part of it.

Only that for Nasurti, it was the Dragon who tempted her, aroused her, entered her, and made her explode with pleasures that felt unworldly—unholy. But in my case, it was the snake. And it was here now.

I didn't see it at first. I felt it—more like a presence than a shape. Something slick against the steam-thickened air, curling into the corners of the room. My breath caught in my throat as something soft and wet brushed against the inside of my ankle. My eyes flicked down, and there it was. It was dark. It was gleaming. It was sinister in the way only beauty could be. The snake moved like a liquid shadow, black with hints of deep emerald glowing beneath the surface of its scales. It didn't hiss. It didn't rush. It slithered slowly, with the patience of something that knew it would be welcomed even if the mind screamed *no*. It didn't ask permission. But it didn't need it, did it?

It slid over the top of my foot, its body cool against the heat radiating from the water, and then slowly wrapped around my ankle. My breath grew heavier, my chest lifting and falling with growing urgency as it made its way up—circling, exploring. Not like a threat. Not like a predator. But like a lover reacquainting itself with skin it had once known intimately. The snake was never meant to be a lover. It was always meant to be an enemy. Nonetheless, it's the forbidden fruit that's always more tempting, capable of making you break free from the shackles of your own cruelly crafted rules, keeping at bay the very pleasures of the world that make you feel *alive.* And the mere thought of something forbidden made me bite my lip. In the midst of the growing heat, my knees softened, my thighs tightened.

The snake wound around my calves, then higher, coiling and gliding, dipping between the inner lines of my legs. The sensation made me gasp—a low, involuntary sound torn from the back of my throat as the fabric of my dress clung tighter, now soaked to every curve of my body. And still, I didn't move. I didn't want it to stop. I was moaning now. Softly. Slowly. With each flick of its tongue near my skin, with each pass along the trembling lines of my inner thighs.

The snake moved with purpose. Not fast. Not slow. Just... deliberate. It wound its way higher as each movement traced over my soaked skin like a memory being written into flesh—but not my memory. His. The memory he wanted to carve into me. A mark of his presence. A mark of his power — the serpent's.

My breathing turned into soft, staggered exhales, my hands braced against the cold tiles behind me as I let my head fall back— not in surrender, but in control. I was letting him think this was his moment. That I was unraveling, let him. He wasn't a friend. He was a threat cloaked in temptation. And still, I opened my legs slightly as his thick, slick body slid higher, coiling around one thigh like a claim. I moaned. Not because I wanted to, but because I needed him to hear it. I needed him to believe he was winning, that he had me. That I was falling under his charm the same way Nasurti once had.

But I wasn't hers. I was mine. I was my own to destroy myself in the process of destroying my enemy. And I had already decided that I would take the pleasure. I would take the invasion. I would let him touch every inch of me if that's what it took. Let him explore the battlefield if it meant I would win the war. This body was not just skin and bone, for it was more than that now. It was bait. And I was holding the leash of the very thing that I thought was wrapping itself around me.

He slid between my legs, uninvited yet expected, his weight resting against the slick, wet fabric of my dress that clung like a second skin. A sudden, involuntary shiver ran up my spine when his cold length pressed where I was already soaked from more than just the shower. My breath hitched, and I tilted my hips forward in an attempt to offer. I wanted him to think I wanted it. I wanted him to think *he* was in charge. So, I allowed him to let his thick coil glide upward, past my hip, across my abdomen, tracing the line of my ribs. My nipples strained against the soaked fabric, aching as they brushed against his cool, glistening skin. The wet silk of my midi dress clung tighter now, outlining every curve, every gasp, every silent intention. And still he climbed. Studying me. Testing me. Teasing the borders of what he thought I would give. Therefore, I gave him more.

Then, as though sensing a go-ahead from me, he reached the strap of my dress, already loosened by water and heat, and with a subtle flick of his scaled snout, made it slip down my shoulder. I didn't stop him. I tilted toward him. I gave him my throat. He found the embrace in the nape of my neck. The other strap slid, soft as a whisper. My dress surrendered, falling to my waist, exposing the rise of my breasts to the cool air and to him—this creature who should've disgusted me, who should've triggered some primal alarm in my mind to run, escape, scream. But none of that came.

Instead, I stood taller, stripping myself to him not in fear but in mastery. I was letting him take me in, explore me, make his silent claims with each gliding touch, because I wanted him to believe he had the upper hand. I wanted him to think I was becoming his. And maybe in some twisted, unspoken way, I was. Not because I craved his affection, but because I needed his presence. Because the moment his mouth touched my neck—a flick of his tongue with a slow, deliberate stroke, I knew I was crossing into territory far darker than I had anticipated, but I welcomed it. The serpent's tongue against my skin was cold and wet, yet the sensation made me burn from the inside. I could feel the heat building inside me, not just from desire, but from the subtle game I was playing. This wasn't just about giving in; it was about control. Every inch he explored, every part of me he touched, I allowed it for a reason. I wanted him to think I was submitting, to think I was just another conquest.

But I wasn't. I was the one with the power, and with every brush of his scales against my skin, every flick of his tongue that left me breathless, I knew that. The serpent wanted to break me, to make me beg, but I wasn't going to give him the satisfaction of that. Instead, I let him think he had me—let him think his touch, his movements, would be what took me to the edge of madness. The slow, sinuous way he moved, the deliberate teasing against my sensitive skin, only made me want to laugh. He had no idea who he was dealing with.

As his body continued its descent, moving like liquid fire over my torso, I arched my back, pushing myself further into his grasp, making sure to press against him, to let him feel the heat of my body against his, to let him feel the intensity of what I was building. My body was no longer mine; it was his to explore, to test, to see how far he could push before I cracked.

I wanted him to feel it—the tension, the electricity. I wanted him to feel the pull of desire that wasn't just about lust, but about power. This was my game. And the more he slid against me, the more his scales brushed over my skin, the more I could feel him sinking into my mind, pulling me closer to the edge of something dangerous and wild. He flicked my dress to the side, his cold, wet body pressing against me, and I gasped. My body was wracked with tremors as his coil tightened around my waist, holding me in place, but I didn't resist. I let him take control, but only because I was still holding onto mine.

He pressed harder, sending a shiver through me as he moved toward my breasts, the roughness of his body against my soft skin creating a maddening friction. I bit my lip, swallowing the moan that threatened to escape, but I couldn't help it. The feeling of him against me was intoxicating, overwhelming. His presence, his touch, everything about this moment was pushing me to the brink of losing myself, but I refused to. I kept reminding myself: this wasn't about pleasure. This was about control. And I was going to take him deeper, farther, until he was tangled up in my web, and I was the one pulling the strings.

As his tongue traced the curve of my neck, I tilted my head back, offering him more, letting him believe he was winning. My pulse raced, not in fear, but in anticipation of what was to come. The snake was relentless in its pursuit, never rushing, always deliberate, each movement calculated to make me writhe, to make me fall into the desire he was planting in me. But the truth was, I was already planted in my own mind. And while he thought he was making me his, I was already making him mine.

His coils slid lower, between my legs, pressing gently, slowly against my inner thighs. My body was trembling, my breath catching, but still, I didn't pull away. I welcomed the sensation, feeling his coldness against the heat of my skin, the contradiction of pleasure and power coursing through me in waves. I wasn't going to resist. Not yet. Because every moment of this—the slow, deliberate dance between us—was exactly what I wanted. The serpent thought he was the predator, but he had no idea who he was dealing with.

The serpent continued its deliberate dance across my skin, its coil tightening around my waist as it traced higher, inch by inch. The slow, sinuous motions felt like a slow-burning fire, starting at my toes and curling upward, building with every brush of its cold, slick body against the heat of mine. It wasn't just the wetness of the water that made my skin shiver—it was the tension, the dangerous arousal building with each delicate movement. His body, cold and firm, pressed against the soft curve of my abdomen, and my breath quickened, each inhalation feeling like a stolen secret.

With every stroke, the serpent teased, coaxing a pleasure from me that I hadn't planned for, but had, nevertheless, welcomed. His scales felt like an unholy invitation, cold against the warmth of my skin, yet sparking a heat that spiraled through my core. I leaned into it, letting my hips push against him as his touch grew more insistent, more purposeful. Each touch sent waves of shivers through my spine, and my pulse quickened, making my legs tremble under the pressure of his advances.

I couldn't stop it. I didn't want to stop it. Every touch, every glide of the serpent's body over mine, seemed to reach deeper into me, igniting a fire that threatened to consume my control. I gasped as his cold coil moved between my legs, pressing against the damp fabric of my dress. I felt the subtle pressure as he slowly moved higher, forcing a breathless moan from my lips, and for a moment, it seemed like I was losing myself.

It was so close. So close.

The serpent continued its deliberate dance across my skin, its coil tightening around my waist as it traced higher, inch by inch. The slow, sinuous motions felt like a slow-burning fire, starting at my toes and curling upward, building with every brush of its cold, slick body against the heat of mine. It wasn't just the wetness of the water that made my skin shiver—it was the tension, the dangerous arousal building with each delicate movement. His body, cold and firm, pressed against the soft curve of my abdomen, and my breath quickened, each inhalation feeling like a stolen secret.

With every stroke, the serpent teased, coaxing a pleasure from me that I hadn't planned for, but had, nevertheless, welcomed. His scales felt like an unholy invitation, cold against the warmth of my skin, yet sparking a heat that spiraled through my core. I leaned into it, letting my hips push against him as his touch grew more insistent, more purposeful. Each touch sent waves of shivers through my spine, and my pulse quickened, making my legs tremble under the pressure of his advances.

I couldn't stop it. I didn't want to stop it. Every touch, every glide of the serpent's body over mine, seemed to reach deeper into me, igniting a fire that threatened to consume my control. I gasped as his cold coil moved between my legs, pressing against the damp fabric of my dress. I felt the subtle pressure as he slowly moved higher, forcing a breathless moan from my lips, and for a moment, it seemed like I was losing myself.

It was so close. So close.

I could feel it—the inevitable release, the pleasure building as his movements became more assured. He was pressing against me, his cool body gliding smoothly over the soft swell of my breasts, and I could feel the coil of tension tightening, the aching anticipation of what was coming next. My body was betraying me, reacting to the serpent as if I had no say in the matter, my legs parting further as I instinctively gave in to the sensations that were pulsing through me. The serpent's body brushed against my thighs, his scales sending jolts of electric pleasure through my skin. I was on the brink.

Just a little more… I was so close. But then, something shifted. A flicker in my mind—sharp, clear, unmistakable. I snapped out of it. It was as though the trance I had been under dissolved in an instant, and in that split second, the tension broke. I could feel the weight of the serpent's body pressing against mine, could feel the coldness of his form as it spiraled higher, but I was no longer lost in the rhythm of his movements. I wasn't caught in the illusion anymore. I wasn't the prey. I was the one in control.

My lips curled into a sensual smirk as my eyes narrowed with a dangerous gleam. The serpent paused, his cold body quivering against mine. He must've sensed the change in the air, the shift in the game, and for the first time, I saw a flicker of uncertainty in his eyes. He had believed he was the one leading this dance. But he was wrong.

The serpent, thinking it had me, now found itself caught off guard. I watched as the flicker of realization crossed his face. It was a moment of confusion, then something like panic. In an instant, his body recoiled, the tension unraveling as his coils loosened. Without a word, without a single glance back, the serpent disappeared, slithering away into the shadows as quickly as it had come.

I stood there, breathless but unbroken. My heart was still pounding from the intensity of what had just transpired. The water from the shower fell steadily around me, but I didn't feel it. My skin still burned with the remnants of the serpent's touch, but I was in control. I had snapped out of the trance when I needed to—just before I let him completely take me. I had dealt quite well with the serpent. It was time for me to deal with Caleb now, wrap him around my finger, make him play right into my fantasy, making him believe that he had me under his spell, only for him to get caught in the very web that he had woven.

XVII:
Oh, To Be Loved…

Nothing could have prepared me for the *things* that came after. From the bathroom to the floor of my bedroom, I drifted myself almost on the wings of the air. I was not on my feet, no. It didn't feel that way. Never did reality feel any different from the dreams — dreams that have kept me awake even amidst a slumber that would make you question whether I was asleep, only to be woken up by the latter hour of the day, or if I had drifted off to a slumber, so so deep that nothing in the world could break me out of it— making you wonder if I was even alive. And now, that steamy, hot encounter with the serpent was making me want to be satiated. I was breaking, but not emotionally, no. I felt like I was breaking piece by piece by the burning desire to be devoured, to be swallowed whole. But not as food, no — as a thirst that could only be quenched by a profound, passionate love. It was within my body — the desire.

Had it only been about my body, I would have had Caleb satiate me, but then… it wasn't just bodily. It was the hunger of my very soul that most people thought didn't exist. My whole body was beaming with the scorching desire of my soul to be touched, to be felt by the soul of another—by the soul of my *lover*. The million-dollar question was: Would I be loved the way I earnestly desired to be loved? Did I have it written in my fate to be loved by someone dearly, passionately, unconditionally? Was it erased because of what I had been doing all my life, surviving and feeding on animal blood — on human blood? Or was it never written for me in the first place?

My body ached in a way it had only ached when I yearned for being held in the arms of a lover who seemed nothing more than a far, distant dream, never to see the light of reality. I had, over the years, grown used to it, satiated with sleeping with men who were morally grey, who were nothing more than a prey in the eyes of the predator that lurked in me, but were also the men who were astoundingly well in bed. They knew what they were doing when it came to pleasing a woman, reaching every inch of their soul and not just their body when they were in bed with them. They had the skill. No men I had slept with could have left a woman unsatisfied, but only yearning for more. For me… well, how unfortunate! Did I suffer all this time because I was… I was Nasurti? Was I never going to experience the burn of a lover's kiss, burying deep into my skin?

I asked myself again. This time, my voice was louder and out there than it was before —muffled and suppressed. This time, it was as if I was speaking to my surroundings than to my own self. *Was I never going to experience the burn of a lover's kiss, burying deep into my skin?*

Alas! For there came no response.

I lay there—half curled, half sprawled—on the cold floor, the tiled surface doing little to calm the heat swelling within me. The silence of the room had a voice of its own. I could hear it. Like a hum. Like a murmur coming not from the world outside but from somewhere inside of me. I wasn't crying. I wasn't touching myself either. I was just there, breathing and burning, the way dry wood burns in slow, crackling fire. My legs were bare. My inner thighs warm. My lips parted slightly. I could feel the ache rising like smoke—soft, thick, fragrant with longing. The air carried the scent of sandalwood. No, not sandalwood. Something deeper. Something that wasn't incense but memory. Something old and masculine and sacred. I pressed my hands to the floor. The coolness didn't reach my palms. Nothing did. And then, in the silence that felt like a breath waiting to be exhaled, I heard it. A whisper.

Douglas.

A single word. No echo. No thunder. Just a breath inside my chest that I hadn't taken myself. It didn't come from outside. It came from within me—spoken as if by a second soul that had lived inside me all along. I sat up slowly, not in alarm, but as if rising from a trance. My body still ached, but the ache had a name now. My eyes widened slightly, not in fear, but in wonder.

"Douglas…" I repeated.

Who was he?

Why did the name feel like it belonged to me long before it had ever been spoken?

I rose to my feet, the ache between my thighs deeper now, not dulled by time or thought but sharpened by that single word. I crossed the room slowly, each step feeling like a dance between realities. I stood by the window. The street below was empty, lamplight flickering on the pavement. I felt his presence before I saw him. When I turned around, there he was.

He didn't knock. The door hadn't creaked. The air hadn't shifted. But there he stood in my living room, tall and still, like a statue made of fire and longing. He was a stranger, but everything about him felt known. His shoulders were broad, wrapped in a black shirt that clung to him like it had grown there. His chest rose and fell with a kind of rhythm that slowed my breath to match his. Bearded. Eyes dark. Hands strong and silent. I didn't say a word. Neither did he.

He walked toward me, his movement slow and deliberate, like he had walked this floor before. My lips parted but no sound came. I didn't need to ask how he got in. I didn't want to. I only knew that he was here now, and my body—my poor, desperate, shaking body— had already surrendered.

He dropped to his knees before me, and without a word, took my foot in his hand—warm, steady, reverent. And that's how he began.

His fingers wrapped around my ankle like he had done it before, in some other time, some other life—like I had once belonged to him and was only now finding my way back. He didn't rush. His thumb moved in slow, deliberate circles, warming the delicate bone just beneath my skin. My breath caught in my throat—not from surprise, but from the overwhelming softness. His touch wasn't greedy. It was worshipful. He raised my foot gently, pressing his lips to the arch. I shivered—not from cold, but from the unbearable heat building under my skin.

Douglas didn't speak. He didn't need to. His mouth said all that needed to be said. One kiss on the arch, then another on my ankle. He trailed upward, kissing the inside of my calf, the curve behind my knee, his lips dragging against my skin as though memorizing it. My legs trembled beneath me, and I reached for the edge of the table beside me to steady myself. But Douglas caught me before I could fall. He stood, lifted me with ease, and cradled me like I weighed nothing, like I was air and shadow and flame all at once.

He placed me gently on the bed, like one would lay down something fragile and precious. He didn't climb on top of me—not yet. Instead, he stood there for a moment, just looking. And oh, the way he looked, not like a man seeing a woman undressed, but like a man beholding the night sky for the first time. Reverent. Quiet.

Consumed. I reached for him, my fingers brushing the hem of his shirt, and without a word, he pulled it over his head.

There he was. Fully. Bare-chested, carved like something made by divine hands, not the gym. There were old scars on his skin. A story I didn't know. A history I hadn't lived. But I wanted to learn every chapter with my mouth. His chest rose as he exhaled, and then, slowly, he climbed onto the bed and kissed my knee. Then my thigh. The kisses trailed higher, and I gasped—not because he touched me where no one had ever touched me before, but because of how he did it. With patience, with quiet, with a sense of knowing.

He hovered over me, his lips brushing my inner thigh. My back arched instinctively. I wanted him. No—I needed him. He kissed the other thigh, then moved upward. His hands found my waist, then my ribs, and slowly, slowly, he pulled my shirt over my head. I let him. I let him see all of me.

My breasts rose with each breath, nipples taut from air and anticipation. He didn't rush there either. He watched. Then lowered his mouth to my left breast, his lips wrapping around the nipple so softly I gasped. He sucked gently, then again, deeper this time. His other hand cupped the other breast, fingers warm and calloused and sure. My hands were in his hair, pulling, threading, desperate without knowing how to ask for more. And he gave me more.

His tongue circled my nipple again, then again, slower, firmer, as if he wanted to draw every shiver out of my spine. He moved to the other breast, giving it the same devotion, the same sacred kind of attention that made my throat tighten. I let my head fall back into the pillows, my eyes fluttering shut as his mouth worshipped me in a way I had only imagined in lonely hours and half-slept dreams. He took his time—his mouth and hands in perfect synchrony, teasing, exploring, memorizing.

Then he kissed up the line of my collarbone, his stubble grazing my skin and sending a ripple down my entire body. My chest rose to meet him. I could feel the weight of his want pressed just above my stomach, but he didn't let himself fall into me—not yet. His lips reached the curve of my neck, the place where my pulse beat like a hummingbird's wings. He paused there, breathed me in. And then he bit, gently, just enough to make my toes curl, to make my hips lift in search of more.

I turned my head to the side instinctively, offering him more space. He kissed the hollow of my neck, the angle of my jaw, the place just beneath my ear where no one had ever kissed me before. My hands ran over the broad plane of his back, down to the muscles shifting at his waist, and I pulled him closer, needing to feel the weight of him against me.

But Douglas had a pace of his own, as though he was listening to a rhythm only he could hear. He slid down again, his lips tracing a path from my throat to the center of my chest, down to my belly. My stomach clenched when his breath hit my skin. He kissed just above my navel and rested there for a heartbeat, his hand splayed across my stomach like he was grounding me in place—anchoring me to the now.

Then his hand moved lower, slowly. Fingers trailing down the line of my hip, curling around my thigh. He pushed my legs apart gently, and I let him, more than ready. My legs parted like a flower unfurling under sunlight. He settled between them, and I watched as he looked at me—his eyes darker now, hooded, his lips parted just slightly. That look was the beginning of my undoing.

He kissed the inside of my thigh again, closer now. My hips rose involuntarily. His tongue followed the same path his fingers had taken. Then he kissed the place just above where I burned for him, and I cried out softly—because he hadn't touched me there yet, but it was enough to make me ache. He pulled one leg over his shoulder and then finally—finally—his mouth met the center of me.

And when his tongue touched me, slow and firm and without hesitation, I shattered.

My fingers twisted in the sheets as his tongue began a rhythm that was maddening in its precision. He didn't rush—not even when my hips bucked against him, not even when I whimpered his name without even meaning to. His tongue moved with such surety, such intimate understanding, like he had known my body in another lifetime. He kissed me like he was fluent in the language of my hunger. Every stroke sent sparks along my spine, building and circling that aching knot in my center that no one else had ever reached this way—not even close.

His hands gripped my thighs, keeping me open for him, keeping me still as his mouth drew out wave after wave of unbearable pleasure. And it wasn't just the act—it was the way he breathed against me, the quiet groan that came from his chest every time I moaned his name, the way his stubble scraped the tender skin of my inner thigh, grounding me even as I felt myself leaving the earth. I felt like I was hovering somewhere between madness and something divine.

I couldn't think. Couldn't speak. My hands let go of the sheets and found his shoulders, his head, threading through his hair, desperate for something to hold onto. I was trembling, heart pounding so hard I thought it might burst, hips moving of their own will against his mouth. And still—still—he did not stop.

Then he slid two fingers inside me with a smoothness that made my body jolt. His fingers curved in just the right way, syncing perfectly with his tongue, and I heard a sound escape me that I had never made before—raw, helpless, gruff. My legs tensed, then shook, and I knew I was close. I was close in a way that felt terrifying because it wasn't just physical. It was emotional. It was spiritual, like the pieces of me that had been scattered for so long were suddenly converging at this single point of heat and touch and want.

My climax came like a storm—slow at first, then building with such violence I couldn't keep still, couldn't breathe. I cried out his name, over and over, as he held me steady and carried me through the intensity of it. My body convulsed against his mouth, waves of release breaking over me in sharp, endless pulses. I thought it would end—I thought it *had* to end—but then a second climax hit, and I felt my body arch off the bed, tears springing to my eyes because nothing had ever, ever felt like this before.

When it finally ebbed, when the shaking slowed and my body began to settle, I reached for him blindly. And he came up slowly, kissing the skin of my belly, the space between my breasts, the hollow of my throat, before finally hovering above me, face inches from mine. His eyes searched mine without saying a word.

I was breathless. Shaken. Changed.

And I wanted more.

Douglas lingered above me for a moment longer, his chest rising and falling in the same erratic rhythm as mine. I could feel the heat of his body pressing into me, the weight of him as if he had imprinted himself onto my very soul. His breath was warm against my skin. His gaze was fixated on mine, never leaving, never ceasing. It was as though he were silently studying me, seeing all of me. But the longer he looked, the more I realized that there was something else beneath that gaze—something unreadable. Something far older than the physical desire that had coursed through us.

I should have been terrified, should have felt overwhelmed. But all I could do was feel alive in a way I had never known before—like I was not just in the world, but a part of it, woven into the very fabric of it with him.

"Don't leave me," I whispered before I could stop myself, my hands gripping his back as if I could anchor him to me, as if the act of holding him would make him stay.

He didn't answer at first. His lips brushed against mine again, slow and deliberate, and it took all of my strength not to get lost in it once more. The taste of him was still on my tongue, intoxicating and warm. But there was something else, something deeper, about the way he kissed me now—a promise, a silent understanding that he wasn't just going to leave. Not yet. Not like this.

And yet, a whisper of doubt began to creep into my mind. The way he held me—so completely—felt like it was more than just passion. It felt... sacred. And though I wanted to bask in the safety of his embrace, my thoughts were clouded with an ache I couldn't quite name. Why had he come to me? Why now?

"Douglas..." I breathed, my voice shaky, unsure of how to ask the question that had been lurking in the back of my mind since he first appeared. "Who are you? Really?"

His eyes softened as they met mine, but there was something about them that sent a shiver down my spine. He didn't speak at first, and the silence between us stretched thin. I felt his hand stroke my hair, pushing it back gently from my face. His touch was tender, almost affectionate, as if he were memorizing the way I felt in his arms. But still, he didn't answer.

"Who are you?" I repeated, more urgently this time.

"I am..." he began, his voice low and almost too soft to catch. But before he could finish, a sudden knock at the door shattered the moment like glass.

The sound cut through the air, slicing through the quiet of the room like a knife. I jumped, startled by the interruption, and Douglas tensed above me. My heart pounded in my chest, a drumbeat of anxiety crashing over me. The knock sounded again—louder this time—urgent.

Douglas didn't move, didn't seem to react, as if he hadn't heard it at all. But I could feel his body stiffen, and something in the air changed, shifted. The heavy intimacy that had wrapped around us was suddenly replaced by an invisible tension. Something was wrong.

Another knock—this time more frantic.

I tried to sit up, but my body was weak, still trembling from the intensity of what we had just shared. My mind was still clouded, the haze of desire clouding my thoughts. But then the door rattled, the sound unmistakable. Someone was trying to get in.

Douglas's gaze flickered toward the door, and for a moment, I thought I saw something cold in his eyes—something dark that didn't belong in this room. His grip on me tightened for the briefest of moments, as if he were considering something.

"Stay here," he murmured, his voice rough, low. He slid off me, his body moving with a dangerous, calculated grace that sent a shiver down my spine.

I reached for him, confused, panic starting to settle in my chest. "No—Don't go. Please."

But Douglas was already standing, his back to me, his expression unreadable as he crossed the room. Without a word, he made his way toward the door. I could hear his footsteps—the quiet click of his boots on the floor—each step a heavy, deliberate echo that seemed to make the air grow even heavier.

He reached for the door, his hand hovering over the handle, and for a moment, everything stopped. I didn't know whether to shout, to beg him not to open it, or to run and hide.

But then, as if on cue, Douglas glanced over his shoulder, his eyes meeting mine one last time. There was a flicker of something in his gaze—something that didn't belong to this world.

"I'll be back," he said softly, his words hanging in the air, weighted with something I couldn't understand.

Then, without another word, he opened the door. The hallway beyond was empty. No one was there. But I could feel it. The shift. The presence. A presence that wasn't mine.

And as the door clicked shut behind him, I was left alone in the silence, my body still burning, my mind racing, and the echo of his departure lingering in the air.

Who was Douglas?

Why had he come to me?

And more importantly... why did it feel like he had left with something of me, something I couldn't quite name but knew was missing from me now?

XVIII:
The Past of Me, The "Me" of Today

The ceiling was all that she could see as she lay still. She wasn't asleep — not quite. But she wasn't awake either. It was as though she was drifting off to a slumber so deep that she could hardly make out anything that lay in her surroundings, but it was a slumber so weak that she couldn't quite let go of what lay in front of her eyes. It was as though she was there, but not quite. Her hands rested softly over her belly like she was cradling something. The dancing flame of the candle along the wall had long melted down into small golden pools, and yet she didn't rise to fix them. Time had thinned itself, become watery at the edges, and in that in-between place, the voice began to stir again. But this time, it wasn't whispering riddles or warning her of change or calling her by names she didn't remember owning. No, this time, it was telling her a story. A story with weight. With blood. With betrayal. And it began the way all old things begin: not with answers, but with a memory.

"Let me tell you," the voice said, slow and dry as bone dust, "how it all started."

And just like that, Iyah was gone. Not truly, not completely — her breath still rose and fell, her fingers still curled slightly as if clinging to some invisible thread — but her mind sank into the voice like it was a river, and it took her far back, to the year 1270, when the oceans were colder and kings were crueler and promises were stitched together with flesh and fire.

King Nerwill was not yet king when he was taken to the Snake Cave. He was only a man with hunger in his eyes, and that was enough. The island had no name, or at least none that mortals were permitted to utter. It sat in the midst of the Black Straits, wrapped in mist and guarded by currents that could pull down entire fleets. Nerwill had gone there not of his own will, but on his knees, chained and bloodied, dragged by those who believed power had to be earned through suffering. They said the cave was alive — that it breathed, that it could smell you. That if it let you live, it would keep a part of you forever. Inside the Snake Cave, it was always wet, not with water, but with something thicker. The stones pulsed. The shadows crawled. And every night, the child was brought to him.

She could not have been more than five when it started. Her skin was the color of rich, deep soil after rain, and her eyes burned gold even in the dark. They said she was born of the vampire king who ruled the southern jungles — a ruler cloaked in silence and immortality, whose blood alone could stitch together heaven and hell. They kept her chained to the wall when she wasn't feeding him, her little wrists bruised, her silence louder than any scream Nerwill ever heard. She never wept. Not once.

Three years. Every day. A small cut on her palm. Sometimes her thigh. Sometimes her neck. The blood poured, and he drank. At first, he gagged. The sweetness of it was too much, like drinking stars, like swallowing dreams not meant for him. But in time, it changed him. Made him faster. Hungrier. He began to see things — things no man should see. And she... she began to fade.

And through it all, the voice continued, soft and unflinching.

"This was the price he paid for the throne. And this was the soul he sold to buy it."

When the third year ended, the child had grown into something else. It was not quite a girl, not yet a woman, not human, not entirely. It was something totally different. Her limbs moved with grace, but they were no longer hers. Her eyes no longer burned; they *glowed*, and her voice, which had been mute for so long, returned with words no child should speak. Her hair thickened, coiling with the weight of magic, and sometimes, in sleep, she sang low, mournful tunes in a language that turned the walls of the cave cold with fear. She was not the only one who had changed in the course of those painstakingly long years. It was Nerwill, too, who had changed — shifted in his entirety, in the very being of himself. His veins no longer let the blood flow as quietly as it would. Now, it thumped as though every ounce of the blood—no longer pure—was beating with the rhythm of his heart. The blood pulsated. His teeth were now sharpened. He no longer needed fire to see in the dark. The island no longer imprisoned him. If anything, it was the island that was now a prisoner. It obeyed him.

And so the vampire king came down from his mountain of bones, from his temple thick with vines and ash, to stand before the man who had fed on his daughter for one thousand nights. The meeting took place in silence, broken only by the hiss of the ocean and the trembling of the ground beneath them. No blood was spilled that day — not because there was no reason, but because there was an agreement. Nerwill would leave the island. He would take the girl with him, and she would be wed to Nerwill's son, who was waiting in the north, pale-skinned and soft-palmed, a boy who had never known hunger or shadows.

The wedding, the king said, would unite their two worlds: the blood of the immortals and the breath of men. And Nerwill, with eyes that no longer belonged to a man and a heart that had hardened in that wet blackness, agreed. Oh, but if only he meant to keep his word. He didn't. He lied.

When they returned to the northern lands, she was given no crown, no silks, no name. The courtiers whispered. The priests spat. Even the animals shied from her. Her skin was too dark, they said. Her silence is too deep. The prince, her promised one, would not even look at her. She was housed in a stone tower with only a single window and no mirrors. Her meals were brought cold. The maids never touched her.

And Nerwill, now King, never came to see her. Not once.

The promise was broken, like a snapped bone hidden beneath velvet. And the girl—only twelve, barely breathing beneath the weight of her magic — waited. She waited for the prince. For the wedding. For the day someone might speak her name again. And instead, her birthday approached. The cursed thirteenth.

She felt it first in her spine — a stretching, a hunger. Her teeth ached in her mouth. Her tongue itched. Her skin pulsed hot, like it remembered things she hadn't lived yet. At night, the tower walls bled. The birds that flew near the window dropped dead from the sky. The maids stopped coming. And still, she waited.

The voice in Iyah's head trembled then, just slightly, like it, too, had once stood in that room, had once touched the stone where the girl sat staring out toward the moon, whispering to herself the only lullaby she knew: one her father had hummed through fangs, under jungle stars.

"Love," the voice said, "was the only thing that could've saved her."

But no one came.

The days folded into themselves like wilted flowers. Time no longer passed, for now it *coiled*. And the girl, unnamed, unkissed, unloved, did not cry. Not once. She sat on the stone sill with her knees tucked up and her hair like night around her shoulders, and she waited for the end of something she could not name. She had heard her body speak in riddles. Her blood whispered to her. The dark told her things. But never once did she speak back.

Until the morning of her thirteenth birthday.

It began before sunrise, before the stars had the courtesy to fade. Her door, which had not opened in moons, creaked. A tray of food was pushed in — untouched. Then a voice. A human one. A young man, trembling. "The king," he said, "has summoned you."

She stood. Not because she obeyed, but because she *knew*. Today, something would be undone.

They brought her down in silence. The courtiers gasped. Her hair now reached the floor. Her eyes were no longer eyes — they were golden stones swimming with shadows. Her steps made no sound. No one looked directly at her. Even the guards kept a distance.

And there, in the great hall, under banners soaked in the blood of old wars, sat Nerwill.

Older. Colder. Crowned.

He did not rise. He did not speak her name. He simply stared, like one might stare at a prophecy they had tried to forget.

"You will leave this place," he said.

She said nothing.

"You will go far, and you will not return. My people will not accept you. My son… he is to wed another. You understand."

She did not blink.

"It was a mistake," he muttered. "You were never meant to come here. Never meant to… be."

At that, her lips parted.

"I was made," she said, "by your hunger."

The room grew colder.

"Your hands drank my blood. Your body stole from mine. And now you ask me to leave."

"You were never my daughter."

"No," she said. "I was your mirror."

She turned then—slowly, like winter turning into spring—and walked out of the hall, past the trembling guards, past the weeping priest who clutched his holy book like a shield, past the courtiers with mouths full of venom and fear. She stepped out into the snow.

And the sky split.

Not with lightning, but with *voices*. Whispers, a hundred thousand strong, wrapped around her bones, humming through the marrow, awakening what had long been buried beneath the surface of her skin. The moon lowered itself. The wind howled like it knew her name. And behind her, the castle doors slammed shut — not by hand, but by command. Something ancient had returned. And as she stepped into the world alone — exiled, betrayed, still unnamed — her birthday passed.

Her thirteenth came, and with it came the beginning of her death. Or her awakening. Or both. In the voice that pressed against the insides of Iyah's skull, there was no pause, no breath, only the weight of time being folded back like silk from an old wound. She did not know if she was hearing it or remembering it-or if, somehow, the boundary between those two things had ceased to matter. She lay still, limbs heavy, mind suspended in that velvet space between dream and possession. And still, the story poured through her. The girl from the past had left the castle, yes — but her journey had not ended. It had only shifted into something colder, lonelier, and far more dangerous than anything she had known in the snake cave.

For weeks, she walked. Through ice fields that cracked beneath her feet. Through forests that refused to name her. Through towns where windows were shut before she approached. The humans feared her — and rightly so. She moved like a rumor. Her shadow came before her. Dogs whimpered and children cried. She slept in hollows of dead trees and drank from poisoned streams that had no power to hurt her. Her body remembered a different kind of blood. Her veins still carried the mountain king's kiss — that strange legacy of immortality, diluted and twisted inside a child's body that had never been allowed to be just a child.

But it was her mind that truly began to unravel. Not with madness. No. But with knowing. Visions came. She would blink and see women weeping over burning cities, would taste iron and honey at the back of her throat. She would wake with mud on her hands and not remember where she had been. Something — someone — was pushing through her. Speaking through her. The blood was remembering itself. And it was *not done*.

On the twenty-third night, she reached a crossroads where the trees leaned in too close and the air hung with a silence too loud. There stood a woman in white. Not old. Not young. She bore no weapons, only a bowl of black water and a veil made of moth wings. The girl did not flinch. She had stopped fearing strange things long ago.

The woman did not speak her name. She didn't have to.

"You carry the sin of two kings," she said. "One who made you. One who broke you."

The girl said nothing.

"They thought you were a child," the woman continued, voice softer now. "But they were wrong. You are a vessel. A door. What you become will change the course of blood and moon for a thousand years."

"I do not wish to change anything," the girl replied.

"Wishes are for the pure-hearted. You are not that anymore."

"What am I?"

The woman tilted her head. "Still becoming."

She gave her the bowl of water. "Drink, and see."

The girl drank.

And what came next was fire. But not the fire that burns — the fire that *awakens*. She saw bloodlines unravel like ribbons. She saw men crowned and beheaded, entire lineages scorched by the touch of one decision made in a cave centuries before. She saw her name — the one no one ever said — etched in ancient bone beneath the sea. She saw her children. And their children. And one girl, far in the future, lying alone, eyes shut, body aching with a transformation she did not yet understand.

Iyah.

The king had not banished her, though. He did tell her to leave, but having her gone meant he was inviting troubles from not just the world of the mortals. He could not kill her. That would have stirred gods he no longer believed in. So he did what cowards do — he erased her. Not with fire, but silence. No one spoke of the girl. There was no record of her arrival or her bloodline. She was not sent back to her people. She was not honored. Instead, they placed her where the forgotten things go — back in the tower. This time, with no pretense of royalty. Just stone and dust and the ghosts that came to keep her company. So, when she was on her way forward, the guards captured her near the crossroads, where she had found the woman dressed in white.

Now back in the tower, she was condemned to live her life, for as long as it was to last, in the quiet of the dungeon that the tower had become for her. Every day nearing her birthday, she experienced change. The change was usually slower. However, ever since she met with the woman at the crossroads, the change came rather hurriedly. Something in her was changing faster now, like a storm chasing itself through her blood. The days before her thirteenth birthday stretched long and slow, as if time itself was reluctant to witness what she was about to become. Her skin no longer held to one shade — it darkened and shimmered like tree bark slick with rain, like oil sliding across glass. Her nails curved into talons in her sleep. Her tongue split at its tip for a few hours one morning, then stitched itself back before dusk. She bled silver once — not red — and the stain left on the cold stone floor hissed until it burned itself into smoke.

The girl stopped eating. There was no food left that her body could hold. She stopped drinking too — but still, her bones grew heavier. It was as if something ancient was growing inside her, threading itself through her organs and coiling around her heart. At night, the tower cracked. Its stones groaned under the weight of her breath. Birds stopped flying over it entirely. The castle below began to whisper of curses and plagues. No one dared come up the steps anymore. But on the eve of her birthday, she awoke to a voice.

It was not her father's, though she begged for that. It was not the prince's, though she had dreamt of his face enough times that she knew it like her own reflection. It was her own voice, but deeper. Older. Like it had traveled across centuries to reach her. It told her what she already knew.

"You will not survive unless he loves you."

And she laughed. Not with joy, but with something sharp and bitter. Love? Love had never visited her, not in the blood she gave. Not in the cage she was kept in, not in the cold prince's eyes or in Nerwill's betrayal. If love were to be her salvation, then she was already condemned.

She walked to the center of the tower. The wind moaned through the single window like a grieving mother. And the girl knelt. She placed her palms on the stone and began to whisper, not in the language of the court. Not in the tongue her mother used when braiding her hair. But in the dark-sung dialect of her father's land — a language that cracked open time itself.

She chanted until her voice bled. Until the stone beneath her glowed with heat. Until a spiral burned itself into the ground — a sigil, a seal, a seed. In that moment, she did not curse them. She did not call for revenge. She did not even ask to be remembered. She did something far more dangerous. She *hoped*.

She sent that hope forward — not to Nerwill, not to the prince, not to the world that had scorned her. She sent it into time itself. She broke herself into stardust and scattered it into the bloodstream of the unborn. She pushed her voice into the minds of women who would one day lie under strange moons and feel something stir inside them. And far, far ahead, in a world where torches had become streetlights, and old magic lived only in dreams, a girl named Iyah would hear it. But first, the girl in the tower had to die, not in body. That would come later — or it may never come, for she was the daughter of the immortal king. But she did have to die — in spirit. She folded her memories into the fire beneath the floor and sealed them with her breath. And in that silence, in that final breath, something ancient opened its eyes.

Iyah had not moved in hours. Her body remained curled on her side, the worn linen beneath her damp with the weight of her stillness. The room breathed around her, if it could be called a breath — not air, not motion, but something more ancient, something thick, invisible, and full of memory. The walls did not creak. The wind did not call. But something in the air shifted as if time itself had grown weary of pretending to be linear. The hum she felt now did not come from the world outside. It came from within. Not within her body, exactly — not her skin or her breath or her belly — but from a place further in, a place she had no name for. It was behind her eyes, lodged deep in the bone, coiled like a serpent along the curves of her spine. It was not music, not words, not silence. It was rhythm. It was memory. It was someone else's breath beating in time with her own.

The voice had changed now, for it was no longer a mere whisper weaving stories into the folds of her mind; it had settled into something more perilous — a steady, persistent force operating beneath her own reflections, like an undertow tugging at her feet. She was not simply hearing now. She was remembering. And not her own memories. The visions didn't dance at the edge of sleep like dreams do. They cracked open inside her. The tower returned — the dust, the scent of rust, the cool stone pressed to a girl's forehead as she knelt and whispered to gods that had long turned their backs. Iyah saw hands in the dark — brown and thin and shaking — carve a name she could not pronounce into the floor with a nail torn from flesh. She smelled blood — her blood, but not her blood. She felt the hunger rise, raw and bright. And she knew, without question, without logic, that she was watching herself from another life, or rather, from a life that had never ended.

XIX:
Into the Realms of Here and There

Oh, there were, but none — no stars at all, for they had all vanished by the time I allowed my eyes to let the light in, enabling them to open. Nor was beneath me the room I once felt. The tower was no longer to be seen, to be felt, or to be lived. There were no stones — no more of them cracking under my feet. Oh, but what was actually there was my present, though once familiar, now seemed unfamiliar in the most peculiar way possible. The quietness that befell the present realm I found myself in felt the most hollow. Could I have known where I was before and where I was now? No, not immediately. For a moment, I knew not where I was. Before I could process my whereabouts or assess the condition I found myself in when I opened my eyes, I could feel my mouth. My mouth was as dry as a deserted land. My heartbeat came more and more shallow. It was slow, as though I was barely alive.

Oh, but I very much was alive. The ache I felt in every inch of my body was the very testament of my being alive. My body winced, I moaned, and before I knew it, the scent of recycled air and a cold that felt unnatural pulled me back. As I blinked, the cabin lights above — dimmed as they were — and the gentle murmur of other passengers stirred like distant waves. I let out a groan that made it evident that I was in pain, and the pain wasn't the kind you'd feel when you've been exhausted for years and the long-sought rest that never came. It was the kind of pain that reeked of years of emotional exhaustion and a yearning that none could explain. So, of course, my body ached and my shoulders felt tense. I hadn't slept, not truly, but I had gone somewhere far deeper than sleep. My arms were stiff across my chest, and my fingers twitched with a memory I could no longer touch.

The plane was beginning to descend as slowly as it could. It almost felt like time had frozen. Outside, through the window, only clouds and the faintest suggestion of earth were waiting. I had almost forgotten that I was headed away from all that chaos. I was headed to Brazil. Or maybe it had never been about Brazil at all. Maybe I had only needed to cross another threshold. My breath caught as I turned my head. Mr. Haruki sat beside me, his face unreadable as always, hands folded neatly in his lap. He looked older since Morocco. Or maybe not older, only heavier, like a man who carried too many truths.

His eyes flicked toward me as though he sensed my stirring, but he said nothing. He didn't have to. He had been there when the first dream came. He had stood beside me after the blood. He had never once asked what I truly was. The silence between us was not cold. It was sacred. And yet, beneath that calm, there was something fraying inside me. It was not panic. There was no way it could have been confusion either. It was a weariness of another kind.

My body felt foreign; I felt as though my skin did not fit. There were moments where I thought I could still hear the girl, Nasarai, whispering from somewhere behind my ribs, not in words, not in phrases, but in the shape of emotions that arrived without permission. There was a surge of various emotions. Grief was one of them, but fire was also part of those emotions. And loneliness, the dominant one of them all. There was hunger, too; it was a hunger that stretched far beyond mere food, far beyond mere desire. It was more of a hunger for recognition, for being seen, for not being left behind again. While I struggled with the emotions that felt foreign but were the very ones that I could feel were my very own, even though they weren't, we landed in São Paulo just before sunrise.

The airport buzzed with a language I didn't know but somehow felt wrapped in. It brushed against my ears and shoulders like fabric I had once worn in another life. Everything smelled damp and living. The air outside hit me like a dream interrupted. Thick, wild, unfiltered. Palm trees leaned into the sky with the laziness of gods who had nothing to prove. Even the asphalt shimmered with a kind of sleepy power. Mr. Haruki kept a close eye on me but gave me space. He did not speak as I moved through the terminal. I was too quiet for conversation. I could still feel something from the other side, as if a piece of the past had followed me through the veil and was now watching from the corners of my eyes. My body carried the weight of transformation, but it had not yet settled. I still didn't know what I was becoming. And then, just for a moment, I saw him.

Not fully — not in a way anyone else might have noticed, but in a way that I couldn't have noticed him. It was a flash on a screen mounted high on the wall above the terminal shop. It was more like a familiar face in motion. He was being interviewed. There was no sound, only the shape of his mouth moving and his hands rising with slow gestures. It was him. It was Dougla. I did not need to read the caption to know who he was. I just… I knew. My body reacted before my mind could form language. I could feel a severe kind of tightness in my chest. There was heat in my face as my stomach trembled that had nothing to do with nerves. There he was, the man from the dream, the one I had never met but somehow already mourned. Oh, but I did meet him, did I not? He was the one who was in my room the other night. The one who burned my body with a desire that was new to me. It was something I had never felt before. Was it a dream or a reality? The difference between the two has already been blurred. I didn't move. I only stared, as though standing still might keep the vision from fading.

The screen shifted, and Dougla's image faded into footage of forest fires and rising waters. The news anchor's face replaced his, lips moving in urgency, but my mind could not absorb the language. That moment, brief and stolen, had left me hollowed in a new way. Not broken, only winded — as if something inside me had been cracked open without warning. The man was real. No longer a spirit conjured from dreams, no longer a theory or figment, but real flesh walking this same earth. It should have comforted me, but it didn't. It filled me with quiet panic, the kind that crawls up from the gut and settles into the throat. What now? What if meeting him wasn't salvation but another kind of death?

I turned slowly, for I was well aware that Harki's eyes were watching. His eyes lingered on the screen too, but only for a second. He had already memorized the man's features, the shape of his name, the lines of his past. Dougla Sousa. The man of waves and ruins, a survivor cradled by loss, loved fiercely by an old woman who still believed in wine and wonder. There was something poetic in that, something dangerous too. A man with so much death behind him would either fear me or feel pulled toward me like a tide to shore. And I, who no longer trusted my own reflection, was in no shape to become someone's hope.

Outside, the city broke from the deep slumber it had fallen into. São Paulo was not kind in its architecture, not gentle in the way its streets groaned under the weight of movement. It was all metal and sweat and open mouths. But in the spaces between, I could feel it — the pulse of the old world beneath the pavement. Brazil held stories that had never been written, myths that had gone to sleep with their tongues still warm. I could hear them if I stood still long enough. Could feel the vines waiting just past the concrete, the hush of trees taller than memory, the pull of the forest calling me to step deeper.

Mr. Haruki led me to the car with the quiet authority of a man who had accepted that love was no longer his to own. He had once held me like a daughter, before Morocco. Before Robert's name turned to ash, he stayed close like a bodyguard who would gladly take the blade, not because he believed in justice, but because he believed in me. There were questions in his silence, but he no longer asked them aloud. He had seen what my presence did to time, how the room itself would breathe differently when I entered. Love, for Haruki, had become something wordless and raw.

The car cut through the thick morning air, its tires whispering over slick roads. I leaned against the window, cheek pressed to the glass. My body still hadn't settled. The spirit of Nasarai, the girl from the tower, had not left. She was woven now into every nerve, every muscle twitch. I could not tell where I ended and the girl began. My thoughts came layered now, not just my own, but echoes, shadows. I would look at a tree and feel the urge to kneel. I would hear a song, and my mouth would form unfamiliar syllables. There were moments my reflection moved slightly after I did, as if something within me was still catching up.

The car stopped at a small inn with fading green shutters and the smell of wet stone. I didn't want a hotel, nor was I looking for luxury. All I needed was to be someplace quiet. Somewhere I could disappear if needed. Haruki handed me the key, eyes meeting mine only once. He said nothing, but the look was enough. *Be careful.* Or maybe it meant something more. Perhaps it was his way of saying what he couldn't—that this was the part of the journey he couldn't follow me into. I took the key, fingers grazing his. The weight of it felt heavier than it should have, like it held more than just a door.

The door creaked open, its hinges worn from age, revealing a room that smelled of lime and damp soil. It was small, not cramped, and the walls were the color of faded apricot, as if they had once been kissed by the sun but now lived in shadow. There was a fan above that spun lazily, uninterested in its purpose. The bed was narrow, draped in white that had yellowed slightly at the corners, and beside it sat a wooden table with a glass of water already placed, sweating quietly in the heat. I did not wonder who had left it there. I was too used to small signs from the unseen.

I closed the door behind me and leaned against it, letting my body press fully into the wood. My spine ached, my knees hummed, and somewhere just beneath my ribs, a tension curled like a thread pulled too tightly. The spirit within me — Nasarai or whatever remained of her — had not spoken since the airport. She wasn't gone. She simply waited. Sometimes I thought I could feel her braiding thoughts together inside my head, weaving fragments of memory and grief into something I hadn't yet dared to name. It wasn't possession. It wasn't madness either. It was more like companionship between souls who had long lost the luxury of separation.

I peeled off my jacket, hung it on the single nail jutting from the wall, and moved toward the bed. My body lowered slowly, carefully, the way someone lowers themselves into a grave they know isn't theirs yet. The sheets were cool, the mattress thin but forgiving, and as I lay there, staring at the low ceiling, I felt a strange weightlessness wrap around my shoulders. Brazil had a softness I hadn't expected. Not in the city itself, but in the air — in the green I glimpsed between buildings, in the way the wind carried stories without shape. It was as if the land itself was trying to soothe me, knowing what I carried.

I closed my eyes and waited for sleep, but none came. Instead, my thoughts stretched across time, across space, back to the screen at the airport and the man who had filled it with light. Dougla. The name tasted old in my mouth, though I had never spoken it aloud.

There had been other men, of course. Marcus. Caleb. Others who had fallen in love with the illusion I wore like perfume, who had claimed me with breathless hunger and broken under the weight of what I truly was. But this one felt different. Not because he was more beautiful or more distant, but because his spirit had brushed mine in a way no one else's had. It wasn't love, not yet. It was recognition. That ancient, unspoken thing that happens when two souls remember each other without knowing why.

I thought of his life. Of the tragedy that had shaped his bones. The loss of twenty-two family members in a single crash — a massacre wrapped in silence, stitched into the fabric of his grief. How did a man survive that kind of devastation? And more than that, how did a man still smile into cameras and speak of healing and meditation and the sacred bond between earth and spirit? What kind of fire had tempered him, and would it be strong enough to hold me?

My hand moved to my chest, fingertips pressing lightly over my heart, as if checking to make sure it was still mine. I feared what would happen when I stood in front of him. Not because I doubted my allure — that was a weapon I knew too well — but because for the first time, I wanted more than seduction. I wanted to be seen, not just desired. To be chosen, not possessed. I wanted love without conquest. A softness without suspicion. A man who would not flinch at the shadows I carried or the names etched into my blood. But the world had never given me what I wanted. Not freely. Not kindly.

And if Dougla was truly meant to break my curse, then love would not come easily. Nothing of value ever did. The morning passed in a strange kind of hush, as if time itself had slowed to match the rhythm of my breath, which was now soft and shallow, curling in and out of my body like smoke from a forgotten incense stick. I had not slept, not in the way most people understood sleep, but I had drifted between veils — sometimes conscious of the room around me, sometimes swallowed in old images I had not summoned, and sometimes in that empty space between wakefulness and memory where only shadows dared to linger. By the time I rose from the bed, the sun had stretched high and lazy across the sky, casting long bands of amber light through the slats in the wooden shutters. The city hummed just beyond my walls, not in chaos, but in a kind of slow, unbothered rhythm, as if São Paulo knew its own weight and had no desire to impress anyone with speed.

I washed myself in silence, my hands moving deliberately across skin that felt too ancient to still belong to a woman not yet thirty. The water was neither cold nor warm, and as it slid across my collarbone, I thought again of the girl in the tower, the one who had once sung to stone and slept with hunger curled inside her ribs like a coiled snake. That girl had never fully died, and now she lived again in muscle and blood, in the softness behind my eyes, in the ache that still gripped me every time I remembered how love had abandoned the girl at the moment she needed it most. But I was no longer a child. I had crossed too many borders, both real and unseen, had buried too many parts of myself to believe that love, even if it came with fire and gentleness, could arrive without a price.

I dressed without ceremony, choosing a simple linen shirt the color of unbleached paper and dark trousers that whispered against my skin when I walked. My feet slipped into old leather sandals that had molded to me over time, and though the world outside pulsed with heat, I carried a shawl in case my body chilled again without warning, as it sometimes did now when the spirits leaned too close. As I stepped out into the courtyard, I was struck by the scent of mango trees ripening in some nearby garden, the fragrance thick and golden and almost too full of life to bear. I paused, eyes half-lidded, taking it in until the sweetness made me dizzy.

The streets were narrower than I remembered from my first visit to Brazil many years ago, before the dreams had grown louder and before Caleb's name had become a wound instead of a memory. The tiles along the sidewalk were cracked in places, and small children ran barefoot through patches of light and shadow, their laughter unburdened, their limbs slick with summer. Vendors called to passersby, their voices rising like birdsong, and the colors of fruit piled in baskets seemed almost unreal — deep purple figs, bursting oranges, mangos split open to reveal their molten cores. I kept my eyes low as I walked, not out of fear, but because I had learned long ago that when you carry a world inside you, it is better not to draw the attention of strangers.

It was Haruki who had given me the address. A small museum tucked inside an older part of the city, known more for its architecture than its visitors. It was not where I expected Dougla to be, but it was a place he had once spoken at, and the woman who ran it — a friend of his aunt, perhaps — had agreed to meet me. I did not trust this lead, but I trusted the rhythm of the path I was on, trusted that the man who had appeared in my dream and then on the television screen would not vanish again without first confronting the thing that pulled us both like water to the moon.

I arrived at the entrance by noon. The building rose like a breath held too long, its pale façade weathered by decades of sun and salt, its doors carved with symbols I did not recognize but instinctively understood. Something old lived here. And it had been waiting.

The woman who greeted me at the museum door was not what I had imagined. She was taller than most women her age, with skin the color of coffee left to cool in a clay cup and silver hair braided thick down her back, wrapped in a ribbon the shade of dried hibiscus petals. Her eyes held something I could not name — not suspicion, not warmth, but the kind of awareness that belonged only to those who had witnessed things others were too frightened to even name. She did not introduce herself, not immediately. Instead, she stepped aside, opening the door wide without a word, her gaze brushing over my face once more before settling somewhere behind me, as if she could already see the ghosts trailing just out of reach.

The air inside the museum was cooler, touched by stone and silence, and carried the scent of books, charcoal, and pressed leaves. The room stretched high above my head, its ceiling made of wooden beams so old that ivy had begun to weave between the cracks. There were no tourists, no chattering voices, no footsteps beyond my own. I followed the woman deeper into the space, where paintings hung crooked and artifacts lay behind glass, not in the sterile way most museums displayed their dead, but as though someone had placed them there with reverence, with the understanding that these things still breathed.

When we stopped walking, it was in front of a small exhibit tucked into a corner of the main room. There were no labels, no descriptions, only a glass case and the object it held — a shard of blackened stone carved with spiraling patterns, smoothed at the edges by time or touch. The woman gestured toward it, then spoke for the first time, her voice slow and measured, with the softness of moss but the weight of iron.

"Dougla brought it here himself," she said, her accent lilting gently through the syllables. "Found it in the Amazon, near a place they say does not exist. He said it sang to him at night. Would not let him leave until he listened."

I said nothing. My eyes were fixed on the stone. I did not know why, but my hands tingled, as if the object recognized me. There was no fear in me, only a tightening in my throat, as if my body understood something my mind had not yet caught up to.

"He has not returned since," the woman continued. "But he calls sometimes. He asks about the air. About the heat. About the trees. I think he is searching for something he lost but does not remember losing."

The words snuggled into my chest like seeds. I felt their truth immediately. I was hit with a sudden realization that Dougla was not just wandering, he was being pulled, just as I was. And the tether, invisible and strong, stretched between us in ways neither of us fully understood.

"Where is he now?" I asked finally, my voice thinner than I intended.

The woman looked at me then, truly looked. Her expression did not change, but her eyes deepened, as if they had widened inward.

"You already know," she said. "You would not be here otherwise."

As I lowered my gaze, I allowed my finger to brush the edge of the display case, careful not to touch the glass, but hover just close enough to feel the cold that it emitted. I had come this far by instinct, by visions, by whispers that slithered through my dreams and kept me awake at night with words in ancient tongues. I could feel it again now — the pull of a path not made with footsteps but with memory. Dougla was in the forest. Of that, I was certain. Somewhere deeper, past the edge of the maps, where vines hung like curtains and the trees mumbled in their own secret language. If he had carried this stone from that place, then it had marked him, just as it had now marked me.

"Tell me how to reach it," I said, still not lifting my eyes. "The place he went. The place that does not exist."

The woman hesitated, but only for a breath.

"Not by road," she replied. "Not by guide or compass. You will find it only if it wants to be found. Or if he is calling you back."

And I, who had lived lifetimes inside a single heartbeat, understood exactly what that meant.

XX:
Tales We Tell In Whispers

That night, the sky above São Paulo was a dull velvet, pulsing faintly with smog-filtered moonlight, the kind that never reached the ground whole but spilled instead like memory. It felt fragmented, unreliable, and soft at the edges. I stood beneath it, having a shawl that I had drawn around my shoulders despite the warmth, and looked up as if expecting the stars to answer for the aching in my ribs. The city was never quiet, not even now. Somewhere nearby, music drifted from a second-floor window. There was a trumpet that wept into the dark. Cars passed at intervals, their lights washing the buildings with fleeting gold, and from deeper in the alleyways, the occasional shout or laughter rang out like sparks struck against stone. Yet none of it touched me. I was apart from it all, as if sealed inside something older than time, older than the woman I had become.

I did not return to the inn. Instead, I walked without aim, my feet following something invisible that dragged me between shadows. My thoughts looped like rivers lost in a jungle, circling around the woman at the museum and her warning, around the shard of stone that still buzzed in my palms, around the idea that I might already be on the path, not because I chose it, but because it had always been mine. There had never been a real choice. Not when the voice had first spoken. Not when Caleb had touched my spirit with his dreams. Not when I awoke screaming with tongues in my mouth. And not now, with Dougla somewhere in a forest that no map dared claim.

There was something sacred about being hunted by destiny. Something cruel, too.

The forest came slowly. Not all at once. First, as trees on the horizon when I boarded the old regional bus that took me east, then as vines clinging to buildings, thick and playful, reaching through the windows of half-ruined homes like lovers forgotten. The road grew narrower the farther I went, the sky heavier, as if even the sun had to fight to exist here. By the time I stepped off the bus, hours later, the land was thick with breath. Not mist. Breath. As if the very earth exhaled and pulled in air with a rhythm all its own. The forest did not begin. It enveloped. There was no edge, no threshold. One moment I was walking a dirt path lined with ferns, and the next I was inside something alive.

I did not hesitate, and my feet moved forward because my blood demanded it. There was no compass, there was no map. All that was the stone memory in my chest and the name that whispered through my veins like a prayer, *Dougla*.

I saw his image again, not on a screen, but in the memory of the girl I once was. Or perhaps still was. A boy sitting on the bank of a river, dark curls damp against his temple, arms wrapped around his knees, eyes watching the water as if expecting it to rise and speak. I didn't know where the memory came from. I could not even tell whether it was mine, or his, or something conjured by the land around me. Nevertheless, it settled behind my eyes like truth.

Hours passed without sound. The forest did not speak the way stories said it would. It did not screech or wail. It listened. And that silence was more terrifying than any growl. Trees arched above me, ancient and wide, their trunks thick with green moss that glistened like skin. Insects darted through shafts of gold light that pierced the canopy in reluctant beams. And always, always, I felt the pull.

The deeper I walked, the less I felt human. The pulse in my wrists slowed. My breath became shallow. My body no longer belonged to itself. Something inside me began to rise, not violently, but with quiet insistence, like the surface of a lake lifting toward the moon. It was not possession. It was merging. I had always known I was more than one soul. Now, the pieces stirred, aligning. I was not just the girl from the plane. Not just the vessel from the tower. I was becoming what they had all prepared me to be — a woman who could walk through a forest that devoured men and still keep her name. I didn't know where Dougla was, but I felt him. Not just ahead, but beneath my skin. And the forest, it seemed, felt it too.

The trees closed around me like memory, but not in a way that would feel rather threatening or cruel. In fact, it felt more like a kind of intimacy that came from something knowing you far too well. Every step deeper into the forest felt less like movement and more like surrender. The vines stroking against my ankles no longer startled me. The strange warmth in the soil beneath my feet no longer felt foreign. Even the silence had changed its weight. It was not absence, but presence, filled to the brim with what was watching. There were no paths now, only instinct, and instinct had begun to feel like truth.

By the time I reached the clearing, the light had shifted. It poured through the trees in long, honey-colored strands, slanting just enough to feel intentional, as if someone had pulled the sun slightly to the left just for me. In the center of the clearing stood a pool, wide and still, its surface perfectly unbroken. It was not water, not entirely.

Not in the way lakes or rivers behaved. It held no reflection. It held only depth, the kind of depth that made my blood pause in my veins, the kind that whispered of old gods and forgotten names. I did not kneel beside it. I stood, barefoot and trembling, and listened. In that precise moment, I felt him. Nothing really came as a warning, for I heard no footsteps. I didn't even hear a breath. There was no sound to be heard either, only something that could be felt — a presence, strange yet familiar.

A ripple beneath my skin. A tug low in my belly. A shift in the air that carried no scent but somehow still smelled like him. I turned slowly, not knowing what I expected to find — but knowing without question that something had arrived. The forest behind me remained still. No figure emerged. No shadow flinched. Yet my body told me what my eyes could not yet see. He was near. And not just in the way two people are near in space. He was near in the soul. The air thickened. My spine tingled as my lips parted with a name I did not speak aloud. In the whispers came *Dougla* out of my mouth. I did not move. I let the moment breathe.

There had been too many times before when love arrived as a storm, crashing through doors it never intended to stay behind. This was not that. This was the air changing shape around me. This was the feeling of being seen, fully and without judgment, by a man I had not yet touched. Somewhere in the distance, a bird cried out once and fell silent. A leaf twisted in mid-air and landed upright. Even the insects had stopped moving.

Then, in the reflectionless pool before me, a face formed. Not on the water, but in it. As if the pool were not made of liquid but of memory. His face, softened by time, ringed with light I did not understand. His mouth did not move, but his eyes met mine. Brown, dark, wide. I had seen them before in dreams I had not dared confess. I knew them. And they knew me. It lasted only seconds. I blinked, and the pool was still again — empty and clear. However, my body refused to forget.

I pressed my hands to my thighs, steadying myself, breathing through the thunder that had started to rise in my chest. It was not fear. It was recognition flooding my nervous system like wine. The kind that made you warm too fast. The kind that unbuttons you before your mind can protest. I thought of all the men who had knelt before me, trembling with desire, hoping I would save them. I thought of Marcus. Of Caleb. Of the ones whose names had not survived my forgetting. None of them had touched this place inside me. This was not lust. It was the beginning of something holy.

I turned, finally, and left the clearing. The forest did not resist. It let me go, as if it knew I would return. My steps were lighter now, more certain. My body carried the memory of his face like a lit candle I dared not breathe too close to.

By the time I reached the curve in the path where the trees thinned, the sun had nearly gone. But the heat in my skin had not faded. He was real, and he had seen me. That was all I needed — for now.

The forest did not close behind me. It remained open, not like a door I had passed through, but like a breath that had accepted my exhale. Each step back toward the village felt heavier than the last, not because of fatigue, but because I carried more than I had when I entered. Something inside me had been cracked open, not violently, but deliberately, as if a key had turned inside my ribs and released what had always been waiting. I could still feel the hum in my wrists. Not pain. Not magic. Something older — something inherited.

The village I had arrived in that morning now looked unfamiliar. The buildings leaned slightly, the roads curved in new directions, and the faces that passed me by held expressions I could not read. Children stopped playing when I walked past. An old man paused his sweeping, eyes narrowed beneath a brow furrowed by the sun. It wasn't fear exactly. It was a reverence touched by unease as though they could smell something on me — not blood, not perfume, but the mark of the forest. They knew, without knowing how, that I had been somewhere most would never dare enter. And something about me now did not fully belong to their world.

I returned to the inn without speaking. Haruki was not in the courtyard. His absence did not surprise me. He had given me space, either because he trusted me or because he feared what I might become. I let myself into the room, peeled off the clothes that had begun to cling to my skin with a desperation I could not explain, and washed my face in the basin beside the bed. The water was cool. It smelled faintly of clay. When I looked up in the mirror, I paused, for my face was the same — and yet not.

The shadows beneath my eyes had deepened, not from exhaustion, but from something else, something ancestral. My cheekbones appeared more defined, my mouth softer at the edges. But it was my eyes that struck me. They looked older. Not tired, but ancient. And for the first time since I could remember, I did not flinch from my own reflection. I stared at myself for a long time, then reached up and touched my lips, not to silence myself, but to feel the shape of what I had become. The night did not bring sleep. Instead, it brought the sea.

Not in sound, but in sensation. A rolling inside my body, a tide that rose and ebbed with every breath. I lay on the bed with my arms above my head and my legs stretched long, my chest rising slowly and steadily, and my mind filled with water. I was in the forest again. Not standing, not walking — but floating. The trees had become silhouettes of themselves, black ribs against a sky made of liquid fire, and in the center of it all stood Dougla.

He was barefoot, shirtless, his skin a deeper bronze than I remembered, his shoulders wider, his face unchanged but more luminous. His eyes met mine and did not waver. He reached out, not with urgency, but with an offering — palm up, fingers open, no words. I did not ask what he wanted. I placed my hand in his, and the moment our skin touched, the forest melted. The sky turned. The world shattered into light.

I awoke gasping, not in fear, not in terror, but in a hunger I could not name. I could, in that moment, feel a strong sense of yearning. My fingers were curled into the bedsheets. My skin was damp. The room smelled faintly of moss and sandalwood. And my lips ached as if they had kissed someone in a place that existed only in the breath between heartbeats.

I sat up slowly, pressing a hand to my chest. There was no mistaking what had happened. This was no dream spun from exhaustion. This was a meeting — one that took place beyond the flesh, in a realm where spirit recognized spirit and longing could not be disguised. Somewhere, Dougla had felt it too. Of that, I was sure.

And now, the distance between us had grown thinner. It had been, but not in miles. In the very essence of it. By morning, my body ached in ways I could not name. It was not the pain that made me feel that way. It was not fatigue either. My body pulsated with an awareness that every cell had shifted. My bones no longer felt entirely like they belonged to me, and my skin, soft as it still was, carried something beneath it that pulsed with memory and the scent of someone I had never truly touched. Dougla had not spoken to me in words, yet I heard him. His silence had a shape, and I knew now what it meant to be chosen without ever having met.

I ate little. Some fruit, torn open and eaten with my fingers, the juice slipping down my wrist. My appetite was dulled by a fullness I couldn't explain. It was as though the dream had fed me more than food could, and even as I moved through the courtyard and out toward the edge of the village again, I felt as if I were carrying his breath inside my lungs. The land was brighter now. Or perhaps I simply saw it differently. Each leaf seemed deliberate. The light that filtered through the canopy of trees had a rhythm, like breath between words. Even the insects crawling over stones looked purposeful, part of some unseen design I was only now beginning to read.

I didn't take the same path into the forest this time. Instead, I followed the call that rose from the soil itself — a vibration beneath my feet that was not sound, not scent, but instruction. I turned away from the busier trails and entered the area where the vines were thickest, where branches clawed at my clothes like fingers, and the air was thick with silence that tasted like soil and held secrets. The trees grew closer together here, and their bark bore strange markings — not carvings, but natural twists in the wood that resembled symbols. Spirals, triangles, mirrored lines. I paused before one and placed my palm against it. It felt warm. Not from the sun. From something older. A memory. A body.

Then I heard it. It was a name that was not spoken aloud, but carried in the rustle of the trees. It was the name I had grown used to repeating to myself in the midst of the night, like it was a lullaby, *Dougla.*

He had been here. I knew it with certainty now. His spirit had passed through this place and left behind a trace of itself, like the warm indent in a bed after someone rises. I moved deeper, letting the forest unfold before me, never hesitating, not once. This was no longer about searching. It was about being drawn. The further I went, the more the world around me changed. There were no birds here. No animals rustling in the undergrowth. Only light. Soft, golden, unwavering — and the strange stillness of a place that had seen something sacred. At the base of an ancient ceiba tree, I found it — a mark. The mark was not on the bark, but it was on the ground. A circle drawn in ash, surrounded by stones in the shape of a star. In its center, a small bundle wrapped in cloth the color of old blood. I knelt, my knees pressing into the softened earth. I didn't question if it was meant for me. The moment my hands touched the bundle, my skin prickled with heat, not from danger, but from recognition.

I unwrapped it slowly. Inside was a small vial, its glass fogged with age, and a slip of paper folded in half. On it, a symbol — not a word, not a name. Just a shape I had seen before. In a dream. In the pool. On the stone. A crescent moon cradling a drop of fire.

I turned the paper over. There was no tale, no long sentences that would make me lose my mind in search for their meaning, but a single one. It was more than enough, though, for in that one single line, a tale was told. It wasn't just told, it was initiated. It was an indication of the beginning of the end.

"He waits where the river forgets its name."

I closed my eyes. I didn't know what river was referred to, but deep within me, I felt the words. They felt very much alive, as though they were a part of me, and I was breathing them in as I breathed and letting them out as I exhaled. They may have been a riddle, but oh, they weren't. If anything, they were a key. The forest was listening. It had always been listening. And now, I knew — it would guide me.

I folded the paper again, tucking it into the shawl tied around my waist, and rose to my feet. My body no longer felt like mine alone. It carried someone else now, not just Nasurti, not just the weight of ancestral women turned to spirit. It carried Dougla. His echo. His hope. His ache. And somewhere ahead, waiting among roots and time, he carried mine.

The forest didn't speak again, but it opened itself to me, with arms wide open. I walked forward, not as a seeker, but as one who had already been found.

The path that unfolded before me now was nothing like the one I had entered through. It wasn't wide. It wasn't clear. There was no signpost, no suggestion of welcome. And yet, I felt no fear. I moved as though I belonged, as though my steps had already been pressed into this soil by a version of myself who had passed here long before, leaving behind just enough breath for the forest to remember. The phrase on the folded paper repeated itself in my mind, not as a sentence but as a chant where *the river forgets its name.*

I spoke it silently, not with my lips but with my pulse, and the forest responded — subtle at first. A shift in the green of the leaves. The sudden hush of insects. A coolness in the air where only stillness had been. The trees began to curve as I passed, their trunks bending not in threat but in reverence, their roots parting beneath my sandals with grace instead of resistance. It was as if the forest had simply been waiting for me to say *yes,* and now that I had, it bowed in quiet permission. The smell of water reached me before the sound.

The scent of places untouched by hands or language. It clung to the air like a promise. And then, slowly, I began to hear it. Not a rush. Not a roar. Just a persistent murmur, like someone whispering a story too old for words. I followed it, my limbs heavy with the weight of visions and the tension of nearing something that lived just beyond understanding. The trees parted into a narrow stretch of forest where the canopy thinned, and light spilled across the floor in trembling pools.

And there — ahead of me — the river waited.

It didn't move like any river I had ever seen. Its surface didn't ripple. It didn't bend around rocks or crash against fallen branches. It moved like smoke drifting just above the water's edge, like a thought in liquid form. It was colorless yet dark, transparent yet impossible to see through. It offered no reflection. It did not offer itself for interpretation. It was simply there, very much alive and watching.

I stepped to the edge as my feet sank slightly into the soft mud. I didn't speak, for I didn't need to. I only closed my eyes and let my breath fall into rhythm with the river's invisible current. Beneath my lids, the world shifted, and I knew I was no longer standing alone. I saw him. It was not just his face that I was seeing. He was there. With me. In flesh. Sure, he wasn't close — not enough, but he most certainly was there. I could feel his presence, and it told me that Dougla wasn't far. I could feel the stretch of his soul brushing against mine, taut like a thread between fingers that ached to close. He was in this forest, though not beside me, at least not yet, oh, but soon. But near enough to shift the leaves, to pull the clouds low, to call the river by a name it had forgotten centuries ago.

I crouched beside the water and dipped my fingers into its surface. The river didn't resist. It curled around my skin like silk. It felt cold, but it did not feel cruel. It wasn't cruel. I swore I heard it sigh. I brought my wet hand to my lips and pressed the droplets there. They tasted of earth and metal and old stars, and then it came. It was not a memory. Nor was it a quiet dream.

I was walking beside the river, not as I am now, but as someone older. My feet were bare, my body clothed in something sheer and gold-threaded, my hair bound in vines, and beside me walked a man. His face was Dougla's, but his eyes… they weren't. They were older. Wiser. Sadder. We didn't speak. We didn't need to. Together, we stepped into the river. Not into the water, but into it — as if it were a doorway, a mouth, a memory, and then there was nothing — just light. Just heat. Just the collapse of time into meaning.

When I opened my eyes, I was still kneeling, and the river… well, it hadn't moved. However, my hands were shaking, while my breath came in short, shallow pulls. I had seen something real, something peculiar, but not something of now, not even of this life. It was more of a pattern that felt like an entwining. It felt older than either of us. Somewhere, he had stepped into the same river, not to bathe himself in the waters of times forgotten, but to remember — or to make the river remember me. It did, now. It reminded me.

I didn't rise right away. I stayed there, hands chilled from the water, my breath light as if it had slipped out of my chest and was learning how to return again. What I saw wasn't just lingering in my mind — it lived in my bones. My ribs carried his name before my lips ever learned it. The forest didn't move. The trees stood sentinel. And the river, quiet and unreadable, hummed with something too sacred to ever be spoken aloud. Eventually, I stood.

I wiped my fingers on the edge of my dress and turned away, not because I was done, but because the river had given all it could. What waited for me now lived elsewhere, somewhere far, somewhere much, much deeper. I walked forward without fear. My steps weren't guided by direction but by surrender. Meanwhile, the forest changed again.

XXI:
It Awakens!

Part I

I did not move for a long time after I stepped into that space. Even though there was no sun above me in the sky, the earth still felt warm beneath my feet, as though it had been exposed to sunlight for a long, long time. It was not just warm; it pulsed, almost as if it were breathing — or maybe it was I. Maybe I had become part of it now. The wind had gone quiet, but the silence was not empty. It was full of memory, and there was a subtle murmuring that I could hear in the stones. Were they speaking to me? Were they speaking *of* me? Did they remember her — Nasurti? Did they remember him? Did they remember me? This was not a place I found. This was a place that found me, for this place had been waiting. And there he was somewhere in these woods, waiting to be found by me. I felt him before I saw him.

There was no sound of rustling brush, no dramatic shift in the air, but just the weight of his presence like a hand placed gently on the back of my neck. And I knew. Without turning, without speaking, I knew it was Dougla. He didn't call my name, and why would he when he didn't need to? Just like that, in the blink of an eye, the distance between me and him vanished, and as I turned around, I found my gaze falling on him. Turning towards him, I let my eyes linger, and as naturally as they could, his eyes met mine with the gravity of an eclipse. All the time between us collapsed into that gaze. I had seen him in dreams, felt him behind the bone of my chest, but this — this was the moment the world had been circling toward. He was real now, and I was in his presence. There was no way I was hallucinating this. Oh, but what now? Was I even worthy? Was he the one who'd relieve me of the curse, or would he be the end of me? From where I stood, I could see his chest rising and falling with a rhythm that felt trance-like. His breath was visible. His skin held the scent of fire and salt. I did not ask how he found me. He didn't ask what I was doing here.

Perhaps because some truths don't belong to language, perhaps some words were better left unsaid. Perhaps, he already knew. Then, swiftly, before my eyes could even blink, he stood right in front of me. He stepped closer, and I felt the earth give a soft sigh beneath us, as if it recognized something ancient reuniting. His hand reached for mine, and I didn't hesitate. When our fingers touched, I felt the surge — not electricity, not magic — something older. It felt more like recognition of some sort — like bone calling to bone. I gasped, and something inside me opened, not gently, but like a sealed door kicked in by fate.

It was my face that he touched next. His thumb brushed just beneath my eye, and in that instant, I remembered who I had been before I was Iyah. I saw jungle shadows. I saw Nasurti's hands. I felt her tears. Her voice came not from the sky but from within me.

It was not an instruction. It was a legacy. Then, as though sensing this conversation between me and Nasurti, Dougla leaned in, and his forehead touched mine. The tips of our noses breathed the same air, and then he kissed me, not like a man who had been waiting, but like a man who had always known. His mouth was slow. It was reverent. It asked nothing. It *unlocked.*

I wrapped my arms around him and felt the shiver of something sacred crawling through my spine. The Earth pulsed again, and just as it did, my body began to tremble, not in fear, but in recognition. His hands found my hips, my back, the line of my spine. Every touch was a ceremony. Every breath, an offering. As our bodies began to move closer, heat curling between us, I felt it— A'zerai, waking inside me.

It began with a breath. One long inhale between the heat of our lips, as if the jungle itself was slipping inside me. His breath, my breath—no longer separate. The air became thick with a fragrance and a smoky scent, like sandalwood scorched under a harvest moon. Dougla's mouth wandered across the curve of my cheek, down to my neck, and I tilted my head not out of submission, but because my body remembered him. Not just in this life. But in the ones before.

Every kiss was a thread being pulled loose. Every stroke of his fingertips undid another knot tied tight in my chest. There was no rush. There was only the rhythm of return. His hands slid beneath the fabric of my dress like water finding its way through cracks in stone. And I let him. I let the earth press its hush against our skin, let the sky bow in silence. Nothing needed to watch. This was not for spectacle. This was sacred.

When our bodies finally met—his chest pressed to mine, his hands lifting me just slightly, as though he feared I might fall apart, there was a flash of light behind my eyes. My breath hitched, and a sound escaped me, low and almost animal, not one of pain or fear, but one of recognition. It had all been about it — recognition! Something inside me—some muscle of spirit—flexed open.

His lips found my collarbone. I curled my fingers into the back of his hair. I didn't speak, but inside I was whispering every name I had ever carried. Every version of me. Every echo of Nasurti's voice, of her longing, her torment, her unfulfilled craving. Her pain was folding into mine, but this time, it would not end in silence. This time, there would be completion.

We moved slowly. Like waves. Like ancient beasts, remembering the shape of one another. My back met the soft moss-covered stone, and the world around us began to flicker. Dougla's hand was over my heart, then over my hip, then across the top of my thigh, his skin on mine like sunlight chasing night. I arched to meet him, and the moment he entered me, it was like a bell rang across every inch of earth that had ever known my name. It was not just a joining. It was the beginning of something else entirely.

And far, far away—so far I could barely sense it, but deep enough that it made my spine twitch—I felt it. A tremor in the dark. A sharp inhalation from some long-forgotten place beneath stone and soil. The serpent. It had stirred. A'zerai pressed against the walls of my womb, not in pain but in power. Nasurti's voice—now louder— spoke through my ribs.

"You were made for this."

And somewhere beyond the forest, in a place wet with blood and sealed with bones, a scream was trapped behind a mouth that had not opened in centuries. I did not stop. Dougla's lips were on mine. His hands wrapped around my thighs. My body had turned to fire, and I would burn for this man who knew how to light me with touch alone. However, the ripple had begun.

There are things the body knows before the mind dares to speak them aloud. As Dougla moved inside me, slow and steady as the pull of a full moon tide, I felt time unravel. My skin no longer belonged to this hour, this day, this century. It felt stretched between lifetimes, some I had lived, some I had only dreamed. His hands had maps in them. And they knew the roads of me by memory.

Our mouths met again, not in haste, but in awe. He tasted like ancient stone and wild honey. I moaned, not from pleasure alone but from the overwhelming ache of finally being seen. Beneath us, the moss turned warm. The trees leaned in closer. The stars above blurred like someone had smeared the heavens with trembling fingertips. This was no longer earth. This was not sky. This was the crossing. And in that crossing, something inside me broke wide open.

It started in my stomach, a twisting sensation, not painful but deep. Primal. A spiral of energy like a wind being born. I clutched Dougla tighter. He whispered something — my name, or maybe a word in a language older than blood. My eyes rolled back, and I gasped. Light poured into my chest, like a sun being resurrected in the hollow of my ribs.

"*Nasurti,*" I whispered, and my voice sounded like hers. My hips moved not from my own rhythm, but from memory — her memory. The motion was sacred. Ritual. The pain she'd carried folded itself into my body and then, like paper doused in flame, turned to ash. And through it, A'zerai stirred again. Not as a child now. As fire. As breath. As something inside me that was neither spirit nor flesh, but both. And far away, the serpent awoke.

His body was buried in the folds of stone — the cave he had been sealed inside for centuries. But her voice reaching fulfillment, the voice of the woman whose womb carried his blood, woke something that should have stayed sleeping. The ancient scales of his skin began to tremble. The veins, dark and poisoned, surged with movement, and he let out a sound, not a roar, but a vibration of sorts. A low, cruel pulse meant to punish. The serpent could not reach me. Not yet. But he had others. He had Caleb. After all, Caleb had always been his pawn.

I didn't see it then, not with my eyes, but I felt it — the echo. Somewhere across the world, a body jolted, a heart began to rupture, and the blood ran backward. Caleb fell to the floor. The serpent had touched him.

Dougla's lips were at my shoulder. His hands gripped my waist, anchoring me in the holy storm between us. But in my mind, something twisted. A cry I had never made escaped me, and Dougla pulled back slightly, searching my face.

"Are you alright?" he asked, his voice hoarse, thick with concern and desire.

I nodded, though I wasn't sure what was rising in me now. Love? Fury? A warning?

"Someone just felt us," I said.

And from the depths of my womb, A'zerai whispered through gritted teeth:

"He knows."

I lay beneath him, breath tangled in the quiet hum of aftershock, my body still trembling where his had just been. The forest had not returned to silence. It had changed. It watched. Every tree stood like a witness, leaves stilled in reverence, and the ground beneath me felt warmer now, as if something ancient had cracked open and spilled its knowing into the earth.

Dougla rested his forehead against mine. His chest rose and fell over me, still slick with sweat, still glowing faintly in the fading blue light. But then again something inside me had changed. It wasn't the way his body had moved with mine — it was the thing it had called forth. I could feel her — *Nasurti*, being fully awake now, her voice laced into my bones, threaded like golden wire through the lattice of my ribs. Her pain had not been erased, but had been absorbed — more like it was transformed. And A'zerai — oh, I could barely breathe through the way his presence surged through me now. No longer dormant, no longer curled like a sleeping child inside the hollow of my spirit. He was fully awake now, but not with anger or fear, but with a kind of watchful intensity. A guardian, maybe. Or something else entirely.

I pulled Dougla closer and kissed him again, not with longing this time but with recognition. I had loved this man in another life. I was sure of it now. The way our bodies moved together wasn't learned — it was remembered. But under all of it, just under the skin of the moment, I felt the pulse again. A second rhythm was felt but not mine, nor was it Dougla's. It was Caleb's. I didn't know exactly where he was. I hadn't seen his face in months. But I felt him now, like a line of smoke creeping beneath a sealed door. A scream caught inside a body that couldn't hold it anymore. There was pain, so much pain that it almost burst through my spine in waves, and I gasped, curling inward against Dougla's chest.

"What is it?" he asked, his voice no longer soft.

"I don't know," I lied. "I think someone's hurting."

Dougla rose slightly, looking around the forest as if expecting to see something crawl out from between the trees. But the trees kept their secrets. They always had.

"Iyah, you're shaking."

I was. But not from fear. I was shaking because something in the world had been tilted by what we just did. The serpent had felt it — the tearing of his line. He was coiled in his cave, thrashing, awakening, and with every tremor of his fury, he sent shards of pain through Caleb's flesh. Somewhere far away, Caleb was screaming. Clawing at his own body. Begging for it to stop. I curled tighter into Dougla's arms, my heart loud in my ears. Because now I knew. Our union hadn't just awakened love or power. It had **rattled the bones of the old gods**. And they were not pleased.

XXI:
It Awakens!

Part II

I did not speak of it again that night. Dougla, gentle even in his silence, held me as the air cooled and the leaves resumed their rustle above us, as though nature had been holding its breath all this time and could finally exhale. His heartbeat slowed against my ear, but mine did not. I lay there, my body warm and aching with everything we had just shared, and yet my spirit was pacing.

Inside me, A'zerai had coiled himself around my spine. Not asleep, not restless — alert. Watching. I felt Nasurti's breath behind my eyes. Her voice was no longer a whisper. It was beginning to sound like my own. And through it all, beneath the quiet rise and fall of Dougla's chest, I could still hear the other one — the one crying out through blood. It was Caleb, wasn't it? Who else could it be if not him? His pain wasn't distant anymore. It throbbed like a wound I couldn't see. I don't know if it was his screaming or the serpent's vibration I heard first — but they were entwined, layered like two chords of a dirge I hadn't known I knew. Caleb's body was failing under the pressure. The serpent had sent something crawling through him, some ancient venom in the shape of a curse. Every inch of our union, every sigh I had exhaled into Dougla's mouth, had reached that cave — and what stirred there was nothing short of vengeful.

I saw flashes. Caleb was on a floor, wet with sweat and spit, his hands curled in fists so tight his fingernails tore his palms open. The veins on his arms were blackening. His throat moved, but no sound came. His mouth shaped one word, again and again:

"Please."

But there was no mercy. The serpent's rage had no language. It had only pain to give. As a consequence, then, Caleb did what the dying always do when the pain outweighs the truth. He began to beg for an end, not just to the suffering, but to the source.

"I'll find her," I heard him whisper.

His voice cracked like a rotten branch. I wasn't there, but I saw him as if I stood over him. His eyes burned red. His ribs stuck out like wings, too long buried. "I'll find her and I'll make it stop." The serpent said nothing. It didn't need to. Its silence was permission.

Soon after, somewhere in the dark, Caleb stood up, unsteady and filthy but alive only because vengeance can animate even the dead. Far away, sensing it all, as though I was a witness, a comrade even, I shivered. Dougla stirred beside me. "You're cold?"

"No," I whispered. "Something's coming."

The forest around us felt too still, like the sky had dipped lower, heavy with something unsaid. Dougla didn't ask questions, and he only wrapped his arms around me tighter, as if he too sensed the shift. Nonetheless, it was too late, for our love had called forth the ghosts, and now, one of them was already on his way.

Dougla's arms were an anchor, but no amount of warmth could shield me from what I had summoned. My body, slick with sweat and divinity, still hummed from the aftermath of our joining, but my spirit could no longer pretend to rest. A wind had passed through me, sharp and invisible, a warning carried between dimensions.

Still, I closed my eyes for a while, letting his heartbeat become my rhythm, letting the scent of earth and man and flame settle over me like a veil. I imagined we could stay here, locked in that holy hush, our bodies marked by passion, our blood mixing like rivers that once forgot they were ever separate. I imagined we could make a life here. I imagined the ghosts would give us that much. But I knew better.

A crack split through the bottom of my spine — not a break, but a flare of sensation so deep it felt ancestral. Nasurti screamed, not in fear, but in warning. She was no longer whispering. Her voice rose from my bones, filled my throat, and I gasped for air, curling against Dougla's chest.

"Iyah?" His voice was low, urgent.

I couldn't speak at first. I clutched his arm, nails pressing into skin, and waited for the wave to pass. When it did, I sat up slowly, breathless. I felt soaked in centuries. My thighs still ached from him, but my mind had gone elsewhere — down through layers of stone and memory, into the cave where it all began.

A'zerai was moving inside me now. Not violently, not cruelly — but with undeniable force. He was waking. My womb pulsed like it had become its own heartbeat, no longer bound by biology or time. It was as if something ancient had uncoiled, unbound by the act of love. I touched my belly, not in fear, but with a sense of awe.

Dougla noticed. "What are you feeling?" he asked.

I didn't know how to explain it to him. This wasn't something words could hold. It wasn't pregnancy. It wasn't possession. It was remembering. It was Nasurti's legacy flowering inside my cells; her cries turned into power. It was A'zerai slipping back into himself — stretching his limbs from a thousand-year slumber, rising within me not as a child, but as what he had always been. **A consequence. A prophecy. A weapon.**

Far beyond the forest, I felt the earth shiver. The image of Caleb sharpened. His legs moved like someone dragged by rage. His feet bled from stones. His mouth foamed from the serpent's toxin. But his eyes—his eyes were clear now. Clear and cold and filled with one thing.

Find her.

Dougla sat beside me in the moss, brushing hair from my cheek. "Are you still with me?" he asked gently.

I turned to him and nodded. But the truth was heavier.

"I am," I whispered. "But something else is too."

The ground beneath me pulsed again, but this time it was not from pleasure or memory. It felt like footsteps, like something heavy walking just beneath the soil, sending tiny tremors up through my spine and into my teeth. I reached for Dougla's hand, and the moment our fingers met, the wind shifted. Trees bent slightly, not as if pushed, but as if bowing. The forest knew. It had always known.

"Something's changing," I told him.

Dougla nodded, eyes scanning the canopy. He didn't speak much, but when he looked at me, I saw no fear — only a kind of reverent certainty, the same look he had given the temple when we arrived, the look of a man who had spent his life reading symbols, only to discover the final page had always been inside him. His palm wrapped around mine, and for a moment, I believed we could hold off the gods just by holding each other.

However, I couldn't have been more wrong, and just then, the whispering started. It wasn't in the wind. It was in me. First, it was one voice, then two, then many—layered and breathless, like voices in water. Some sounded like Nasurti, others like echoes of women I had never met but somehow still carried. They spoke not in words, but in warnings. I felt them rise into my ribs, pour down into my legs. My knees buckled slightly, and Dougla caught me before I fell.

"Iyah," he said. "Tell me what to do."

I pressed my forehead to his shoulder, not because I was weak, but because I needed to be held by someone who had not died yet. "Just stay," I whispered. "Stay until I understand what's happening to me."

And then the burning began. It started in the pit of my stomach, a heat that curled inward, spiraling upward, like fire trapped in glass. My skin prickled. My teeth ached. I gasped, clutching my abdomen as A'zerai twisted inside me, not in protest, but in power. The love had awakened him fully now. He was no longer drifting in the ether of my bloodline — he was here. Present. Expanding.

Dougla placed both hands on my waist and looked into my eyes. "Your body," he said quietly, "is glowing."

I looked down and saw it too — a faint shimmer beneath my skin, like something golden had been stirred in the marrow of my bones. My veins shimmered as my heart roared, and far away, the serpent knew.

Caleb dropped to his knees in a field soaked with rain. His back arched, his mouth opened in a silent scream. The serpent had dug into his spine, wrapping itself like smoke around each nerve, filling his vision with fire. His eyes bled. His jaw locked. But through it all, one word thundered in his skull:

"Iyah."

He whispered it like a curse. And he began to rise.

Something in me clenched. I reached for Dougla's arm and whispered, "He's coming."

Dougla didn't ask who, for he already knew. The wind shifted again, not as a gentle breeze or playful stirring of the leaves, but as something sentient, purposeful, curling cold and serpentine through the branches as if sniffing for a scent only it could recognize, and for the first time since Dougla had touched me, the forest felt like a stranger. The trees, which had seemed earlier like guardians of our moment, now creaked and rustled with unease, no longer bending in reverence but shuddering with withheld warnings, and every root beneath my feet began to hum with a warning I could not fully translate, though my bones understood it well.

Dougla moved slowly, the way one does in sacred places where anything sudden might anger the spirits, and he came to stand in front of me with his hand instinctively pressed over the hilt of the blade he always carried though rarely acknowledged, the one he had once told me belonged to his grandfather, forged not just for hunting or protection, but as a symbol of oath — one forged in blood and silence, a blade that had waited, perhaps like him, for this moment. His eyes met mine, and in them I saw no fear, only recognition, as though everything I had never explained to him was now fully known, as though the bloodline I had hidden beneath my skin had awakened some ancient truth in his own, and it terrified me how easily he accepted the change in me, how he had not asked once about the golden glow beneath my veins or the shift in my voice when I whispered the names of the dead in my sleep.

"Iyah," he said, softly but with the weight of steel, "we are no longer alone."

I knew that too well. The pressure in the air had thickened, not with moisture but with memory, and somewhere just beyond the ring of trees I felt it — the vibration of something not human dragging itself forward with hatred in its breath and a name carved into its mouth, and the worst part was that it wasn't the serpent itself but the one it had sent who terrified me more. I could see Caleb, even though he was far, his movements unsteady but sure, his body battered but moving with unnatural purpose, his skin cracked and bleeding but still hot with venom, and every step he took toward me felt like a tear ripping through the thin veil that separated the sacred from the damned.

Dougla reached for my hand, and though I placed mine inside his, it trembled slightly, not out of weakness but from the force that had begun to coil inside me, something older than Nasurti, something deeper than A'zerai, a presence that had not yet spoken but was pressing its mouth against the walls of my soul. My belly ached with fire, my breath grew short, and I whispered without meaning to, "He is close," and Dougla didn't ask who, because by now he had come to understand that knowing wasn't nearly as important as being ready.

The leaves around us suddenly froze in the air, suspended for a breathless second, and from the direction where the darkness was thickest, a voice spoke, not loud but whispered with such intimacy that it felt like it came not from outside but from inside my very skull. I turned sharply, my heart rumbling in my ears, and I knew with a clarity so sharp it hurt that the voice belonged to the one I had once tried to save, the one who had tasted death but returned with something far crueler in his chest.

"Iyah," the voice said again, and this time it was louder, clearer, closer, as if he stood just beyond the veil.

XXII:
The Final Battle

Dougla stepped forward, but I stopped him with a hand, not because I was brave but because I knew what was coming. The forest around us exhaled once, long and low, and then everything — trees, wind, earth, even the stars — went still. That was the moment I noticed it. It wasn't a clear shape or figure, just a dark shadow that didn't seem to belong to any tree or person, creeping toward us in silence, as if the night itself had turned into something dangerous. And it was headed straight for me. I felt frozen in place. Next to me, I could sense Dougla's breath hitch, his body tense and ready, the knife he held catching the faint glow of the moonlight that peeked through the leaves. However, I couldn't bring myself to move. Something in that shadow, in the way it drifted across the ground without sound or shape, pulled at me, not with fear, but with an eerie recognition — as if some part of me had known it would come, had been waiting for it all this time.

The serpent's current had traveled far. It wore no skin, no cloak, and yet it carried the stench of rage soaked in centuries. I could feel the venom humming against my ribs, threading itself through the last of my breath. My name had been spoken not with love, not even with vengeance, but with hunger. The kind of hunger that is not for flesh, but for annihilation. For undoing.

Dougla stepped forward, blocking me with the full breadth of his body, blade lifted. "Show yourself," he growled.

The shadow paused as if amused, and then it began to lengthen and grow. Slowly, it rose, transforming not into a beast, but into a boy—or was it a man? He appeared gaunt and hollow-eyed, trembling with an air of desperation. His lips were cracked, and he whispered something repeatedly, though the words eluded my understanding. And then I looked into his eyes and knew. It was Caleb. He was not the boy I remembered. Not the one who once spoke to me in dream-tongue. Caleb's body was no longer his. The serpent had seeped into his bones. His back curved with unnatural bends, his skin pulsed with dark veins, and his hands… his hands were shaking with something he couldn't hold inside anymore.

"Iyah," he said again, voice low, broken, pleading. "Please… help me."

Dougla stepped toward him, but I grabbed his arm.

"Wait."

The wind went quiet. I stepped forward, slowly and carefully, as I felt something ancient tighten inside my belly. A'zerai stirred again, and Nasurti's voice grew louder in my skull. This wasn't a boy anymore; it was a warning. "Caleb," I said, my voice barely above a whisper.

His lips quivered as he struggled to form words. "He's inside me. I tried… but I can't… I have to…"

His mouth twisted in anguish, his eyes rolling back until a primal scream erupted from him. It was not a human sound; it tore through the forest like a blade through silk, a scream so loud and raw that even the stars seemed to flicker in response. Dougla lunged toward him, but Caleb's body convulsed violently. In that moment, I felt something inside me begin to break open, a profound shift that mirrored the chaos unfolding before us.

I had never seen a human body unravel the way Caleb's did. His scream echoed across every inch of the forest, shaking the branches, sending birds scattering into the ash-colored sky. His spine cracked loud enough to tear through the night, and from his mouth poured not words but something dark, something slick and ancient, as though the serpent inside him had finally decided to take the stage. The shadow I had seen earlier no longer loomed behind him — it had become him.

Dougla stepped between us without hesitation, holding the blade not as a weapon but as a line drawn in the sand between man and monster. He said nothing, but the resolve in his stance was enough to still the wind. Caleb's eyes locked on mine, hollow now, glowing faint green from within as if something pulsed behind them. His jaw moved slowly, cracking as he tilted his head.

"You gave yourself to him," he said. "You were meant for me."

Dougla did not wait. He rushed forward, swift and grounded, the blade raised high, and I watched him move like a storm — fluid, powerful, the echo of centuries guiding his body. But Caleb's limbs responded like a rope pulled by invisible hands, twitching and jerking without logic. He caught Dougla mid-swing and hurled him backward into a tree with such force that the bark exploded. Dougla hit the ground and didn't rise.

I screamed his name and ran forward, summoning the fire in my gut, but Caleb turned to me, lifting both arms. The ground beneath us split open, a thin line at first, then wider, glowing from within with a dark, pulsing red. From it came the voice — not Caleb's, not the serpent's, but something else, deeper, a groan that had once cracked through stone temples and made women's wombs tremble.

"She wakes," Caleb said, his smile both eerie and unsettling. His voice twisted in the air, echoing as if two mouths spoke in unison from a single throat. "She is almost here." The serpent, ancient and dreadful.

I felt its coils turning deep beneath us, slithering through dark tunnels carved with blood and the fervent cries of worshipers, rising from the pit where it had been imprisoned for far too long. The air around us thickened, heavy with the weight of sins long past, pressing down like a thick fog. I took a shaky step back, not from fear, but from the raw intensity of it—the undeniable gravity of a being that had tasted the divine and hungered for more. In that moment, I realized I had no weapon to fight back, only the echoes of memory and the bitter taste of pain that lingered in my heart. My eyes locked onto Caleb, who drifted just above the ground, his skin cracked open to reveal glowing threads that pulsed with an otherworldly light. His mouth stretched wider than humanly possible, and as the earth beneath us trembled, I understood what had to be done. Yet, deep down, I was acutely aware of the truth: I would not survive this confrontation.

The earth roared beneath me, trembling like it remembered its own birth. Caleb was no longer fully visible—he shimmered, not with light, but with something darker, like smoke held together by threads of memory and hate. I moved toward Dougla's body, crawling more than running, my hands digging into the soil like I could anchor myself to the present moment, as if I held on tightly enough, I wouldn't lose everything.

He lay crumpled at the base of the tree, eyes closed, a thin line of blood trailing down his temple into the collar of his shirt. I touched his face and felt warmth, but no stir, no breath. Not yet. I shook him gently, then harder, my voice cracking as I whispered his name again and again, but the world around us didn't wait. Caleb's laughter rose above the chaos, fractured and layered, like many mouths were laughing from one throat.

"You love him?" he said, stepping closer, his feet never touching the ground now. "That fragile, breakable man? I was made from your curse. He was made from nothing."

I stood, trembling but upright, and turned to face him. The glow in my skin had begun to pulse again, dim at first, but growing brighter with every breath I took. I raised my chin and looked him in the eye.

"You were made from the serpent's fear," I said. "You were never mine."

His smile vanished. For a moment, just a moment, something human flickered behind his eyes—grief, confusion, a memory of being a boy who once dreamt in his own voice. But it vanished as quickly as it came, drowned in the hiss that slipped from between his teeth.

He raised his hands again, and the ground beneath Dougla split open, not enough to swallow him, but enough to shake the tree, enough to loosen more blood from his temple. I cried out, but it was too late to reach him. Caleb moved faster than I thought, his hand tightening around my throat before I could react, lifting me off the ground.

I kicked, clawed, but he was stronger than before, his grip cold and hard as bone. My vision blurred at the edges, and somewhere far beneath me, I felt the serpent stir. It was close now. I could feel its weight in the cave below us, feel its skin brushing the inside of Caleb's soul, feel it pressing against the very veins of the earth.

"You'll die here," Caleb whispered. "Your body, your name, forgotten like the rest."

But then something shifted within me, deeper than just the air around me. A sound echoed in my chest—not a voice or a scream, but a resonant hum that felt both ancient and sacred. It was the call of Nasurti, a presence that wrapped itself around my soul. Alongside it, another voice emerged, one that felt warmer and wilder, like a dance of fire and freedom. A'zerai stirred within me, alive and vibrant. In that moment, they awakened, and I could feel their power coursing through my veins. My eyes flared to a brilliant gold, a reflection of the passion sparking within me. Caleb's hand, where it rested on my skin, burned with an intensity that matched the heat within. And in that sacred moment, a smile spread across my face, a reflection of the strength and exhilaration that surged through me.

The pain should have destroyed me. His grip around my neck had tightened so brutally that I could hear blood drumming against my ears, and yet it wasn't death I tasted. It was heat—like coals igniting in the hollow of my spine. There was no longer just me inside this skin. I felt Nasurti rise within my lungs, pressing against the breath I had nearly lost. She was not screaming, she was singing—softly at first, like a mother rocking her child in the middle of a war, and then louder, more forceful, until the song felt like it wasn't coming from me, but from the sky, from the soil, from the wound in the earth where the serpent waited to be born again. I couldn't breathe, but I could hear her. And beneath her melody came another sound, deeper, slower, more ancient than even she. It was A'zerai, whose blood now surged through mine. His awakening did not come like a cry. It came like thunder. It came like every god I had never prayed to stepping forward to kneel at my feet.

My hands, once dangling in Caleb's grip, began to move, not by my choice, but by something older than choice. They rose not to strike, but to burn. My fingertips glowed, the skin split open to reveal threads of gold light winding through the veins underneath. I looked into Caleb's face and saw confusion twist across it—not fear yet, but uncertainty, as if something inside him had been shaken loose and didn't know where to settle.

He loosened his hold just enough for me to gasp, and in that gasp, the world turned.

I reached for his wrist and did not pull it away—I pushed deeper, pressed my palm against his skin, and let the light pour out. It wasn't an attack. It was a revelation. I let him see it all: Nasurti's scream as she gave birth alone in the dark; A'zerai's heartbeat echoing through centuries; the trail of blood I had followed since the day I first dreamed of tongues I never spoke. I let him see the cost of his betrayal and the weight of the serpent he had welcomed.

His eyes widened in shock, and his mouth opened as a scream surged from deep within him. But this time, it wasn't anger—it was pure fear. He dropped me and stumbled back, clawing at his own arms as if the memories I'd shared were toxic. I collapsed to my knees, coughing, then crawled over to where Dougla lay motionless, the dirt around him soaked with his blood. When I pressed my face against his chest, I could barely hear a weak breath. He was alive, but just barely. I gently touched his cheek and whispered to the spirits swirling inside me—Nasurti, A'zerai, and the others I'd never known. I sought their strength, not for battle but to keep him safe. I would destroy everything else, but he had to survive. Behind me, Caleb got up again, but this time something sinister trailed him, a shadowy smoke that seemed to writhe beneath his skin. He screamed my name—not out of anger, but of desperation—as he began to claw at the ground with his bare hands. He was going to awaken her, truly awaken her. Time was slipping away for me.

I stood on the trembling edge of the earth, the heat rising from the cracked mouth of the cave as if the world itself was exhaling centuries of rage. It smelled of rust and bone, of prayers long forgotten, of the blood of women who had once dared to walk into temples carved by gods who did not listen. Caleb had become something else entirely now, crouched before the rupture, his arms outstretched as though welcoming the return of a lover. His mouth was open, his eyes rolled back into his skull, and his voice was no longer human. It had dropped into something ancient and guttural, echoing across the trees like a chant taught in a time before language. His body pulsed with veins of greenish-black, veins that writhed with the same rhythm as the serpent's stirring far beneath us.

And I—I felt everything. I felt the ground bend beneath me, not with weight, but with memory. I felt the spirits moving within me like birds breaking free from the cage of my chest. Nasurti rose first, proud and still, her voice not trembling but clear, not screaming but humming a war song from the belly of time. A'zerai followed, and the ache in my spine became a flame, climbing up my bones like ivy kissed by lightning. He was no longer a dormant thread within me. He had risen now, his pulse intertwined with mine, his strength braided into my limbs. And beyond them, too many others to count—spirits who had suffered in silence, who had carried secrets beneath their tongues, now returned to lend me what little they had left. I knew what was to come.

Caleb opened his arms wider, and I saw him lift his face toward the sky. From his chest rose the hiss—the true voice of the serpent. It wasn't a sound, it was a storm. A vibration that cracked through the air and sent the birds flying, the trees leaning, the clouds recoiling. The serpent was almost fully here, its power leaking into the living world through the man it had chosen as a vessel. He was not Caleb anymore. That name belonged to someone who once dreamt of love. This thing standing before me was a shrine of hatred, crafted by betrayal and baptized in obsession.

I stepped forward, barefoot on scorched earth, my skin glowing with an inner heat that was no longer entirely mine. I reached toward the sky, not in surrender, but in summoning. The fire I carried had grown heavy in my hands, too full of truth to remain caged inside. I called to every voice within me. I told them to rise. I gave them permission to burn. My fingers splayed, and the light rushed forward—not a beam, not a flame, but a wave. It swept around me, through me, into the cave's mouth where the serpent began to unfurl its true form. I did not wait for fear. I gave them everything.

Caleb turned just as the light struck. For one fleeting heartbeat, his face was his again. His lips parted like he wanted to speak, like somewhere inside him a part of the boy who once loved me still remained. But the light would not be held back. It tore through him like he was parchment, peeling back skin, memory, and the illusion of control. His scream was not a cry of pain. It was the death wail of the serpent itself.

He stumbled backward into the cave, his hands clawing at the air as though he might still be able to stop what was coming. But it was too late. He fell. And the serpent met him.

I did not look away.

Its tendrils curled around his body, piercing it, fusing with it, claiming him fully. The cave groaned, not from pressure, but from satisfaction. Caleb convulsed once, then again. Then his body collapsed inward—imploded—not like a man, but like a star. The serpent consumed him completely, and for a moment, I thought that might be enough. But it wasn't. I felt the hunger still pulsing from the cave's core, reaching now toward me. It had not come only for Caleb. It had come for me, too.

I fell to my knees, pressed my hands to the ground, and called upon the last names, the ones without names, the silent ones, the women never given a grave, the children swallowed by temple stones, the ones forgotten by time. They responded. I felt their energy surge through me, igniting each part of my being with their pain. With the last bit of strength I had, I sent my fire downward, not as light, but as fury. The cave's roots cracked, the earth's bones splintered, and the serpent hissed again as I screamed into it, louder than I ever had before. The sky twisted, the trees trembled, and the fire reached the heart of the serpent—then there was nothing but silence. Then dust. I felt the cave give way, the mountain crumbling around me, turning to ash from a fire that didn't belong in this world. I had done it. But I was left with nothing. My arms fell limp, my skin faded away, and as the warm, soft ash poured over me, I leaned back into the earth. Eyes shut, heart still. I had saved the world, but in the process, I had lost myself. Did I die? Was I dead? Was that all for me? Was it where my story ended?

Oh, but wait, this wasn't all. As I lay there with my eyes closed, my heart suddenly started to beat faster, the rhythm wild and untamed. I pressed my hand to my chest, feeling it rise and fall with every breath I drew and released. The battle with Caleb had drained every ounce of strength from me, and I lay there spent, my limbs heavy as stone, my spirit barely clinging to wakefulness.

But even in my exhaustion, my senses stirred. I heard the faint sound of breathing coming from somewhere close by, just within reach of where I lay still. My eyelids fluttered open, and I turned my head toward the sound, and there, half-buried in the earth, I saw the hand. It was caked in dirt, and blades of grass clung to it stubbornly. My senses sharpened as if the fight had awakened something primal in me. I caught the scent of the tiny pieces of crushed grass and soil. Beneath the layer of earth, my recognition came swift and sure.

As I inhaled deeper, I could smell his sweat, mingled with the familiar scent of his body wash—the same he had used earlier that day. Just hours ago, that very hand had moved across my skin with a tenderness so fierce it had set my soul ablaze. I sprang up with a sudden rush of energy just as he pushed himself up from the soil that seemed reluctant to let him go. And there he was—the one who could bring me peace, salvation, and a love so deep it trembled through my bones.

He lay no more than a hundred feet away, maybe less, still on his back, staring skyward as if silently praying for rain. My heart tightened as tears welled in my eyes, blurring the edges of everything around me. My legs carried me toward him before my thoughts could catch up, my mind racing through memories and dreams I had barely dared to claim.

Dougla would be my light, even when my eyes were closed—like a soldier who loses an arm in battle, yet still finds a hand to hold. He would guide me through darkness, love me without condition, soothe the raw wounds of my spirit, and calm the tremors in my heart. I loved him before I had ever heard the sound of his voice. And in that moment, running toward him, I felt something deeper than hope; I felt the quiet acceptance of self-love stirring in my chest like the softest promise.

But my thoughts broke, fragile as glass. Something shifted in the air, and dread slid icy fingers down my spine. I froze mid-step, a shiver rippling over my arms, goose bumps lifting the fine hair on my skin. "There is something awful in the air," I whispered, so faint only my own ears could hear it. My eyes lifted to the towering Amazon trees above, their ancient limbs stretching high into the sky. The fragrance of crushed leaves and wildflowers swept into my senses, but underneath it, an uglier truth hid.

I watched as a single leaf fell slowly, bearing seeds red and orange, landing softly on the earth. The smell thickened, clung to the back of my throat. My pulse roared in my ears as I felt it run through my veins, seeping into my blood. Beneath the sweetness of rosewood and earth, I smelled it unmistakably—death. The sour reek of rotting flesh, the rusty tang of dried blood.

Panic squeezed my chest tight as I realized Dougla was still lying there, just out of my reach.

My breathing grew ragged; my chest rose and fell so quickly it hurt. I forced air into my lungs as if it might be my last breath on earth. My gaze lifted again to the towering trees, some reaching three hundred feet above me, ancient sentinels that had watched countless lives pass beneath their branches. My left hand clutched at my chest, and my mouth hung open, pulling the damp forest air deep into my lungs, desperate to calm the rising terror.

And then I saw them.

They sat perched at the highest branches, hidden from ordinary sight—but my eyes, sharpened by something older than memory, saw them all. My head spun slowly, turning in cautious circles. They watched me silently, a strange, unsettling beauty etched into each face. Their hair—black, some wavy, some straight, some brown kissed with a reddish hue—fell to their shoulders in effortless grace. Features carved by lineage unmistakably Indigenous, yet their forms were something more: taller, stronger, as if the forest itself had shaped them into ideal guardians of ancient secrets. Their skin bore no flaw, sun-kissed brown, like bronze held up to the light.

A breeze struck my back with sudden force, carrying the sharp scent of moss and earth. I turned quickly, and my breath caught. More had descended behind me. They sat there, each cross-legged, black wings spread wide like those of ravens, their feathers glinting darkly in the shifting light. Stern faces regarded me—not with hatred, but a solemn respect, as though I were something they could neither dismiss nor fully claim. But behind that restraint, I saw it: the raw glint of hunger, a gnawing that reached deeper than fear itself.

And I knew, as sure as the pulse in my veins, that their hunger outweighed their fear.

A sudden scream tore itself from my throat, raw and unrecognizable even to my own ears. "DO NOT TOUCH HIMMMMMMMM!" My voice echoed through the forest, sharp enough to send birds darting from the trees, insects scattering in startled flight. "Father, help me," I whispered next, pressing my trembling hands together in prayer, holding them close to my lips. The words scraped from my throat as softly as broken glass. "Please help me, Father," I breathed again, my lips brushing my cold knuckles.

I lifted my tear-soaked gaze to the treetops, then turned to face the winged figures behind me. "Do not touch him," I repeated, my voice low but edged with something ancient and unbreakable. "I will destroy each one of you." As those words crossed my lips, a piercing ache twisted through my chest—a painful, almost beautiful ache that rooted itself deep in my heart and belly.

Then something stirred inside me, rising like a tide, stronger than the power I had summoned against the serpent—stronger than anything I had ever felt. My tongue felt heavy, each word a weight of fire. The words tumbled from me in the ancient tongue of flame, words that only the Holy Spirit and those gifted with understanding could comprehend. Head lifted to the heavens, voice ringing out in defiance and devotion, I cried, "Glory be to God!"

A blinding pain shot through me, searing every nerve, folding me into its grip. It swallowed every thought, every breath. My body arched, hands trembling in the air as if I could somehow rise above it. A searing ache tore through my back, sharp as steel, deeper than bone. And then, without knowing how, I felt them unfurl —wings!

Wings white as winter's first snow, tipped in shimmering blue along their razor edges—edges sharp enough to slice through darkness itself. They matched the stormy blue of my eyes, as if born from the same ancient spark. And from deep within, I felt my fangs extend, long and sharp like a wolf awakening from a thousand years of sleep. This was me. The real me. The one they should fear. The one the world had waited for—and with that, a new beginning had cracked open, bright and terrible. And as I spread my wings wide, heart pounding like thunder, I saw them descending—drifting downward through the dense canopy—toward Dougla.

Epilogue

The sun in this land did not scorch like it did in the stories of war-torn deserts or blood-soaked mountain passes—it warmed, gently and insistently, like a long-lost friend slipping back into your life without explanation. It filtered through the tall grasses that swayed beyond our porch, kissing the eaves of the little house Dougla built with his own hands. Not a house of magic or prophecy or divine interference—just wood, mud, the sweat of a man who had known ruin and chosen peace. The walls were thick, not to keep out spirits or whispers, but to hold in our laughter, our warmth, the kind of quiet that can only come after storms. I hung bells on every doorway—not to warn away evil, but to remind joy it was always welcome here. And joy did come. In the chirp of unfamiliar birds, in the scent of baking bread, in the soft, rhythmic breath of a newborn sleeping on my chest as if the world had never been cruel to anyone.

We named him Osei. His name meant noble birth, though we never shared the full truth behind it—not with the villagers who brought bundles of grain and embroidered blankets, not with Haruki, who visited more often now, and certainly not with the midwife who said she'd never seen a child born so calmly, as if he simply chose to arrive. Dougla had held him first, arms trembling, face cracked open with awe, and something old in me began to unravel, something I hadn't known was still wound tight. Osei didn't wail the way babies often do. He blinked, observed, and reached out as though measuring the shape of the world. At three months, he reached for fire and didn't flinch. At six, he giggled when a neighbor's ox kicked a stone that nearly grazed him. At nine, he said his first word—not mama, not baba. Just "stone." We laughed nervously, then brushed it off when he pointed at a pebble near the door. Just a pebble, we told ourselves, not a sign or a memory.

Haruki took to him like a second grandfather, bringing small gifts and stories from the northern plains, always staying longer than he claimed he would. Dougla frowned at the tales of fire gods and children of starlight, muttering that our son needed a soft life, not legends. But even he could not deny that Osei seemed drawn to the old things—not just fascinated, but familiar as if he had already walked those paths once and now returned to find them altered. Still, life moved with a sweetness I did not question. I let my hands forget the heat of spirit-summoning and learned instead how to knead dough, how to hum lullabies without remembering the sound of wailing, how to laugh without glancing over my shoulder. The past softened, folded into the soil like ash turned to bloom. I let myself believe that maybe we had finally outrun the blood, the cave, the gods.

But one evening, just as the sky spilled lavender over the trees and the earth exhaled that slow breath it saves for twilight, I found Osei in the garden, his fingers deep in the soil, his eyes closed as if listening to something that didn't belong to this world. I didn't call out. I stood in the doorway, heart snagged in a memory I hadn't summoned. The wind curled past me, heavy with the scent of stone and old flame. Then he spoke—softly, almost to himself. "Mama, I dreamed of a cave. It was on fire. And something inside screamed until it turned into light." I crouched beside him, brushed the dirt from his hands, held his face between my palms as if I could press the dream out of him. "That's just a dream, my love," I whispered, and he looked at me with those wide, blue eyes like the color of the ocean that always seemed too deep for his age. "No, Mama. It's a memory."

I carried him inside, tucked him against my chest, and rocked him as if he were still a baby who hadn't yet spoken, hadn't yet remembered what no child should. That night, Dougla's breath rose and fell against my back, grounding me, but my mind drifted beyond the walls, out to the forgotten land where the Snake Cave once lay buried beneath ash and soil. I stepped outside, barefoot, the moon low and red against the hills, and there—beneath the quiet hum of sleeping things—I heard it. A thrum. Not a voice, not quite. Just something deep, like the earth still remembering its pain.

Haruki was already there. He stepped out from the tree line as if summoned by thought alone, his arms folded, his eyes clear. "You know," I said to him, not needing to explain what. "I see things," he replied softly, "but I never pretend to understand them." I asked him the question that had begun to burn a hole inside me. "Do you think it's him? A'zerai?" Haruki didn't flinch, didn't offer comfort or denial. "Maybe not. Maybe just a piece of him. A shadow. Or a spark. But he's yours now, Iyah. He's here to heal, not destroy."

I wanted to believe him. And for a while, I did. I clung to it like bark to tree. But a few days later, I caught Osei drawing in the dirt—concentric circles, jagged eyes, tongues of fire. Symbols I had not seen since the cave had nearly claimed my life, symbols that should not have survived in a child's mind. And when I asked what he was drawing, he looked up and said, not with fear, but with certainty, "The stone still remembers."

I held him tightly that night and told him stories of stars instead of spirits, of gentle creatures instead of dragons, of rebirths that did not begin in blood. He smiled, tucked a dried petal behind my ear, and whispered that he dreamed of wings—black ones, wide enough to cover the sky. I kissed his forehead and wished upon every ancestor I'd ever known that his dreams would never become prophecies.

But I have seen enough to know that peace is never forever—it is borrowed. And some debts, no matter how lovingly paid, leave behind their trace.

Osei slept soundly, curled beside me, his breath warm against my collarbone. But even in sleep, he held a closed fist against his chest as if guarding a secret. And I? I stayed awake and listened—to the wind, to the soil, to the faint, rhythmic beat of something ancient stirring far beneath the surface.

Maybe the gods were done with us.

Or maybe they were only just beginning.